Emma Berry Mystery series

*Saddled with Death*
*A Gem of a Problem*
*A Body in the Woodpile*
*Murder at the Mill*
*Death in Disguise*

# A GEM of a PROBLEM

An Emma Berry Mystery
Book #2

Irene Sauman

Jakada Books

PERTH WESTERN AUSTRALIA

A Gem of a Problem: Format (novel)
Irene Sauman / Jakada Books / Perth Western Australia

Paperback ISBN: 978-0-6459954-0-4

# Dedication

This book is dedicated to my friends
and critique partners
Helena Holton and Jacquie Garton-Smith
who have provided support, encouragement, and
positive feedback throughout,
lighting a solitary journey

# Author's Note

The Emma Berry mysteries are set in the eighteen-seventies on the Murray River, the third longest navigable river in the world, surpassed only by the Amazon and the Nile. Its great navigable length was responsible for the development of the riverboats, the side-wheel paddle steamers that opened up the Australian countryside along the river's length to settlement and sheep farming, in much the way railways did in the wider countryside.

Indeed, it was the railways that eventually ended the glory days of the paddle steamers, though they continue to ply the waters in the twenty-first century, carrying tourists and holidaymakers. Two generations of my father's family produced working riverboat captains. But this story is strictly fiction.

*A Gem of a Problem* is the second title in this series.

# Main Characters

<u>At Wirramilla on the Murray</u>

Edward & Rose Haythorne: pastoralists

Emma Berry: their widowed daughter

Eleanor Haythorne: Edward's mother

Lucy Wirra: housekeeper

Sal, Jacky & Janey Wiira: Lucy's adult children

Nella Brackett: Lucy's eldest child, married to
  overseer Jeff Brackett

<u>At Nettifield on the Murray</u>

George Macdonald: pastoralist, widower

His adult children: Matty, Beatrice (Bea), Jim

Thomas Quilp: overseer, Bea's betrothed

<u>The PS *Lisette*</u>

Daniel Berry: Captain, Emma's brother-in-law

Crew: Mr. Shankton, Mr. Wilson, Fred Croaker,
  Shorty Mason, Blue Higgins, Ah Lo (Charley),
  Willy Bowman,

<u>At Merrim on the Murray</u>

Mr. Fraser: Scottish station manager

Deirbhile (Deelie): Irish housekeeper

Brendan O'Neill: Irish station hand

Mort: elderly gardener

<u>At Echuca</u>

Nathaniel (Nat) Pickles: Echuca Wharf office

Charity Pickles: his sister, Pickles Boarding House

Old Mr. Pickles: their father

Henrietta Pickles: Nat's estranged wife, owns the
    Primrose Tearoom

Janet Pickles: Henrietta & Nat's daughter

Alex Thompson: retired jeweller

Clarice Thompson: his ward

George Knowles: boatbuilder at Dutch's slip

*The Argus, 19 January 1876, p 6.* The shipping on the Murray is now assuming considerable proportions, and new steamers and barges are constructed every year. There are now 23 steamers and 25 barges Victorian owned, which make Echuca their port; and there are 16 steamers and 19 barges South Australian owned, whose port is Goolwa. The firm of Messrs. W. McCulloch and Co. are interested in a large number of these steamers, but there are many owned by the captains, or by merchants in Melbourne or Adelaide.

---

# Chapter 1

## Major Barnaby Poses a Problem

*Wednesday 8 September 1875*

EMMA WASN'T relishing the idea of meeting with Major Frederick Barnaby. What possible information could he have about the sinking of the PS *Mary B* and Sam's death? Nothing she didn't already know, surely. It wasn't something she was likely to forget anytime soon.

"This is very odd," her father said, when he found Emma in the stillroom with her grandmother. "Said he was just passing by but wasn't explicit about what he wants to discuss with you, just mumbled something about the riverboat business and Sam's death. Would you like me to sit in with you?"

"Oh, I don't think that will be necessary, Father," Emma replied, immediately on guard. If the Major had something to tell her about Sam, she wanted to hear it alone. Her marriage to Sam Berry had not been universally approved of among her family. She would decide later if it were information she could share. "Thank you, all the same, but I will speak with you if it's anything important," she added.

Concern was etched on Edward Haythorne's face, but he nodded. "Very well, if you are sure."

Emma understood her father's disquiet. The Major had never graced Wirramilla with his presence before. They didn't move in his social circle, although her grandmother was friendly with his wife. Eleanor Haythorne was known to almost everyone along the Murray for her herbal remedies, so there was nothing unusual in that.

But Major Barnaby wouldn't have travelled two hundred miles from his sheep property on the Murrumbidgee in New South Wales just to speak with her. He must be in the area on other business and saw an opportunity while here. Perhaps he thought he could buy the *Mary B* cheaply because it was still wait-ing for repairs. It would fit with his reputation.

When Emma entered the drawing room, leaving the door open as propriety dictated, she found the Major pacing in front of the fireplace. He was a short man, running to corpulence. He compensated his lack of height by holding himself stiff and upright, hardly surprising in a military man.

"I'm sure you would welcome some refresh-ments, Major, so I've had tea brought in for us," Emma said, as Lucy preceded her with the tea tray. Emma's fox terrier Floss followed on Lucy's heels drawn by the scent of chocolate cake. "Please take a seat."

She indicated an armchair and sat herself gracefully on the sofa, swirling her skirt at her feet with a flick of the hand, the way she'd been taught during her year at Miss Eunice Marshall's School for Young Ladies. She didn't normally behave with such aplomb, but the cool look she had received from the man seemed to call for it. Lucy gave an odd cough which Emma suspected had started life as a laugh. She ignored it and waited quietly until the tea tray was ready.

"Thank you, Lucy. I will deal with it now."

"Yes, ma'am." Lucy left the room with a swirl of black skirt around her brown ankles. She had done that deliberately, Emma was sure. It was fortunate the woman hadn't curtsied.

"Do you take milk, Major?" she asked as she poured.

He gave a grunt which Emma took as an affirmative. Floss, who had taken up a position on the floor beside her, responded with a 'huh' deep in her throat. Not a good sign.

"I hope Lady Annabel and your daughters are all well, Major," she said politely as she handed him his cup. She knew his womenfolk were in London for the season, trawling for a husband for Julia. It had been a coup for the Major, a younger son of minor gentry, to marry into a titled family but Lady Annabel was the Earl's seventh daughter. Even the well-off landed gentry had their limits. "When are they due home?"

Major Barnaby took the proffered teacup but gave her a hard look. "I didn't come all this way for social chit chat, madam," he said. "I am here concerning a small packet I had entrusted to your husband. I want it returned."

"A packet?" Emma said, taken aback as much by his attitude as his statement.

"Do not play games with me, madam. You were on board the boat when your husband took delivery."

"Was I?" Emma felt annoyance replacing confusion at his accusing tone. "That may well be so. I did reside on the *Mary B* after all, but I don't know of this item. Please explain."

"Don't give me that. You witnessed the meeting."

Emma shook her head. She caught the Major's eye across the tea table and her heart hammered at the hostility in his gaze. The air crackled between them. Emma found she was clutching her cup tightly with both hands and carefully returned it to the table for fear of breaking it. She sat back, forcing herself to relax. The silence lengthened.

"I see," the Major said at last. "You think you can play me with your arrogance, this quaint little tea-party." He leaned forward in his chair and put his own cup, none too gently, on the table. "If you think you can blackmail me into paying for its return you had better think again, very carefully. It wouldn't be only the Berrys who lose here. They are of no importance anyway, just trumped-up carriers." He snapped his fingers. "The Haythornes now, they are another matter."

Emma felt her face flush. Her hands clenched in her lap.

"I'm no more arrogant than yourself, Major," she retorted. "As I have already said, very clearly, I know nothing of any packet and an accusation of blackmail just makes me wonder what underhand business you are engaged in." The Major's face reddened at her words, but he hesitated, as if no longer sure of his footing. Emma took the opportunity to attack, always believing it the better part of defence. "I don't know how many ways I can say it, but I did not know Sam was carrying any item for you, or that he had any association with you whatsoever. My husband did not take me into his confidence about every little piece of cargo. Most men don't usually discuss business details with their wives, do they? So why don't you tell me what this is all about."

He stared at her. "Hmph. The packet I entrusted to your husband is missing," he said. "It went missing when your boat sank. Someone must have it and that someone is likely to be yourself, whatever you may say to the contrary."

Emma ignored the implication she was lying. "All the cargo the *Mary B* was carrying was salvaged and any damage was covered by insurance. All you need do is put in a claim to the insurers for your loss."

"I will not be making any insurance claim."

"That doesn't make sense. Oh." Light dawned. "It wasn't on the cargo list, was it? You were smuggling something. You had Sam smuggling something for you."

Had Sam been that stupid? She didn't believe he was dishonest, but he could have seen it as a lark to outwit the customs men. Larrikin had been her father's word for him. The customs duties payable at the colonial borders were flouted every day, not always on purpose, as people crossed the Murray River between New South Wales and Victoria, moving stock and goods. A traveller could be fined, or even forfeit an item, for not paying duty on something carried unwittingly in their pocket.

"Oh no. I gave your husband the fee for the customs duty," the Major said. "If he decided to smuggle the packet across the border and pocket the duty that was his risk. It matters not. The item is still missing, and I want it returned."

Emma frowned. The customs duty for jewellery crossing the river border into Victoria was substantial. What was the Major doing that would require him to pay such a sum? But if this was a mess Sam had got them into, she was going to have to sort it out. Quietly, if possible. Perhaps Daniel already knew about it. Her brother-in-law hadn't been on the boat when it sank, but he had dealt with the aftermath. Right now, he was captaining the PS *Lisette*, a McCulloch Company steamer, while the *Mary B* languished at the boat builder's yard at Echuca, awaiting repairs.

Best she discover what she could from the Major though, because curiosity had now turned into suspicion.

"If you expect us to locate this item, we need to know what it was," she said.

"A small flat box, wrapped in oilskin."

"And does it have any identifying marks?"

"A red wax seal with my initials stamped. That should be sufficient to identify it."

"Possibly. And the contents?"

"You don't need to know that. You just have to locate the packet."

"But if by any chance the item and its wrapping have become separated?"

He pounced. "Have they?" he asked, his words sharp as a whip.

"I don't know!" Emma's suspicions multiplied tenfold. "The *Mary B* was under water for several weeks before it was salvaged, Major," she argued. "The cargo was retrieved much earlier, but the packet could have been seriously compromised. The box could have swollen and cracked, the wrapping come undone, the contents spilled. Anything could have happened to it." Including being lost in the mud at the bottom of the river.

The Major leaned back in his chair, considering. "I was sending a necklace to a jeweller in Echuca," he said at last.

"For what purpose?" she asked.

"That is of no concern of yours."

"I don't believe there was a packet at all," Emma scoffed.

"I would be very careful what I said if I were you," the Major warned.

"I am being careful. That is the point. You expect me to find an item I know nothing about. An item, clearly expensive, that you refuse to give details about. Little wonder I should be sceptical of the whole thing. Why the secrecy?"

"There was no secrecy on my part, madam," he shot back. "The necklace belongs to my wife, Lady

Annabel, of course. I was concerned some of her jewellery wasn't insured for its proper value, so while she was away in England, I decided to have this piece looked at and have it cleaned at the same time. I didn't have time to make the journey to Echuca myself, so I arranged the delivery with your husband."

Emma's skin prickled. She could hear her grandmother's adage that if it didn't make sense, it likely wasn't true. "Why wouldn't you send the necklace to Sydney for valuing? Why pay to have it taken across the border?"

"Why I choose to do something is no concern of yours. Your concern is to locate and return the item."

His words did nothing to dispel Emma's disbelief in his explanation. "It may still be on the *Mary B*, of course, but if not... you must consider the possibility that it has been lost in the river."

"In which case, I would have to sue you for its value," he blustered. "If you choose not to keep your bookwork up to date that is not my problem. Personally, madam, I do not believe you have no knowledge of it."

"Tch. I hardly think you could sue for something of which there is no record and only your word that it even existed. Be that as it may, I would gladly hand it to you if I had it, Major, I can assure you. Please, we both want the same thing. Perhaps as it is such a small packet, it has gotten mixed up with someone else's cargo in the confusion. A description of this piece of jewellery is essential to my mind."

The Major got to his feet and paced, hands in pockets, then stood facing out the window. Emma waited, wondering what he was about to reveal.

"It's an emerald necklace with a large drop and graduated stones set in gold on platinum," he said at last, still with his back to her.

Emma gave an involuntary gasp. "The Montague emeralds?" They were famous. Or infamous. A hereditary piece belonging to the Earl of Ellsworth's family. Lady Annabel wore the emeralds to the Governor's Ball each year. The event, and what the women wore, was reported in the newspapers in detail.

"You can't be serious – it's a valuable family heirloom. Irreplaceable."

"In which case, you had better find it, lady," said the Major, turning back to her, his eyes glittering. "Before my wife returns from England. If not, someone will pay for it. And I can assure you, it will not be me."

Emma found herself lost for words at the audacity of the man. Good emeralds were worth more than diamonds. The Montague emeralds had to be worth, what? Six, eight thousand pounds?

She rallied. "I don't believe the Montague emeralds were in the packet. No one in their right mind would pay hundreds of pounds in custom duties to send a piece of jewellery for valuation. This is pure extortion from top to bottom."

Floss barked as if in agreement as Emma got to her feet and started for the door.

"I'm going to call my father and expose this."

"Go right ahead," challenged the Major. "I'm sure he would be extremely interested to hear my side of the story. Seems to me there has been some nefarious goings-on. An arrangement I have recently discovered between a person in my employ and your husband to steal the emeralds. A clandestine meeting somewhere late at night. On the riverbank, perhaps. The necklace smuggled across the border and disposed of in Melbourne."

Shock at his words caused Emma to stop and turn to stare at him. A meeting, late at night, on the riverbank? A memory stirred. One night she had woken to find the *Mary B* stopped on the New South Wales side of the Murray somewhere near the junction with the Murrumbidgee.

She had looked out the window of the cabin she shared with Sam and seen two men on the bank by a fire, quickly doused. One of the men had been Sam. The other she had barely glimpsed. Sam had returned to the *Mary B,* and they had moved on.

When she asked him about it next day, he'd given some mumbled explanation about a fellow by a fire hailing them, wanting information about the nearest station where he might get work. 'Just some tramp,' he had said.

Emma thought it odd Sam would leave the *Mary B* to talk to a tramp when he could just as easily speak from the wheelhouse window. And why douse the fire? It had puzzled her at the time.

But now – had the other man been the Major? It was possible. The Barnaby property, Honey Hills, was only five miles up the Murrumbidgee from the junction. He could have seen her in the firelight that night, her face at the cabin window.

Major Barnaby nodded, a look of triumph on his red face. "Yes, you know what I'm talking about, don't you? So much for your husband not speaking to you on business matters. Not as honest as you pretend, are you?" Emma was too stunned to speak. "Of course, no one will believe I'd hand over thousands of pounds' worth of jewellery on a riverbank in the middle of the night, so you can forget that little idea."

"You can't expect to get away with such a story. You know it isn't true."

"Such a trite phrase, Mrs. Berry. I can get away with whatever I please. Your husband is not around to claim otherwise, and I can always find someone to confess to being party to the theft. Oh, they may escape justice, but that is of no concern. Now you have several choices. You can stop lying and hand the necklace back now, locate and return it if it truly has been misplaced, which I very much doubt, or pay for it. The latter wouldn't be too difficult, of course, if you have already disposed of it."

"Only a fool would steal such a well-known piece of jewellery. It would be recognised," Emma managed to say, her hand going to her chest, her breathing tight.

"Ah, but not if it was broken up into separate gems and sent overseas," the Major said, shaking a finger at her. "Very clever. And the scandal. How would your father feel about having his daughter involved, hmm? We'll see how respected the Haythorne name is then."

Emma's stomach churned; the gloating look on the Major's face showing he had got his message across.

"Enough talk," he snapped, taking up his hat. "I want the necklace returned or paid for. My wife returns in less than two months. If I don't get satisfaction, you know what to expect."

He marched past her, and Emma heard the front door slam, heard his tread, heavy on the verandah. A cold fear clutched at her heart. What had Sam gotten them into now?

# Chapter 2

*Out in the Cold*

SHE NEEDED space to think, clear her mind. There were going to be questions about the Major's visit. Out on the front verandah she stared down across the grey-green haze of the Mallee scrub disappearing into the northern distance. The Murray River flowed below, winding around the base of the plateau, the glimpses of its waters blue in the distance between the trees where it reflected the sky. She had spent months travelling that stretch of water on the *Mary B*, living with the feeling of motion and freedom, of being part of the world.

To the west and south her view was truncated by garden plantings and farm buildings, but the landscape was the same. It was, after all, one God-made country. It was only men who made life complicated with their silly rules and regulations, designating the river as a trade barrier between the colonies. Power and control. It was always about power and control. The Major was no different.

What was he up to? Whichever way she looked at it, it made no sense for him to pay the exorbitant custom duty to send the necklace for cleaning and valuation. And why had he contacted her about it and not Daniel? Did he think he could frighten her more easily? Well, he was right about that. And of course, the Haythornes were the ones who would come up with the money if the necklace couldn't be found. Her family had a reputation to protect.

"Emmaline? Where are you, child?" her grandmother called from the hall.

Emma managed with an effort to put a smile on her face as she went back into the homestead.

"Here I am, Grandmama."

Eleanor Haythorne, still tall and straight despite her growing years, looked at her, the green eyes, that Emma had inherited, assessing. Under that cool gaze Emma felt as if there were two of her, one part afraid and worried, the other behaving as if all were normal. Like a duck, paddling madly but serene on top. Though she preferred the idea of a swan.

"The chamomile soap is ready for shaping," her grandmother said. "Are you done here?"

"The Major has left," Emma replied.

Her father, hearing their voices, appeared from his study. "What did the Major want?"

Her father and grandmother looked at her expectantly.

"Oh, he was asking about the *Mary B*," Emma said, trying to answer calmly and without lying. Too much anyway. She crossed her fingers behind her back. "I think he's interested in getting involved in the river trade, at least that's what I gathered."

"He didn't come here especially for that, though, surely?"

"He didn't say, Father. I wouldn't have thought so. Anyway, I told him I would have to speak to Daniel. As far as I'm concerned, the *Mary B* isn't for sale."

"Hmph. It seems like a roundabout way of doing business if you ask me. Why didn't he have his Echuca agent handle the matter?"

Emma shook her head. "I've no idea, Father."

Eleanor Haythorne sniffed. Emma believed her grandmother had a built-in lie detector, something Emma had discovered at an early age. She steeled herself for more questions. Floss chose that moment to come out of the drawing room, tongue flicking around her mouth.

"What have you been up to?" Emma asked, bending down to the little dog and putting a hand under her chin. She glanced in at the tea table. The cake plate was upside down on the floor. "You're going to have one awful tummy ache if you've eaten all that cake," she scolded, relieved at the interruption as she went to investigate. Fortunately, most of the pieces of cake were trapped underneath the plate and Floss had gotten little more than crumbs.

"Don't be long, Emmaline," Eleanor called, as Emma cleaned up. She took the tea tray to the kitchen and headed to the stillroom. Steam was billowing from the washhouse as she passed.

"What's going on, Emma?" Janey Wirra popped her head out, dark damp hair sticking to her brown forehead. "That one angry mowmi leave here. I hear him shout at Jacky."

Emma pulled a face. She doubted the Major would appreciate being referred to as an old man, but it wasn't as bad as the names she was calling him in her head.

"He wanted something I couldn't give him," she said.

"Huh. All men the same. You give me a hand with the wash?"

"Grandmama needs me in the stillroom right now. Where's Sal?"

"Helpin' Nella with the kids. She been there all night."

Nella, married to overseer Jeff Brackett, was the daughter of housekeeper Lucy Wirra and Emma's grandfather, born before the Haythorne women arrived at the newly established Wirramilla station many years ago. Janey, Sal, and Jacky were Lucy's younger children by stockman Jimmy Bango. Emma had grown up with them all. Right now, Nella's three had chicken pox. Emma planned to lend a hand with them later.

The warmth generated by the stillroom fire was welcome when Emma entered the room located at the back of the washhouse. The air was sweet with the scents of chamomile, rosemary and half a dozen other aromatic herbs, bunches of which hung from the rafters. On the bench were several metal soap moulds and a large pan of warm Chamomile soap mixture.

Her grandmother was already at work, with several formed bars of soap on the bench. Floss was curled up on her cushion in the corner. She didn't even lift her head as Emma entered. Miffed at missing out on a sweet treat in the drawing room no doubt. How did you explain to a dog that it would have given her a stomachache – or worse?

Emma dipped her finger in a bowl of chamomile oil and ran it round the inside of a mould, then took a spoonful of soap mixture and pressed it in. Firming it into the corners, she smoothed the top with more chamomile oil before tipping the bar of soap out onto the bench. They worked in silence for several minutes, Emma relaxing into the repetitive work as her grandmother remained silent. Perhaps Eleanor was satisfied with her answers after all. Or perhaps not.

"What was that man doing here, Emmaline?"

Emma struggled to answer. She didn't want to talk about Sam, and she didn't want to answer questions about the Major's visit.

"Oh, some business he had with Sam. Daniel can sort it out," she said dismissively trying not to sound rude.

Her grandmother methodically filled another mould.

"Why did the Major speak to you, then? Why not Daniel?"

"I really don't know, Grandmama. Perhaps he hasn't been able to catch up with Daniel."

Another bar of soap landed on the bench. Emma tensed. She was sure her grandmother spaced her questions in order to build suspense and weaken her resolve.

"It must be something important to bring the Major all the way up here."

"If that was the only reason he was in the area," Emma said. The mould she was filling slipped from her oily fingers and skittered across the bench. She held her breath for a moment to calm herself before reaching for it.

"I see."

Emma was afraid she probably did, but thankfully her grandmother said no more. Could Eleanor be giving her some privacy on the matter of her late husband? She would be thankful for small mercies. Just so long as Eleanor didn't share her thoughts with her son before Emma had a chance to speak to Daniel.

<>◇<>

THE SOUND of sheep down in the shearing yards floated up over the farm buildings as Emma went across to the Brackett's cottage after lunch. Nella, a year older, was her friend and confidant, but even with her she didn't intend to discuss the Major's ultimatum. Nella soon dispelled that notion, however.

"What's going on?" she asked when she opened the door to Emma.

Emma thought she should be used to Nella sensing how she felt, but it still came as a shock most of the time when she did. Emma greeted her friend with a hug but didn't answer the question.

"I've brought some more olive oil." It was the best remedy for itchiness.

She could hear Billy crying, and Agnes Lilley, the blacksmith's wife, appeared from the children's bedroom with him in her arms. Elly, the eldest, ran to greet Emma, but Jack clung to Agnes' skirt, red-eyed and tired.

Nella, looking almost as tired as Jack, raised her eyebrows at Emma. "Why aren't you answering me?"

"Because you need to get some sleep. I'll help Agnes with the children for a few hours while you rest."

Nella tried hard to prevent the yawn that overtook her, but she wasn't fooling anyone. "All right, but then we're going to talk."

With Nella safely tucked away, Emma sat with the boys on the kitchen floor and had them draw pictures of animals while she told stories she had heard from Lucy. Billy's drawings were jagged lines scored across the paper with fingers that could barely hold the crayon. Jack's work wasn't much better, but the distraction worked while Agnes baked ginger snaps with Elly.

After eating some of the biscuits washed down with glasses of milk the children were settled for a nap, helped by the soothing effect of ginger and copiously anointed with olive oil. When Nella emerged, Agnes went home to the cottage next door for her own much needed rest.

"So, what is going on with you?" Nella asked over the inevitable cup of tea at the kitchen table. "Does this have anything to do with that man who was here earlier? I heard him shout at Jacky in the stable."

"Janey heard him too."

"So she said."

Of course, she had. Emma sometimes wondered if the Wirras communicated by some sort of thought process. Perhaps it was cultural. Nella gave her a look that clearly said stop stalling.

Emma sighed. "It seems Sam has left a problem."

Nella's brown eyes grew rounder as Emma told her what the Major had said, including his threat to claim Sam had received stolen goods. She didn't seem concerned with Sam's reputation, seeming more interested in what might happen to Wirramilla if the packet wasn't found.

"That's an awful lot of money," she said, when Emma had finished. "I can't even begin to imagine it. What does your father say?"

"I haven't told him."

"Why not?" There was an edge to her voice.

"You know how he felt about Sam, Nell," Emma said, wondering why she needed to explain herself. "I need to sort this out myself." If she could, but she wasn't about to say that out loud.

Nella put a hand on her arm and leaned toward her. "Em, you need to tell him. He could advise you on the best way to go. You can't handle this on your own. Not with so much at stake."

"I don't know enough about it yet, Nell."

Nella looked at her as if she were speaking a foreign language. "You're taking an awful lot on yourself, considering what could happen. You can't solve everything, Emma."

What was Nella getting so upset about? She should have been sympathising with her, offering comfort and ideas.

"I need to speak with Daniel," Emma explained. "He may know where the packet is. I don't want to cause alarm and worry for nothing."

"What if Daniel doesn't know where it is? And when are you going to ask him? He was here only a couple of days ago. He won't be back for weeks."

That was a slight exaggeration, but it was bothering Emma too. How long would the Major wait? Time was ticking away with Lady Annabel due to return in two months.

"You need to tell your father, so he can do something about it right now," Nella insisted. "Surely you can see that. Not that I think it's likely," she all but muttered, looking away.

"What's that supposed to mean?"

"You didn't listen when I said you were making a mistake marrying Sam and now see where it's got us. I don't know why I should think you'd listen to me this time."

"When did you tell me I was making a mistake? I don't recall you saying anything like that."

"You had stars in your eyes. You thought you'd found the answer to that promise with Matty Macdonald. And Sam was charming, I'll give you that. But you weren't listening, like I said."

Emma stared at her. "So, this is all my fault because I married him?"

"Well?" Nella's teacup met the saucer with a definite clink. "You're not perfect, Emma. You don't always get it right."

"And you do?" It was a childish response, Emma knew, but she already knew this was her fault for marrying Sam Berry. She needed Nella to tell her it was all right, everyone makes mistakes, and then they would talk over how to fix it.

But Nella stood abruptly, gathering up both her cup and Emma's and carrying them to the wash bowl without checking to see if Emma had finished. Which she hadn't.

"Wirramilla is my home too, remember," Nella said turning back to Emma, her face taut. "This place matters to me just as much as it does you. Just because my name isn't Haythorne doesn't mean I don't know who my father is."

"Don't you mean was?"

Nella gasped, her hand going to her mouth. Emma wanted to cut off her tongue as soon as the words were out. Her grandfather had died seven years earlier. She didn't know if he had ever openly acknowledged Nella as his daughter. It was one of those things known but never mentioned.

"Nell... I'm sorry, I didn't mean…" But Nella had walked out.

What on earth had just happened? They didn't argue. Not like this. Nella's reaction was out of proportion. Where did that come from? Emma heard one of the children wake, disturbing the other two, and heard Nella's voice.

When she didn't come back to the kitchen, Emma went to find her only to discover the cottage was empty. Nella had quietly taken the children out the back door. When Emma let herself out at the front, she saw them on their way down to the river, Nella carrying Billy and the older two running along in front.

Later that day the PS *Consul* called in, delivering supplies from John Egge's store thirty miles down-river at Wentworth. The delivery should have lifted Emma's spirits, giving the usual feeling of plenty when the storeroom was well stocked, but it didn't have that effect today. Not even the thought of one of Lucy's fruit cakes made with the fresh supply of dried fruits helped ease the miserable ache in the pit of her stomach.

The *Consul* also collected orders for her grand-mother's herbal remedies which would be delivered on the journey upriver. That required restocking the depleted shelves with the most popular remedies and kept Emma busy in the stillroom.

She tried twice to see Nella, but both times Agnes told her Nella was resting, the children were doing well, and thanks very much, but her help wasn't needed right now.

# Chapter 3

## *It's Not All Cricket*

"THEY'RE HERE," Sal announced, rushing around to the back of the homestead to alert Emma.

"Already?" Emma thrust the Grevillea blooms she had been gathering into Sal's arms and hurried to wash her hands and tidy her hair.

The mob from neighbouring Nettifield, two hours ride downriver, were coming for lunch and a cricket match. It was the first such event arranged between the two stations since Margaret Macdonald's death two years before, although there had been numerous individual visits over the time.

Emma hurried to the stable to greet their guest. Her father was already there welcoming George Macdonald and Matty and Jim, as Jacky Wirra attended to their horses. She was just in time to see Thomas Quilp lift Bea from her side-saddle, smiling at her as she melted into his arms. Envy and longing coursed through Emma's body. It was moments like these that she really missed Sam, but she was happy for her friend.

Thomas was a man of few words but a definite presence. Big and burly with a bushy black beard and a mouth made for smiling. Well, he had something to smile about with Bea by his side.

"How lovely to see you," Emma said, hugging Bea and smiling up at Thomas who stood protectively by her friend's side. Even at Emma's five foot seven he towered over her, and Bea was half a head shorter than her, petite and pixie faced.

Emma greeted the Macdonald men in turn, giving them each her hand. The Nettifield cart rolled up at that moment, packed with station hands, several accompanying it on horseback. Tillie, the little Irish maid, made a beeline for the kitchen, her basket full of foodstuff, while Jeff Brackett herded the station hands to the men's quarters and the pig on a spit that was waiting for them.

Emma took Bea off to her room to freshen up, leaving the Macdonald men to gather on the front verandah with her father and grandmother, Janey in attendance serving tea and cake. Her mother would still be in the kitchen harrying Lucy or rearranging the flowers or the napkins on the dining table. She would have been out on the verandah socialising if Margaret were still alive.

"So, when are you and Thomas going to announce your engagement?" Emma asked, as Bea washed the dust from her hands and face. "He has asked you, hasn't he?"

Bea pulled a face. "Yes."

"So?"

"He wants to take up some land of his own."

"That's wonderful, Bea. Your own place."

"How can I leave Dad and the boys, Emma?" Bea reached for the clothes brush.

"Here," said Emma, taking the brush from her. She busied herself at the back of Bea's skirt. "You can't spend your life playing housekeeper to the men in your family, Bea. You have your own life to live."

"Dad expects me to."

"Hmm?" Emma felt a pang of annoyance at George Macdonald, not for the first time. Perhaps life would have been different if Bea had had her time at Miss Eunice Marshall's School for Young Ladies. It might have given her the confidence to be more assertive, but George liked his womenfolk compliant. "Has your father said so, in as many words?"

"No, but..."

"There you are, then. Anyway, what about Matty? You told me ages back he was courting Dotty Keogh. When he marries Dotty, she'll want to take over the house and that will solve your problem. You'll be free then. There, that's better." She put the brush down on the dresser. Only then did she see Bea's face. "What is it?"

"Matty hasn't seen Dotty for some time. I think something must have happened. Oh, Emma, I was hoping it would work out the way you said, but now…I don't know."

A little seed of concern took root in Emma's mind. "How long ago?" she asked.

"What, since he's seen her?" Emma nodded. "A couple of months. And he used to ride to Wentworth almost every week before that."

Surely, he wasn't thinking… "Have you spoken to him about it?"

"I did ask once, but he said it wasn't the right time, and I've never asked again."

Not the right time to talk about it, or the right time for committing to Dotty because of that old promise?

"I might speak to him. See what he has to say," Emma told her friend, not wanting to make it sound as important as she thought it might be.

Bea, who didn't know about the promise, just shrugged.

AFTER LUNCH, Emma discovered she didn't have to worry about finding a moment to speak to Matty. He asked her to take a walk with him in the garden.

"I'm looking forward to this cricket match," he said as they wandered across the lawn to the arbour. "It's been a while."

"It has. I'm glad to see your dad is getting out and about more." It wasn't just Margaret's death George was recovering from. Losing a brother and having a sister-in-law charged with his murder would knock anyone's faith in life.

"Hmm." Matty rubbed his eye. "Em, I wanted to clear something with you."

Emma didn't see any point in beating about the bush. "About that old promise we made, you mean?" she responded idly plucking a dead leaf off the hibiscus as they passed.

Matty looked at her sharply. "You've been thinking about that too, then?"

"I hadn't been, until I spoke to Bea."

"I didn't know you'd told her. She hasn't said anything."

"Not about us. She was telling me about you and Dotty Keogh."

"There's nothing in that, Emma," Matty hastened to assure her, clearly not understanding her thoughts on the matter.

They had reached the arbour. Emma brushed off a seat with her hand and sat, looking out at the garden. Spring was her favourite time of year with flowers in the garden and the bush brightening the surroundings with bursts of new green. Unless, of course, you were handed a huge bouquet of wildflowers and a marriage proposal as Matty had done almost ten years ago.

"You know Thomas wants to take up land of his own and marry Bea, don't you?" Emma said. "But she won't leave Nettifield until there is another woman there to take over the household. She was hoping that would be Dotty." Could she make it any plainer?

"This isn't about Bea or, or Dotty," Matty said, as if he had rehearsed it and couldn't, or wouldn't, detour from the script. "We agreed, if neither of us were married in ten years – and you aren't married now – so I'm keeping to our promise."

"But I did marry."

"You know how sorry I am about Sam."

More than you are prepared to admit, perhaps? Emma looked up at him. He seemed just as usual, his grey eyes studying her with serious intent, his blonde hair a little too long around his ears. It would be a safe option, marrying Matty. He wouldn't make stupid decisions based on ego, wouldn't be reckless. Perhaps there was some safety in liking rather than loving. Loving someone hadn't ensured the best choice in the past.

She tried to picture herself taking over the Nettifield household, doing the same things day after day, dealing daily with George, but the image kept slipping away. And their private moments... She shivered. No. It simply wouldn't work.

"Em?"

Emma nodded slowly. "We were still playing at life when we made that promise all those years ago, Matty. Caught up in a pretty moment on a lovely spring day. I was only seventeen and you, not much older. We're not those innocent children anymore."

"I know, but..."

"Matty, I've married and lost a child." Her voice hitched on the last word, and he caught her hand, sympathy in his gaze. "And you've lost your mother," she said, giving his hand a gentle squeeze, "not to mention that dreadful business with your aunt and uncle. Her voice softened. "And as I've already mentioned, you've been seeing Dotty Keogh."

Matty flushed. "Not recently I haven't. I thought it was all right because you were married, you know. I thought that was the end of it."

"It was all right, Matty," Emma assured him. "It still is. You'll be able to pick up with Dotty again, won't you?" What reason had he given for not seeing her? Heaven, she hoped her name hadn't come into it. The poor girl would feel like second best choice if she knew.

"If you're sure, Em. I thought everything was settled between us else I never would have called on her."

"They are settled, and the sooner you see Dotty again the sooner both you and Bea will be settled too. I can't wait to see that."

"I don't like to see you unhappy, Em."

Emma noticed he wasn't denying his feelings for the girl. "I know, dear, but it isn't your job to fix it." Matty gave a heartfelt sigh. "I'm not sure I ever will marry again," she told him." It was how she felt right now and saying it might help Matty move on.

"If you need more time, I'd understand," he said.

"No, Matty."

"You're not really intending to be alone for the rest of your life though, are you? I mean, there must be heaps of fellows who'd jump at the chance of having a great girl like you."

"Ah, but would I want them, now?" Emma responded lightly.

"Old Sam meant that much to you?" Emma didn't reply and let Matty come to his own conclusion. "That's settled then, old girl, is it?"

"Yes, Matty. Finally, and forever settled. You go and marry your Dotty. She seems like a lovely young lady, and I wish you joy of it with all my heart."

Emma was glad to see the look of relief that he couldn't quite hide. She hadn't wanted to break his heart two years ago, and she was glad she wasn't doing so now. It did leave her feeling a little bereft though, a part of her past firmly closed off.

EVERYONE HAD gathered at the back paddock below the plateau. The playing field was ready, the grass scythed, and a pitch rolled. Benches scavenged from around the farm buildings had been cleaned off and set along one side of the ground for seating. With the teams selected, blacksmith Bert Lilley as umpire and Eleanor recording the score, the game got under way.

The Haythorne team batted first, and Emma was caught out on the second of George Macdonald's slow balls she faced. He wasn't above jeering her off the field with a comment on lady batters, which irked. She was forced to sit out and join the spectators, everyone vocal with much cheering and advice. She tried to congratulate Nella for her score of twelve runs when she came off the field, but Nella acted as if she hadn't heard.

A lavish afternoon tea was served up after the first innings. Lucy made the most of it, showing off her kitchen talents with curried egg sandwiches on fresh baked bread, and cream filled jam sponges, washed down with lashings of tea.

When the Haythorne team took to the field, Emma was determined to give George Macdonald a taste of his own bowling medicine. She was annoyed at him, too, if he really was keeping Bea from getting on with her life.

She had her father give her the ball when George took his place at the crease. He put her medium paced balls out to the boundary on her first over and the team was all for taking her off, but she argued for another over.

"I'm just getting my eye in. I'm sure I can take him given the chance."

"Keep the runs down," her father instructed.

She wasn't as successful at that but was rewarded for her confidence on the fifth ball when he snicked it and Janey's man, Abe, took a flying catch. She mentally thanked her grandfather for tutoring her. He'd considered cricket a healthy sport for women, popular as it was in England.

At the final tally, George Macdonald's team was the winner by twenty-three runs, but to Emma it had been a highly satisfactory game and a lot of fun, something she had needed to take her mind off her worries. For parts of the day at least she had been able to forget about Major Barnaby and her disagreement with Nella.

Matty put an arm around her shoulder and gave her a sideways hug. "You still have it, Em," he congratulated her. He was looking relaxed and happy, Emma noted.

"You made the best score," she replied, smiling up at him, glad they were still friends. "I must thank you all for a very pleasant day."

Still smiling, Emma looked past Matty – straight at the glowering face of Daniel Berry. Her smile faltered under his glare.

"This is the way you mourn my brother, is it?" Daniel greeted her coldly.

# Chapter 4

*Daniel Vents His Displeasure*

MATTY REMOVED his arm from her shoulder and took a step forward. Emma grabbed the back of his jacket and tugged before he had a chance to speak. She didn't need his protection. Daniel ignored him, continuing to glare at Emma.

"That is hardly reasonable, Daniel," she responded, trying to keep down the surge of annoyance his words induced. "You go about your own life as usual."

"I don't have much choice. I don't have this," he said, with a sweep of his hand. He turned to walk away.

Of course, propriety demanded women shut themselves up and mourn while men got on with life, but it wasn't as if she were gallivanting about town. This was her home, and she wasn't about to shun her friends because she was in mourning. One could carry sadness in their heart without pouring it out on others. Daniel would be even more annoyed if he knew she and Matty had been discussing marriage, but she needed to get him to listen, or none of them would have all this, as he called it. It could all go to pay off the Major.

"I need to speak to you," she said, hurrying after him. He didn't break stride. "It's about Sam."

Daniel turned to say something, seemingly dismissive by his expression, but stopped when he saw her face. Emma's heart did a flip. He and Sam had been so alike, tall and well-built, good-looking in a rugged way, though not so alike in personality. She moved closer to him so she wouldn't have to speak too loudly.

"I had a visit from Major Barnaby of Honey Hills, on the Bidgee," she said urgently. "He claims Sam was carrying something for him that wasn't on the cargo list." She paused, the disquieting thought that Daniel may have been involved in this thing with Sam entering her mind for the first time. Where would that leave her and her family? Daniel frowned, not comprehending. "It's missing, Daniel, and we've no record of it for the insurance. He's demanding we find it or pay for it."

"What was it?"

"Something extremely valuable," Emma said looking around, not wanting anyone to overhear. The hands from both stations had started a rematch while her older family members were making their way up to the homestead. Matty was watching her, and Thomas and Bea stood by waiting. Bea gave her a questioning look. Emma turned back to Daniel. "I have to deal with our guests. Can we talk on the *Lisette* when they've gone?"

"I can't wait around, Emma. I have a timetable to keep to, you know that."

Emma did know. Every hour had to be accounted for in the logbook. Time was money on the river, and the Company expected its captains to adhere to that philosophy. Daniel must hate not having his own boat under his feet and control of his own life.

"Bea," Emma called, "I'm just going to see Captain Berry back to his boat. I'll be with you shortly."

Bea acknowledged her with a lift of the hand and started on up with Matty and Thomas. She saw Matty give a glance back as if unsure about letting her go on with Daniel.

"Let's walk slowly and talk as we go." She could give Daniel the gist of the story in minutes, as they angled their way up to the plateau behind the cottages.

"You saw them meet on the riverbank?" Daniel asked, interrupting her as she told him about Sam meeting the Major.

"I saw Sam with someone, and the Major intimated he was the one."

"Go on."

"So, according to the Major, he gave Sam this packet containing an item of jewellery that he was to deliver to a jeweller in Echuca for valuation and cleaning. He claims he gave Sam the money for the customs duty, but Sam didn't list the packet as cargo."

"This sounds like a lot of flim-flam to me," Daniel said. "Did you ever see this packet?"

"No, I didn't know anything about it until the Major called in and spoke to me."

"So, we only have Barnaby's word that it even exists."

Emma was half afraid of that herself. Was Major Barnaby trying some elaborate extortion? There had to be some truth in it because he'd known about the meeting on the riverbank. Unless the story about Sam receiving the necklace as stolen goods was the true one and the Major had uncovered the story at his end. No, no, she'd heard the Major tell that story. It was clearly made up, his backup story for Lady Eleanor if the necklace wasn't found, and a way to ensure her family paid.

"What is he claiming this piece of jewellery is worth, exactly?" Daniel asked.

Emma told him. Daniel stopped and stared, open mouthed.

"How much?"

"It doesn't get any better with repetition, Daniel."

"Are you sure you heard it right?"

"If the Montague emeralds were in the packet, as the Major claims, that is what they are worth according to all the newspaper reports I've ever read."

Daniel rubbed his head and muttered a few curses under his breath as he walked on. Emma had to hustle to keep up with him. She was already feeling the effects of the cricket game.

"There's a place in the wheelhouse where we keep small valuables," Daniel said. "That's where Sam would have hid... where he would have put it for safe keeping."

Small valuables. That was the last thing Emma would call the Montague emeralds. And why had Daniel corrected himself? He had almost said hidden. Had they been in the habit of smuggling small items? Is that why the Major knew who to contact? That made sense.

And instead of giving Sam hundreds of dollars for the customs duty, as he claimed, the Major would have paid him something much less to smuggle the packet. Sam would have thought it all a lark, meeting on the riverbank in the middle of the night, hiding the item, sneaking it off the boat at Echuca. He liked to have money in his pocket, too.

They had reached the bridge at Sheep Wash Creek. The *Lisette* was steaming gently at the riverbank on the other side, the crew lounging on the deck, the barge *Oxley* pulled in alongside. Emma gave the crew members a wave, Shorty Mason saluting her, and Blue Higgins lifting a hand in acknowledgement. She didn't know them well. They had been part and parcel of the *Lisette* when Daniel was taken on by the Company as her Captain. The old crew of the *Mary B* had taken up other jobs, not all of it on the river. Some people took an accident like the one to the *Mary B* as a warning.

Daniel turned to Emma. "I'll stop in at the boatyard when I get to Echuca and retrieve the packet. It'll be there on the *Mary B*. I'll sort it out."

"I'm going with you to Echuca," Emma said. "When you come by on your way back upriver. I need..."

"That won't be necessary."

"Yes, it is, Daniel." Hadn't she explained it well enough for him to understand? She'd had to be brief.

"Haven't you done enough, already?" Daniel all but snarled.

"What?" Emma's head went back as if she'd been slapped.

"I don't suppose it's even occurred to you that you could be responsible for this mess?" Emma stared at him. What in heaven...? "You with your privileged upbringing. How do you think Sam felt not being able to provide that kind of life for you? If he was trying to do extra work on the side, it was to create a future for you and the child."

"Sam thought I wanted something better?" Emma managed to say through a throat suddenly dry. She'd been happy with life on the *Mary B* so long as she was sharing it with Sam. The injustice of Daniel's comments rankled. "I never asked for anything, Daniel. If Sam felt that way, it was about what he wanted." It would have been about his pride, how he saw himself, not about her.

"He felt you were used to better," Daniel insisted, "the daughter of a squatter, educated, with servants, who never had to lift a hand herself."

"You have no idea what you are talking about." Emma almost laughed at such a ridiculous statement. "I refuse to take responsibility for Sam's behaviour. If he had told me what he was planning I would have counselled him against it. Though whether he would have listened is another matter. He didn't listen when I asked him not to race Hargreaves."

"We were doing fine until you came along," Daniel said stubbornly, turning away. "And now I don't even have my own boat."

Emma drew in a quick gasp of air. So that's what was irking him. She stared after him as he walked away to the *Lisette*. She'd been as surprised as Daniel when they discovered Sam had signed over his half share of the *Mary B* to her shortly after their marriage, the share Daniel had given him in an effort to instill a sense of responsibility and provide a stable future.

Emma had taken the gift as acknowledgement of Sam's love, but more recently she had begun to wonder if he'd done it as insurance, because he really hadn't wanted the responsibility and didn't trust himself with it. Had he, even then, been thinking that one day he might want to walk away? From her and the *Mary B*?

She wrapped her arms around herself, suddenly chilled, her steps slowing as she made her way back to the homestead and their guests. Had Sam regretted their marriage after all? A movement caused her to look up. Jacky Wirra had stepped out the stable door.

"You all right, Em?"

"Yes, Jacky, thanks," she told him, swiping her hands across her face. "Just feeling a little chill. Should have grabbed a shawl after we finished playing."

"Go in 'n warm up," he instructed.

"Yes, moondoondi," she said, picking up on an old joke as she called him elder brother. Jacky was a few years younger, but he had always been protective, treating her the same as his sisters. He looked just like his father, regardless of Lucy's own half-white parentage, whoever her father had been.

There weren't so many of his people left now. The smallpox epidemic of the eighteen-fifties had devastated the Murray River blacks. It was little short of a miracle the Wirras had survived. Jimmy Bango had not, preferring to keep in contact with his people than remain isolated.

Jacky nodded but didn't smile. He had seen the tears. This was one of those times she wished her life was more private, but then you wouldn't have people caring about you, she supposed.

So, Daniel resented her half ownership of 'his' boat. She could understand his feelings, but it gave her another reason now for going to Echuca when he returned. The last time she had seen the *Mary B* it had been sinking beneath the waters of the Murray. She needed to get the boat back on the river for both their sakes. Nothing would be mended between them until that was done and some normality returned, and she had as much right to deal with the matter as he did. Emma didn't understand why it was taking so long for the boat to be repaired. It had been insured.

The other reason she needed to go to Echuca was to make sure the necklace was returned to the Major before Lady Annabel returned. Emma didn't trust the man, and it was making her uneasy.

# Chapter 5

## *Emma takes Matters in Hand*

"I DON'T BELIEVE IT. How could he do this?" It was mid-morning on the second day after Daniel's visit. Emma stood in front of the stillroom, hands on hips, with a clear view of the river, as the *Lisette* steamed by without so much as a whistle.

"Who was it, Emmaline?" her grandmother asked from inside the stillroom, the chug-chug of the steam engine having alerted them both to a passing vessel.

"The *Lisette*."

"Daniel?" Eleanor joined her outside, shading her eyes. "Why hasn't he stopped?"

"Why indeed," Emma muttered.

Her bag was packed in readiness, hidden under her bed to avoid questions from Sal or Janey until she was about to leave. All she waited for was for Daniel to call in on his way back upriver from Wentworth. At least that had been her plan. Daniel obviously had other ideas. Well, if he thought this would stop her, he had another thing coming. His wasn't the only boat on the river.

"I'll be back in a minute," she told her grand-mother and strode off, hurrying down across Sheep Wash Creek and past the landing on the lower level. At a large red gum, right on the edge of the bank, she unhooked a rope and hand over hand, sent a white cloth skimming along to the end of the branch, where it fluttered high above the water. The flag would signal a boat going upriver that it needed to call in. Such a signal was never ignored. It could be a matter of life or death.

That was the easy part. Now she had to explain to her family why she was going to Echuca. And why she wasn't travelling with Daniel. It couldn't wait either, as she had no idea how soon another boat would be by. Emma caught up with her grandmother as Eleanor was heading in for morning tea.

"What is going on, Emmaline?" Eleanor asked, as Emma hooked an arm in hers. "Why didn't Daniel call in?"

"He might be running behind schedule," Emma said, hoping to avoid further questions. "And he was here only two days ago."

"But you were expecting him back, weren't you? You've been like a cat on a hot tin roof all morning, listening for every little sound."

"I was surprised," Emma admitted. "I told him I wanted to go to Echuca to check up on the *Mary B.*"

"So why would he not call in for you?" She gave Emma a shrewd look. "Does this have anything to do with Major Barnaby's visit?"

They had stopped on the back verandah. Emma looked up at the iron roof, fighting back the lump that appeared unbidden in her throat as she relived Daniel's accusation.

"Daniel says the accident is all my fault. He says anything Sam was doing was for me and… our future. He says Sam shouldn't have married me. Which is pretty much what everyone else in my family thinks, isn't it?" She looked back at her grandmother, daring her to disagree.

What Eleanor said instead caused Emma's eyes to open wide.

"Men! They can never accept responsibility for their own actions. And if there's a woman involved you can be sure the blame will fall on her. It's like a conspiracy among them. Honestly, it makes my blood boil sometimes."

"Grandmama?" Emma didn't remember when she'd heard her grandmother sound so fierce. Did this attitude have anything to do with her late husband and Lucy? Had her grandmother not been as accepting of that situation as she made out?

"It was Daniel Berry's choice to leave the *Mary B* in his brother's hands, Emmaline. And Sam Berry's choice to race another boat. Don't let anyone convince you otherwise." She reached across and squeezed Emma's hand where it rested on her arm.

"Who put the boat signal out?" Edward Haythorne asked, coming up behind them. "Is anything wrong?"

Emma opened her mouth to speak but her grandmother got in first.

"Emma has to go to Echuca and see about the *Mary B*," Eleanor replied in a voice that brooked no argument, "and do some shopping for me."

Feeling more than a little stunned but grateful at her grandmother's determined support, Emma held the back door for them to enter. Her mother, unsurprisingly, was not as supportive when she heard Emma's plans.

"You can't possibly go to Echuca on your own. What will people think?" Rose asked, pausing in stirring her tea.

"What people, Mother?" It had always been the best answer to that complaint.

"Edward?" Rose Haythorne appealed to her husband.

"What's this about seeing to the *Mary B*?" he wanted to know. "That's Daniel's responsibility, surely."

"Daniel has his work to do," Emma replied, "and he is only in Echuca for a few days at a time before he has to take another trip downriver. He hasn't time to chase up the boatyard. He didn't even call in this morning, he's so busy," she added, and then wished she hadn't as her mother picked up on it immediately.

"He's been by already?" Rose asked. "Why didn't you arrange to go with him instead of travelling with strangers? At least Daniel is family."

"Daniel, like most men, doesn't think a woman can do something he can't," Eleanor said tartly.

Edward gave his mother a wry look, but Rose had no answer to her mother-in-law's comment. She couldn't very well disagree with it. Emma decided she needed to say a little more in the interest of leaving on good terms with her parents.

"The *Mary B* is half mine," she reminded them, "and it just seems like good business to get involved. The boat's been sitting there for several months already. I don't want it rotting away."

"You should take Sal or Janey with you," Rose persisted, though half-heartedly.

"You need them here, Mother," she said. Someone looking over her shoulder and querying what she was doing was the last thing Emma needed. "I'll see Daniel when I get to Echuca, and I'll write and let you know I've arrived safely."

"She'll probably be delivering the letter herself," Edward commented to his wife, no doubt expecting her speedy return with Daniel after failing to achieve anything. "I don't like the idea of your travelling alone, any more than your mother does," he said to Emma, "but the steamers are safe enough, and as you say, Daniel will be at the other end. If you need any help with anything you just have to call on Tuckett."

"Thank you, Father." If only calling on her father's agent could locate the Montague emeralds.

EARLY NEXT MORNING, Emma was sitting in the bow on the lower deck of the PS *Orion* enjoying the changing scenery and the sense of movement. She felt herself properly relaxing for the first time in a week. She was on her way now, and there was nothing she could do until she reached Echuca.

High above her in the wheelhouse, Captain Dickens was marking his course by the long linen charts unrolled along the shelf in front of the wheel. All forms of obstacles and dangers – rocks, snags, sandbanks, shallow reaches, and sharp bends – were shown on the hand-drawn charts, as well as homesteads and woolsheds and other habitations.

The sound of a man's voice drifted down to her. Though unable to make out any words, she knew one of the crew members would be standing at the wheelhouse door talking to the captain, keeping him company and available in case an extra pair of hands were needed on the wheel.

Emma had company of her own, a woman in her thirties who had introduced herself as Maureen Riley. Mrs. Riley had been visiting family in Adelaide and was now on her way home to Riley's Hotel located just past the Murrumbidgee junction. Emma knew the place but hadn't met the woman before. Hotels were not a place she frequented after all. The pair chatted about life and families and inconsequential things as they shared a pot of tea.

The countryside they were passing through comprised of high red cliffs on one side and low-lying swamps on the other, alternating from one side of the river to the other at various points. Flocks of ducks – black, grey, teal – rose ahead of the boat, their wings slapping the water. Ibis and water hens waded in the shallow swamps.

Emma saw the 768-mile tree as the *Orion* rounded a bend. They didn't have as far as that to travel. The mile trees marked the distance between Wentworth and Albury, but their destination, Echuca, was still some four hundred and sixty miles off.

Ahead of them, they could just make out a paddle steamer moored below the cliff at Bingallion Station on the New South Wales side of the river. As they drew closer, they could see the crew of the boat were busy taking on the two-hundred-pound wool bales using a rope and pulley to lower them to the barge one at a time.

"I'm always afraid the rope will break when I see that, and drop the bale on someone's head," Maureen Riley said with a gay laugh.

Emma barely heard her. The moored boat was the *Lisette* and staring across at her over the intervening yards of water was Daniel. Emma couldn't resist waving. Daniel didn't wave back.

"Do you know him?" Mrs. Riley asked.

"Vaguely," Emma replied, feeling a trifle smug. It would be one in his eye if she reached Echuca before him. "Would you like some more tea, Mrs. Riley?"

"I would, Mrs. Berry. Why don't we go see what sweet treat the cook might have to go with it?"

"An excellent idea, even if it's only store-bought biscuits."

TWO DAYS LATER Emma was on her own again when the *Orion* pulled in at Sorenson's woodpile, one of a series of stops made every day to take on wood. Most times the wood was available from the piles set out by the wood cutters, but occasionally the crew had to cut it themselves from the surrounding bush. It was at Sorensons where the *Mary B* had met up with Captain Hargreaves and his stern wheeler *Invincible* on the day of the accident.

Emma decided to stretch her legs while the crew loaded up the three or four tons of wood they needed. She put several humbugs in her pocket along with a small knife she kept for collecting plants and let Captain Dickens know she was stepping off for a few minutes.

"Don't you wander too far," he cautioned. "Could be blacks around about."

Emma assured him she wouldn't, and he'd sound the whistle if she were late back. The woodcutter's shanty was deserted, the two men who lived there out at work. Emma wandered among the trees. She noticed a small green shoot poking through the leaf litter in a patch of sunshine and recognised it as a Murray lily, *Crinum flaccidum*. If she dug it out carefully, she could pot it later and set it out on the verandah at home. It bore flamboyant orange-red flowers. She could keep the bulb in a moist bag until then.

As she stood, plant in hand, she caught a movement in the bush nearby. She kept still and watched. It could have been an animal, a wallaby perhaps, but she suddenly felt vulnerable. The crew on the *Orion* wouldn't hear her over their own noise if she shouted. She gripped her knife tightly. Perhaps she had imagined it but even the birds were silent.

A female voice called from a little way off and a small dark head popped out from behind the tree where she thought she'd seen the movement. Large brown eyes surveyed her curiously before a body followed from its hiding place.

The boy was about three years old and wore a possum skin cloak reaching his knees. Almost immediately a young woman appeared from the trees behind, similarly dressed in a cloak, but worn this time over a print cotton dress. She was carrying a baby in a bag slung across her back. An older woman joined her. They surveyed Emma silently. Were any of their men nearby? They were probably wondering the same of her.

There was something familiar about the younger woman. One of the women in the group that day had been with child, and they were only a few miles from the place where the accident had occurred. Did they recognise her? Did they remember the shattered riverboat, the white man whose body their men pulled from the river?

She didn't know how much English they spoke, and she wasn't sure if any of the words she knew had the same meaning here. There seemed to be a different dialect every fifty miles or so along the river. She dropped the knife into her pocket where it would be out of sight, but easy to reach if needed.

"I've been gathering," she said, holding out the lily bulb. The women came closer, and Emma saw the scars of smallpox on the older woman's face. The boy reached up for the bulb.

"Wadi," the older woman warned, her voice husky. The boy withdrew his hand. Emma knew the bulb wasn't edible. She remembered the humbugs in her pocket. She took out two, popping one in her mouth and offering another to the child, indicating he suck it.

Her facial contortions drew laughter from the women which increased when the child copied her. The younger woman insisted on trying the humbug for herself and the child was forced to give it up. It was passed between the two women who mimicked Emma amid much glee. Emma gave the child another humbug when it became clear he wasn't getting back the first one. It was time she left before anyone else arrived drawn by the sound of their voices. She was out of humbugs.

"I must go," she said, turning away with a smile and a wave of her hand. A whistle sounded from the river. The child copied it in similar tone as Emma began to walk quickly back. She hadn't meant to be away for so long. The child trotted beside her and the women followed. They reached the edge of the cleared area at the woodpile and stopped.

Emma stared. The *Lisette* had arrived. Daniel had caught up with them. Emma turned back to her companions but discovered they had silently disappeared. The crew of the *Orion* were still loading wood, passing the cut logs up the boarding plank in a chain of hands. She watched as Daniel made his way to the *Orion* and spoke to Captain Dickens.

Emma was too far off to hear what was being said, but she saw Captain Dickens summon a crew member and send him off on an errand. Then they both turned and looked at her. Feeling foolish and annoyed under their gaze she crossed the open space to the *Orion*.

"You should have let me know you were planning to travel," Daniel said smoothly. "I would have picked you up on my way by."

"You obviously have a very poor memory, Daniel," Emma responded, refusing to play. "It hardly matters. One boat is as good as another. Captain Dickens is providing a particularly good service."

"I have no doubt, but I can take you the rest of the way. Thanks, Tom."

The crew member had handed Emma's bag to Captain Dickens, who in turn handed it down to Daniel. Daniel touched his cap in farewell and turned back to the *Lisette*.

Emma stood and stared after him for a moment then, fuming, realised she had no choice but to follow her bag. To add insult to injury she was sure Captain Dickens had winked at Daniel.

Without another word to her, Daniel took her bag up to a cabin on the *Lisette*'s upper deck and placed it on the bed. Then he walked out again, ignoring her. Emma went into the cabin and dropped down beside her bag, wondering if she had just been kidnapped, and why.

# Chapter 6

## *Kidnapped*

EMMA'S INCREDULITY at Daniel's behaviour mounted. It would be all along the river in no time how Daniel Berry had hauled his sister-in-law off the PS *Orion* as if she were a runaway child.

She felt the *Lisette* bump gently along the edge of the bank as it moved to take the place beside the woodpile that the *Orion* had now vacated. Below, Shorty Mason's baritone rose in a rendition of 'Hi Ho and Up She Rises' as the *Lisette*'s crew began loading the wood. The lively tune did nothing to allay her growing fury.

Steps sounded on the upper deck and Daniel appeared in the cabin doorway. He stopped, hands on hips. His pose brought Emma to her feet in a flash, chin up.

"What are you now? My jailer?" He looked momentarily taken aback at the bite in her words. "You have no right to treat me in this cavalier fashion. It's none of your business what I choose to do."

"Of course it's my business. You're my brother's widow. I have a responsibility..."

"To do what? Treat me as a piece of baggage?"

Daniel glared at her. "Sam's been gone barely four months and here you are gallivanting about on your own, associating with lord knows who. I can't believe your father let you do this. It isn't proper behaviour for a newly widowed woman, Emma."

"I don't need reminding how long ago my husband died," Emma replied, her voice suddenly shaky. She steadied herself with an effort. "And if you're going to talk about what's right and proper, you might want to consider what Sam was doing, smuggling that necklace for Major Barnaby. It's his improper behaviour that's forced me to make this journey."

"I don't know that he was smuggling anything," Daniel countered, "and I told you I would find the thing on the *Mary B*. You don't need to involve yourself."

"After you've blamed it all on me? I don't have any choice but to be involved. Stop pushing me aside, Daniel. It's more than a little annoying."

"When I find this packet on the *Mary B*," Daniel replied with deceptive calm, his words clipped, "and deliver it to wherever it was meant to go, I will deliver you back home and that will be the end of it."

Emma's fingers curled into her palms, nails biting. She had an urgent desire to punch him on the nose and knock some sense into him. She suddenly understood why men hit one another. They were impossible to talk to. Daniel turned on his heel and she heard his feet on the stairs to the lower deck.

EMMA WOKE next morning to the motion of the steamer and plash of the paddles. The sound of birds squawking and calling from the trees and water punctuated the air. If she listened carefully, she could identify ducks and warbling magpies beneath the screech of the cockatoos as they flew from the treetops at the boat's approach. She lay for a moment savouring the movement and the sounds. A patch of weak sunlight on the opposite wall of her cabin indicated it was not long past dawn.

Daniel seemed to be in a hurry to complete the journey with this early start after travelling the previous night until eleven. Perhaps he was a little more anxious about the missing packet than he was letting on. There was no reason for her to be up at this hour. Emma pulled the covers higher. When she next opened her eyes, the cabin was awash with light, and someone was knocking on her door.

"Missus Berry." It was Ah Lo, the "r's" in her name rolling into something like "l's" on his tongue. "I bring tea."

"Leave it outside the door, Ah Lo. Thank you," she called in reply.

"Very good, Missus. I leave."

Emma pulled on her wrapper and collected the tray, setting it on the folding table beside the bed. She drank two cups of Ah Lo's strong black tea, well sweetened. She would have to ask him to include some milk. It would be powdered, of course.

It was mid-morning before Emma had a chance to speak to Daniel. They had stopped at Murray Downs Station just past Swan Hill to take on wool. Mr. Wilson, the load master, was overseeing the stacking of the bales on the flat-bottomed barge. If the load wasn't balanced the barge could tip when rounding a bend. Emma had watched Sam do this job countless times. She found Daniel alone in the saloon, updating the logbook as he drank his tea.

"Everything all right?" he asked, barely glancing up from his work as she slid into a chair.

"Yes, thank you. Daniel, I need to talk to you about this missing packet. I can't have explained it properly before. If we find it, we need to get it back to the Major as quickly as possible, not send it on to whoever it was addressed to."

"Why is that? Surely it would need to be delivered?"

"The Major said he wants it back immediately. Before Lady Annabel returns, apparently. That's what he told me."

Daniel shrugged. "If you're sure that's what he wants."

Well, that was easy enough. "Do you really think you'll find it on the *Mary B* after all this time?"

"Why wouldn't it be there?"

"The *Mary B* has been at the boat yard for months. Anyone could have gone through it by now, surely."

Doubt flickered across his face, quickly extinguished. "You're making too much of this."

She shook her head. "Daniel, you do realise it could ruin us all if it isn't found." The more he said the more she wondered about his involvement. "You do remember it's been smuggled across the river? We would be in even more trouble if we're found with it." Though it paled in comparison to the financial threat.

"Well, I have to admit I won't be happy about being in possession of the thing at Echuca. That was why I wanted to get rid of it as quickly as possible."

Emma nodded. "I want to talk to the jeweller it was being sent to, as well. I want to know what the Major was planning to do with it."

"Why would you bother with that?" Daniel asked, taking a gulp of his tea.

"Call it insurance," Emma said. "I've listened to the man, remember? I don't believe a word he says, and I certainly don't trust him. I'm wondering if he may be rather desperate for money right now."

"And you believe this why?"

"The social pages, of course. The Major had a new house built at Honey Hills in recent years, and he's having a townhouse built in Sydney. Lady Annabel's trip to England for Julia's season will be costing an awful lot. I'm just not sure how the Montague emeralds come into it." She had her suspicions but that's all they were right now.

"So, you know who the necklace was being sent to then?" Daniel asked casually, sitting back in his chair, and tapping his pen on the logbook.

"No, but there must be an address on the packet." She frowned. The Major hadn't mentioned an address. Perhaps he had just given Sam the directions for delivering it. That could be awkward. She shrugged. "There can't be more than one jeweller in Echuca – two at most. We should be able to find him."

"If he knew the Major was sending it," Daniel pointed out reasonably. "If he was expecting it. He may know nothing about it." That was not a comforting thought, but no, the jeweller had to be a main player in the Major's game, surely.

"Perhaps there's a letter in the package telling him what to do with the necklace. I mean, he would have to know what the Major wanted," Emma pointed out. Daniel looked doubtful. She still hadn't convinced him of the seriousness of this. "Look, I think he wants the jeweller to break up the necklace and sell the gems off in Melbourne. You couldn't sell it as a piece. It's quite distinctive after all. Perhaps the Major asked around quietly and found a jeweller who was most likely to be able to help him with whatever it was he wanted."

"You seem to know a lot about underhand disposal of jewellery."

"I read a lot."

"I'm sure you do." There it was again. A snide reminder of how he saw her idle life. She did enjoy reading, and not only the Trollope books. Recently she'd found stories about lady detectives which had appealed greatly to her sense of adventure. They'd also awakened her enjoyment in a good puzzle.

"There's just one problem with your theory," Daniel said leaning forward. "How would Barnaby account for the necklace being missing when his wife returns?"

Emma had to admit her theories weren't perfect. But she did have an answer of sorts.

"He could use his story of a theft and of Sam being involved."

Daniel stared. "The hell he would." At last. Now he was taking her seriously.

Emma nodded. "He's covered himself, whether we find it or not. Actually..." She hesitated as a thought came to her. "Golly, you know, he's better off if it doesn't get found at all. All he has to do is blackmail us into paying up or he tells everyone about Sam's involvement in the theft. And implicates you and me as being part of it all, I'm sure. He doesn't even need to involve a jeweller and run the risk of him talking."

Daniel stared at her. "That's…" He shook his head. "No, this is getting out of hand. There could be a perfectly simple explanation. Sam didn't have to be smuggling the thing at all. He might have just not gotten around to putting the packet on the cargo list. I mean, one doesn't expect the sort of behaviour you're suggesting from someone of the Major's standing."

Emma didn't see much difference between the honesty of the upper classes and those of the lower orders. The only difference seemed to be in the type of activity they indulged in, and that was governed largely by the opportunities that presented themselves.

"But whether I'm right or not," Emma urged, "it doesn't change the fact that we're still missing one extremely expensive piece of jewellery that we have to find or pay for. So, we need…"

"Missus." It was Ah Lo at the door of the saloon. "I look for you. I have tea and special cake. English lady tea-time."

He put the tray on the table. It contained a plate with four brightly iced cupcakes beside the teapot. More than she would eat.

"And milk for your tea," he said proudly, indicating another cup full of a thick, creamy mixture.

"Thank you, Ah Lo. It's lovely, it really is, but please don't go to any extra trouble for me."

"No trouble, Missus. No trouble." Ah Lo bobbed himself out of the saloon.

"You seem to have a habit of picking up admirers," Daniel said sourly.

Emma frowned at his tone. "I'm not sure what admirers you're referring to." As for Ah Lo, she always called him by his Chinese name and not Charley, as everyone else on the boat did. Perhaps he appreciated that.

"Your neighbour, that Macdonald fellow from Nettifield. You were pretty friendly with him from what I could see at that cricket match. Doesn't seem like you're missing Sam much at all."

Emma's heart seemed to stop for a moment. Not missing Sam, when she saw him, heard him, everywhere?

"You're determined to find fault with me, aren't you?" she said, getting to her feet. "No matter what I do, or why. I'm beginning to believe Grandmama was right."

"What has your grandmother got to do with it?"

"She said men have trouble taking responsibility for their own actions, preferring to blame a woman." She picked up the tea tray. "I suppose you blame your fiancée for luring you away from the *Mary B* that day, too."

It had been a letter from Daniel's fiancée breaking off their engagement that had sent him rushing off to Castlemaine that fateful week. If he hadn't gone, the boat race would not have taken place, and Sam would still be alive.

The stunned look on Daniel's face now was worth it. Serve him right for his constant accusations.

Back in her cabin, she drank the tea and managed to eat all four of the cupcakes. They were small consolation for the sadness she felt. Sam and her child were gone, and now she had alienated two people she considered as friends, Nella and Daniel.

She ate dinner in her cabin that evening. She couldn't face any more disapproval from Daniel, and she wasn't in the mood for the company of the *Lisette*'s engineer and loadmaster. She would have liked to take her meals down with the crew on the lower deck but that wasn't fitting either.

It was raining next morning, the steamer passing from wet to dry as it travelled through localised showers, the *Lisette*'s whistle punctuating the journey at every bend. Outside, the overhanging grey-green trees dripped disconsolately. Even the sunshine-yellow bursts of the ever-present wattle failed to cheer, while the steady hiss and clack of the engine and thrash of the paddle wheels refused to lull as they usually did.

After having lunch in her cabin, Emma ventured down to the galley to return her dishes. She paused at the open stoke-hold.

"Good afternoon," she said, politely.

Young James, wood for the boiler fire in his arms, ducked his head shyly. He was a gangly youth of sixteen, properly named James Young, but that had been turned on its head by the other crew members.

The engineer, Mr. Shankton, square of body and head, with square cut whiskers, was Young James' uncle. He responded to Emma's greeting with a brief nod, before turning back to check his gauges, oily rag in hand. Emma felt Mr. Shankton was one of the old school who thought a woman on board ship was bad luck. He must really hate having female passengers. Or perhaps it was just her.

She passed on down the deck, reluctant now to return to a solitary seat in her cabin. She'd run out of reading matter. Squeezing through the narrow passageway between the paddle box and a stack of crates she found deckhand Fred Croaker sitting on a cask splicing rope. There was a quietness about middle-aged Fred that Emma found restful.

She perched on the corner of a crate and watched as he quietly and deftly twisted the rope strands to make a strong join. An unlit pipe hung from the corner of his mouth. When he had finished the splice, he took up the pipe and began to scrape out the bowl with a penknife.

"You're not the only one keeping out of the captain's way, lass," he said. He pulled a packet of tobacco from his pocket and tamped some into the clean bowl. "Got something bothering him."

"I'm not..." but of course she was avoiding Daniel. It was ridiculous to deny it. It must be obvious she wasn't taking her meals in the saloon. "I didn't know he was in a bad mood with everyone," Emma amended. "I'm sorry if he's making life unpleasant. I suppose it's my fault."

"Why would that be, now?"

"Seems he has to blame someone for what's gone on, you know, and I'm the one he's aiming at." She didn't need to explain what it was that had gone on. Everyone on the river knew what had happened to Sam and the *Mary B*, although she was sure she wasn't Daniel's only irritation right now. The possibility of not finding the packet on the *Mary B* must be part and parcel of his concerns, despite trying to sound positive about it.

"That's it, is it?"

"Well, I suppose he must blame himself at least a little," she said, trying to be generous. "He must feel he could have prevented the race and the accident if he'd been there." Unless he really did blame his fiancée because he wasn't.

Fred Croaker lit his pipe and got it drawing nicely before he spoke again.

"True enough. There's something in that, I guess. But Sam Berry, now. Not as responsible as one might have liked for a boat captain. Sorry, lass, but that's the way most of us saw him." Emma wanted to defend Sam, but the words wouldn't come. It wasn't as if Fred was wrong.

"It's early days yet," he went on. "The Captain'll come round in time. Sometimes a man don't rightly know what he's upset about. Could be he's got feelings he's not even realised himself yet."

"What do you mean?" Emma asked.

Fred shook his head and got to his feet. "You look after yourself, lass and don't go worrying about us," he said, slinging the coil of rope over his shoulder. "We can look after ourselves well enough. He's a good skipper. I've sailed under far worse."

# Chapter 7

## *At the Boatyard*

EMMA PUZZLED over Fred's enigmatic remark until a shower of rain drove her to find shelter. She went along to the stern and found the other three deck-hands perched among some bales of wool under the canvas awning, engaged in a game of cribbage.

She sat down to watch, squeezing into a space far enough from the water dripping from the edge of the awning. Behind on the long tow rope the barge followed, the pilot and his mate slick in their wet weather gear.

"Don't mind me," Emma said. "I'm getting cabin fever."

"This weather can do that," Shorty replied, staring at his cards. The game came to an end with Willy Bowman the winner. Shorty dug into his vest pocket and handed over a coin. Red-haired Blue Higgins did the same before standing to stretch his long, lanky frame.

"I've never known anyone with such luck as you, Willy boy," Shorty said, "and barely a word to say for yourself. What are you doing on the river, anyway? You could be making a fortune in the hotels."

"Nah," Willy drawled, as he pocketed the coins.

"You must be a deep thinker then. Must be something going on in that head of yours," Shorty persisted.

Emma had the feeling this was an ongoing conversation. She wasn't sure cards and betting were the best occupation for people who were cooped up together. Willy ignored the jibe and shuffled the cards. He offered them to Shorty to cut, but the Welshman shook his head.

"That's enough for me today, boyo." He pulled out a packet of roll-your-own papers and a tobacco pouch and proceeded to fashion himself a cigarette. Willy put the cards back in their box and stowed them in his jacket pocket.

"Capt'n says you're going to see the *Mary B*," Blue put in, somewhat shyly.

"Yes. I haven't seen her since she was brought up out of the river."

"Bad business that," Willy said. Shorty asked if the *Mary B* was going to be repaired or sold off.

"Oh, repaired, definitely. As soon as we can get the boatyard working on it." She frowned. "I don't know why it's taking so long."

"I hear there's new boats and barges being built all the time, can't keep up with demand," Shorty said.

"Mmm. I suppose the yard is busy," Emma said, "but it wouldn't take as long to get the *Mary B* back on the river as it would to build a new steamer, would it, and then there'd be one more boat working."

Shorty rubbed his thumb and index finger together. "It'll be about the money, you can bet the cargo on it," he said. He gave Willy a look through a haze of cigarette smoke. "It's always about the money."

"Capt'n will be happier when he gets his boat back," Willy said.

Perhaps that was what Fred Croaker had been referring to.

THE *LISETTE* pulled into the bank below the Echuca wharf, laden with the wool, hides and tallow they had collected on the way. They joined a string of boats waiting their turn at the long wharf, which was crowded with steamers and barges loading and unloading, the cranes clanking and straining, rail cars waiting to disgorge goods and carry the wool bales to Melbourne.

As soon as the plank was let down to the bank, Emma slipped out from her cabin intending to find a boarding house to stay in for a few days while she went about her inquiries. She would take another boat back home when she was ready.

"Where do you think you're going?" Daniel's voice came from behind as she stepped onto the lower deck.

"I'm going ashore," she replied, glancing back at him on the stairs above.

He sighed. He looked and sounded tired. He came down the remaining stairs to stand with her.

"Look, I'm sorry I said what I did, about us being fine until you came along. I'd hoped once Sam married, he might settle down a bit, be less impetuous, I guess. I just," he sighed again, "I just don't think you were the right one for him."

"Well, thank you for your honesty, I'm sure."

"Where are you going?" he asked again, ignoring the sarcasm.

"I'm going to find a place to stay for a few days."

"There's no need. You can stay on the *Lisette* and return with us. Your father will be expecting me to look after you."

"I don't need looking after Daniel, and I won't be returning with you. I have work to do here."

"Emma..." He put out a hand, palm face up. She drew a deep breath and let it out again. It was as much of an apology as she was going to get. They had coexisted before without argument. She'd considered him a friend, an older brother, and there was too much at stake now to continue with the antagonism.

"I would appreciate being able to see the *Mary B* if you would accompany me," she said, trying to meet him partway. "But I will be staying, Daniel."

He nodded. Whether that meant he agreed or not about her staying she didn't know or care right now.

"We can go to the boatyard now if you want. I won't be needed here for a while. It'll take the rest of the day to clear those ahead of me in this queue. We can talk about you leaving later."

Not that it would make any difference to her decision. Emma looked down at her travelling bag.

"I'd best leave this, then," she said.

Daniel handed the bag to Willy, who was nearby and told him to return it to her cabin. Mr. Shankton gave her a look she couldn't define as they turned past the stokehold. Perhaps he'd been hoping to see the last of her. Daniel handed her down the boarding plank then tucked her hand under his arm as they made their way up to the top of the bank. They reached the Esplanade and passed Shakell's Bond Store, and the grain stores and shipping company offices.

The street itself was lined with wagons and carts, some with cargo to ship off, and others waiting to collect from the Bond Store. Foremost among the latter were the carriers for the hotels, of which Emma knew there were a large number in the town.

At Hopwood's Hotel corner, they turned left into the High Street. The sweet smell of beer mingled with the sour smell of sweat, and the sound of voices assailed them through the open doorway of the saloon bar as they passed.

On the street, they were greeted with shop fronts adorned with colourful hoardings advertising everything from ladies' boots to nerve tonics, Bee Tea to Military Pickles. The street, muddy between the footpaths sheltered by the verandahs, was alive with buggies and horses. A newspaper seller's cry reached them from the opposite corner.

Emma kept a lookout for a jeweller's shop as they walked but when, after a mile or so, they turned left again back toward the river she still hadn't seen one. They crossed the railway line, and the unmistakable sound of a sawmill reached their ears, the high-pitched whine of the steam-driven saw growing louder as they approached. Her mind turned with some trepidation to what lay ahead.

As the street dipped toward the river in what was still a largely bush area a half-timbered hull rose above them on the slip alive with activity. A boy carrying a bucket of hot rivets on a bed of glowing coals was passing among the workmen who were hammering the rivets into the three-inch thick redgum planks. Someone else was working an engine funneling steam along a plank bending it into place for the bow. Emma wondered, not for the first time, how a snag could penetrate such a construction.

Daniel led her down to the riverbank past a shed where she glimpsed the shadow of someone watching their progress from an unglazed window. Pulled up onto the bank was an upturned barge and next to it the battered form of the *Mary B.*

She lay on her side, a ragged hole in her hull, the stokehold a shattered mass of bent metal and splintered timbers, part of the upper deck missing above it. Paint had peeled and cracked, the wood dry and shrinking. The door of the cabin she and Sam had shared hung drunkenly on one hinge.

Her mind clouded over with another image. Sam, in the wheelhouse leaning over the shelf behind the wheel, the scroll map unrolling to the floor.

*"Sam! Come on!"*
*"She's snagged. Get off. Go. Now, Emma."*
*He all but pushes her away. She wants to argue, tell him there is nothing he can do, he must leave as well. But she has a child to protect and there's no time...*

"Emma? I said I'm going up to have a look in the wheelhouse."

She nodded, unable to speak, the memory too real. She knew now why Sam didn't leave the steamer in time, before the boiler exploded, the thing that had puzzled her these past months. She watched as Daniel disappeared around the far side of the leaning boat, the upper deck more accessible from there. She heard him scrambling on the timbers, saw his head through the wheelhouse window, knowing what he would find. He didn't take long.

"Whatever was in there has gone," he growled when he returned. "The shelf is open. Someone knew where to look, anyway." He glanced back toward the shed.

"No, Sam must have taken it out. I remembered. He had a screwdriver in his hand. He was opening the shelf. I saw it when I ran to the wheelhouse, and he sent me off to get in the dinghy."

"He did?"

Emma nodded. "That's why he took so long to leave, Daniel. I'd forgotten. He must have been retrieving the packet from where he'd hidden it."

His hand went to his head. "So where is it?"

His face loomed before her through a watery haze, and she felt the tears on her face, as if her eyes were soundlessly leaking of their own accord.

He touched her cheek. "I'm sorry." His voice was not entirely steady.

She brushed her cheeks with the back of her hand and stepped across to an upturned wooden box in the shade of a eucalypt. She sat down, elbows on her knees, chin in her hands. Daniel followed and squatted beside her. She stared at the wrecked boat, her wrecked dreams. She remembered how Sam had looked that last time in the wheelhouse. As if he couldn't believe something like this could happen to him.

"Where could it be?" she asked. A life had been paid for that necklace. Her stomach clenched as a bitter wave of anger at Major Barnaby swept over her.

"Perhaps he lost it in the river, after all," Daniel said.

"Someone could dive for it?" she suggested, half hopeful.

"If it's in the river it's gone, buried in the mud."

"Or swallowed by a Murray cod perhaps?" she suggested, biting down hysteria. "Perhaps we should go fishing."

Daniel grunted. "Hargreaves should have had more sense."

There he was, blaming someone else again. She imagined Sam would have made it impossible for the other captain to refuse. Especially as there'd been a rematch promised when the *Mary B* lost in their previous race at Echuca. But that had been under controlled conditions. Emma didn't want to voice her next thought. That the packet had been buried with Sam. She waited for Daniel to suggest it.

"Hargreaves handled the burial, didn't he?" he said at last.

"Yes."

"If Sam was carrying anything, he would have found it, wouldn't he?"

Emma nodded. "He did, but there was no packet among the items he left for me afterward."

"Hargreaves wouldn't have kept anything?"

They looked at one another and then both shook their heads at the suggestion. Captain Jeremiah Hargreaves was well known up and down the river. An American gentleman of about sixty, he was also an enthusiastic lay preacher whenever he could find an audience. His only weakness was his pride in the *Invincible*.

"He would have given Sam a decent burial at least," Daniel said wryly. "With a very long sermon."

Emma forced her thoughts back to that night at Merrim station. It had been dark when the *Invincible* arrived. Sam hadn't been buried until the morning, and she had been in no condition then to attend his interment or to see anyone.

"Perhaps he delivered it," Emma said. "If there was an address."

"What, to this jeweller it was supposed to be going to?"

"Yes."

"All right. That makes sense. If Hargreaves found the packet on Sam," Daniel mused.

"But surely the jeweller would have been the first place the Major checked before chasing me up about it," Emma said, playing devil's advocate.

"Perhaps he has, and the jeweller has denied receiving it."

"That wouldn't be very smart if we could show Hargreaves delivered it."

"No, it wouldn't. Whatever else, we need to find out if Sam had the packet on him when they pulled him out of the river. We need to talk to Hargreaves. We'll ask at the wharf office, see where he is."

"Everything all right, Capt'n?"

The man approaching them from the shed was stocky, muscles bulging. He spat a stream of tobacco off to one side and wiped his mouth with the back of his hand before glancing at Emma. Daniel stood and introduced her.

"Mrs. Berry, my sister-in-law. This is John Knowles, owner of the boatyard."

The man nodded. "Very sorry I was to hear about your husband, ma'am. This here river's a dangerous place even for men."

And no place for a woman, he may as well have added as she inclined her head in acknowledgement of his words of condolence.

"When are you going to get to the *Mary B*, Knowles?" Daniel asked. "I'm missing the whole season."

Knowles shrugged. "This here boat we're building for the Company, then that barge, then yours," he ticked them off on his fingers. "I lost two good men to the goldfields this month. Darn fools." He spat to the side again. "Soon as someone comes to town flashing a few nuggets off go a few more thinking they can get rich easy. No use telling 'em they'll work harder and longer in worse conditions and no guarantees of seeing so much as a glint." He paused for breath. "Darn fools," he repeated sourly.

"I'd appreciate if you could get to it as soon as possible."

"Always do my best, Capt'n. Ma'am." He nodded and turned back to the shed.

"For those who pay something under the table," Daniel muttered.

"Why don't you take her to someone else if Knowles is so slow?" Emma asked, as they took the shorter route back to the wharf along the railway spur line that ran beside the river.

"Not my choice. He got the job from the insurance company because his quote was the lowest. He'll do it and do it well, but only when he has no better paying jobs on hand."

"Should we pay something extra then, to get it done? How much would he want?"

"You'd have to talk to your father about that. I don't have anything extra," Daniel replied shortly, and Emma realized his grievance with her supposedly comfortable life continued to niggle.

At the wharf, Daniel went into the office to make inquiries about the whereabouts of the *Invincible*. Boat captains were required to telegraph their arrival at every town with whatever information they had to impart, including river levels. They also received instructions and any other items of news that needed to be sent on to them. This procedure was especially required of McCulloch Company boats, as they needed to be in constant contact with their fleet of vessels for efficient operation.

Modern communication was a wonderful thing Emma considered, taking in the bustling atmosphere as she waited. Her skin tingled at the thought of being part of that movement and purpose again. She took a deep breath. The air at the wharf was redolent with the smell of smoke and oil, wool and men.

The *Foxy Lady* was moored in front of her, a boat she was familiar with. Mrs. Barnsdale, with her two small children, often accompanied her husband. And there were women on the fishing vessels and hawking steamers that were family owned.

Once the *Mary B* was back on the water, she would negotiate something with Daniel. If they didn't find Lady Annabel's necklace, she would be needed to offset the wage of another crew member. They would need every penny they could scramble together. Daniel reappeared at her elbow.

"The *Invincible* is on the Murrumbidgee, heading for Hay. She's not due back for some time."

"Did we pass them on the way up?"

"No. He must have made the Bidgee by the time we reached the junction. He's passed through Balranald, so I've sent a telegraph to Maude. It will be relayed to Hay if it misses him there. We should have a reply in a day or two if he's not held up somewhere in between."

He showed her a copy of the telegraph.

*Require news of items Sam had on his person.*
*Daniel Berry.*

"It's going to generate some speculation, but that can't be helped," he said.

"No," Emma said, as she handed the paper back to him, "but you aren't likely to be here when the answer comes, are you?"

"They'll send the reply on down river. We'll probably get it at Euston, or even as early as Swan Hill."

"Someone should be here to act on it," she said. "Even when you receive it you still have to continue your run."

"It would depend on the answer."

"Which we won't know until we receive it," Emma pointed out patiently. "We need to cover all possibilities. I'll stay until we get the answer."

"You think I'm going to leave you here in Echuca on your own?"

"You're not my keeper, Daniel. I'll decide for myself what I do. I'm sure there's a very respectable boarding house where I could take a room until we know what our next move is."

Daniel cursed under his breath. "What will your father think when I turn up at Wirramilla without you?"

"Don't turn up," Emma snapped. "You didn't have any trouble sailing by last time." They glared at one another for a moment. Emma was the first to turn away. "I'm going back to the High Street to look for a jeweller's shop."

"I suppose I'll have to go with you. If this jeweller is part of the deal, he could be dangerous. And lord knows what trouble you'll get into."

"Suit yourself." If this were a truce, Emma didn't care to know what open warfare would be like.

# Chapter 8

## *Talking to the Jeweller*

BACK AT HOPWOOD'S Hotel corner, Emma looked up and down High Street. There hadn't been a jeweller's shop along the section of street they'd already walked, and she couldn't see anything promising in the opposite direction, so she decided to ask someone. She chose a millinery shop across the street and came out a few minutes later, holding a scrap of paper in her gloved hand.

"Did you notice the empty plot at the corner of Radcliffe Street?" she asked Daniel.

"Yes, looks as though there's been a fire there. Not the jeweller, surely?"

"Hmm, about six weeks ago. Several shops were burnt to the ground. I've got directions to the jeweller's home address." She waved the paper she was holding. "A Mr. Thompson. He was the only jeweller in town. I think I should go alone, Daniel. I'm sure I'd get a more sympathetic hearing."

"Not if we're dealing with thieves and scoundrels, as you seem to suppose."

Emma didn't argue. She wasn't as keen on wandering alone away from the relative safety of the busy centre when all was said and done. The directions took them east again along High Street, and after a few twists and turns, into Percy Street.

"Here," said Emma, indicating a comfortable looking timber clad house with a large garden at number twelve.

Daniel opened the gate, and she proceeded him up the path. The rose bushes lining it on either side were heavy with blooms giving off their heady scent. She raised the brass knocker and rapped on the door. The neat maid who answered bade them wait in the hall while she conveyed their names. Emma admired the tasteful decoration, from the richly oiled redwood floorboards and regency stripe wallpaper to the highly polished brass lamps hanging at intervals down the long length of the hallway. There had been no expense spared for the decorating. Emma hoped none of this wealth came from the missing emeralds.

The maid reappeared, followed by a young woman of about seventeen. She was soft and rounded, dressed in a white gown trimmed with Honiton lace, with its classic flower and leaf design, and wearing white cotton gloves. Emma surmised she had probably been arranging flowers. She realised she was thinking like Mrs. Paschal, the detective from Hayward's *Revelations of a Lady Detective* she had been reading recently. It might be a good idea to emulate that lady.

"I'm Clarice Thompson," the girl introduced herself. "Please, come this way. Uncle Alex is in the garden."

She led them through the drawing room and into a conservatory that projected onto a lawned area edged with shaded shrubberies and sunny flower beds. Lattice-patterned wallpaper, white cane furniture, and exotic palms in brass pots completed the picture.

"What an absolutely delightful room," Emma exclaimed.

Clarice smiled her pleasure at the compliment. "Uncle Alex spends most of his time in here, when he isn't out in the garden." She opened the French doors. "Uncle, you have visitors," she called.

"Be right with you," a voice answered from the nearby shrubbery. A small wiry gentleman, grey haired and stooping emerged pump spray in hand. "Those hairy black caterpillars are into the hibiscus," he said, wheezing slightly as he came in, "and Mrs. Campbell's cats have been rolling in the alyssum again and making a mess."

"Uncle, this is Captain and Mrs. Berry," Clarice introduced them as she took the pump spray from her uncle and set it aside.

"We haven't met before, have we? I don't recall..." He peered at them shortsightedly, a result of working on intricate items of jewellery, perhaps.

"No, sir. We've come about a business matter," said Daniel.

"You do know I'm not in business anymore?"

"Yes, but we are enquiring about some past business you may have had."

"Sit down, sit down," he said waving them to a seat and dropping into a chair. "Get us some tea, would you, Clarrie, there's a good girl. I'm mighty parched." Clarice reached for the bell to summon the maid. "Yes, not in business any more since the fire."

"How did that happen?" Emma asked.

"Started in the shop next door. Stupid woman left a candle near a curtain. Lucky she wasn't burnt to death, though daresay she may have wished she had been given her injuries." Emma was taken aback at his lack of sympathy. "I suppose it was time I retired anyway. Clarrie has been urging me to slow down for some time. I must admit I do enjoy having more time for the gardens."

"They are a credit to you," Emma said. "The roses along the front path are really lovely."

"You must get Clarrie to cut you some. Clarrie, make sure you cut some roses for Mrs. – er – Berry before she leaves."

"Yes, Uncle. Tea will be in shortly."

"Good, good."

"It's very kind of you," Emma said, "but I really couldn't accept the roses. I'm not sure where I'll be staying after today, so I may have nowhere to put them." She had that problem now with the lily bulb. She should have left it where it was.

"Well, if you are sure."

"Perhaps just one, Mrs. Berry?" suggested Clarice.

"Of course," said Emma quickly, as Mr. Thompson looked as disappointed as a small boy refused a treat. Best not to upset him until they had the information they wanted. "One I could accept, thank you. They really are lovely."

"We did need to ask you something in your professional capacity, Mr. Thompson," Daniel said, bringing the conversation back to the reason for their visit.

"Oh yes. A Captain, you said? On the riverboats?"

"Yes, sir. My brother Sam was a boat captain as well. It's to do with him that we are here. He was carrying a packet on our paddle steamer the *Mary B* several months back, which we understand was consigned to your shop, but the steamer met with an accident in which he lost his life."

"Oh, indeed. I'm sorry to hear that. Dangerous place, the Murray. I avoid it, you know. Trains and coaches are good enough for me."

"Here's tea, Uncle," said Clarice, as the maid came in with the tray.

Clarice was still wearing the white cotton gloves as she poured the tea and handed it around. Was it an affectation, some new fashion Emma didn't know of, or did the girl have some reason for hiding her hands?

"Thank you." Daniel accepted a cup. "The consignment we are asking about was being sent privately," he said, addressing Mr. Thompson. "Only my brother and the client knew about it. And, of course, the person it was being sent." Emma was impressed. Daniel was trying a bluff about how much they knew. Unless it wasn't a bluff at all. "We are trying to confirm if it reached its destination and was delivered to you."

Emma was sure Mr. Thompson's hand stilled for a moment as he lifted his cup. She cast a quick look at Daniel but couldn't tell if he had noticed.

"I'm not sure I follow," he said. "What consignment are we talking about?"

"The consignment sent you by Major Barnaby of Honey Hills on the Murrumbidgee."

Mr. Thompson seemed to be struggling to formulate a response.

"Haven't received anything from any Barnaby. I'm sorry, I know nothing about it, whatever it is."

"The item is missing, Mr. Thompson. Somewhere between the sinking of the *Mary B* and your shop it has disappeared."

"Disappeared, eh? Well, it's nothing to do with me. You've obviously mistaken me for someone else."

"I do apologise," Daniel said smoothly. "There's another jeweller in Echuca then?"

"Ah, no. No, there's no one. Yet anyway. There's sure to be someone opening up to take my place... One of, one of the major operations in Melbourne could be interested... Kozminsky perhaps. You would need to see them." Mr. Thompson put his cup down carefully using both hands. "Was there anything else? No?" He got to his feet. "You'll have to excuse me then," he said. "So much to do. Nice meeting you. Clarrie will see you out." He opened the door to the garden and stepped out.

"Thank you for seeing us, sir," Daniel said to Mr. Thompson's retreating back.

Clarice was full of apologies. "He's not been himself for some time. He gets upset so easily." She was rubbing surreptitiously at the back of her left hand, the promised rose forgotten.

"He knows about it," Emma said with certainty, when they were back on the street.

"Guilty conscience," Daniel said. A man of few words.

"But did he receive the packet? That's the question."

"Only if Hargreaves found it on Sam and it had an address."

"Yes," Emma agreed.

Daniel sighed. "And if he didn't find the packet on Sam it hasn't been delivered, and it must have been lost in the river."

Emma didn't want to believe that. The thought Daniel might have been complicit in the arrangement reared its ugly head once again. Did he know how to word his questions because he already knew all about it?

"How do you suppose the Major contacted Sam in the first place?" she asked as they walked back. "Where did they arrange it all? And why Sam? Why him?"

"I've no idea."

"Haven't you even considered it?"

"Of course, I have. I didn't keep track of where Sam went or who he spoke to every time we stopped somewhere. Why would I?"

"And Sam didn't give you any hint of what he was planning to do?"

"No. He did not. Do you really think I would have agreed to it?"

"I don't know any more," Emma said quietly.

"I see. Guilty by association. In that case, you should have known about it, shouldn't you?"

"I suspect you think I did," Emma challenged.

"It had occurred to me."

They were back on the High Street before either spoke again.

"How would Sam have explained what he was doing when he met the Major on the riverbank," Emma asked, "if you had been there? As you were expected to be, after all. No one knew you would get a letter and go rushing off. What would he have told you?"

Daniel grunted. "Tell me to get some sleep and he'd pilot for a while. Say he thought he'd stop and check if the fellow by the fire needed help. He never had any trouble finding reasons and excuses for what he did."

Daniel was glib with the answers himself. She wished she could be sure he hadn't known what Sam was up to any more than she had but thinking along those lines wasn't going to get her anywhere. She needed to work out how to get Mr. Thompson to talk to her, because she was certain he knew exactly what they had been asking about. And if the necklace had really been sent for cleaning and valuation, why hadn't he wanted to discuss it?

THE *LISETTE* took her place at the wharf to discharge the wool she had brought up and receive cargo to deliver on the way back down river. While Daniel was busy with that Emma paid a visit to the wharf office to enquire about a suitable boarding house.

"Our Mr. Nat Pickles may be able to help you there, ma'am," the smart young lad behind the counter told her. "His family has a boarding house nearby. Many of our lady passengers choose to stay there when they are travelling alone, rather than at an 'otel. Mr. Pickles, sir," he said to a thin, ascetic looking middle-aged man poring over a ledger at a high desk behind. "The lady is looking for a room in a quiet boarding house."

Mr. Pickles looked over his spectacles and gave Emma a keen assessing look then carefully marked his place in the ledger before climbing down from his stool and approaching the counter. Emma explained she would want a room for perhaps a week, and Mr. Pickles assured her she could be accommodated and gave her an address in Connelly Street with directions. She had obviously passed inspection and so, she found the boarding house when she visited it shortly after to secure her room.

It was a commodious two-storey house with surrounding verandahs and a formal layout inside. Emma was shown to an upstairs room furnished sparsely with an iron bedstead, a set of drawers, several hooks for hanging clothes, and a basin and pitcher on a small table. The linen and furniture were all white and the walls were painted a dull cream, Emma's least favourite colour. The room was without any personality except for one item that stood out like a beacon in the bland space – a peacock blue brocade-covered armchair in front of the window. Emma couldn't help but feel a statement was being made. By someone.

The landlady, Miss Charity Pickles, was so like her brother Emma thought they might be twins. She informed Emma breakfast was served between seven and eight o'clock in the dining room, unless required earlier by request the evening previous, although she could do tea and toast to the room before nine as some ladies preferred it. Dinner was sharp at half past six. The house didn't do a midday meal but there were one or two nice tea shops in the High Street. She recommended the Primrose. The back verandah was for lady guests and family only, and the side verandah for the men.

"I run a respectable house," Miss Pickles assured Emma in her thin, grey voice.

Emma said she did not doubt it and would be happy to have breakfast in the dining room next morning. She paid three days in advance for the room, which greatly satisfied Miss Pickles, who became a little less grey.

Later in the evening Emma watched as the *Lisette*, with the barge *Oxley* loaded with cargo for stations down river, pulled out from the wharf, its lamps already lit for a long night haul. She had made a point of being there when it left to assure herself Daniel was far away and not likely to interrupt her half-formed plans.

Dusk was falling as she returned to the boarding house. Gas lights cast a friendly glow along High Street which was as busy as it had been during the day but with more men looking as if they had come out for the night and fewer families. She passed the Primrose Tearoom. Above the door she noted the name of the proprietor, Mrs. Henrietta Pickles. So, Miss Pickles' recommendation had nothing to do with the quality of the food. This was a family business.

Back at the boarding house, Emma went up to her room and found the maid folding down the covers on her bed.

"I've just left some hot water for you," the girl said, indicating the wash bowl.

Emma thanked her, not expecting such level of service and asked the girl's name.

"Janet, ma'am," she said with a bob of her head. "Janet Pickles."

Emma opened her mouth to enquire about Janet's relationship to Miss Pickles when that good lady was heard to call the girl's name. With another bob, Janet hurried away.

Surrounded by Pickles Emma thought with some amusement. As she washed her face and hands and used the thick towel, she had to admit every care seemed to be taken for the comfort of guests in the Pickles' boarding house. In the dining room a fire crackled in the corner, and she was surprised to see a woman with a child of about eight years and three other gentlemen, one of them elderly, as well as Mr. Nat Pickles and his sister.

The guests were introduced to one another and Emma thought giddily she was glad there were no Pickles among them.

"And our father, of course," Mr. Nat Pickles said belatedly, referring to the elderly of the three men.

Emma managed to change her urge to giggle into a fit of coughing, which drew concern from Miss Pickles until she assured the lady that no she hadn't caught a chill from the night air, it must have been smoke from the fire tickling her throat.

The elderly Mr. Pickles did not say a word during the meal, though Emma several times caught him looking at her. At such times his gaze lingered a little longer than she found comfortable before returning to his plate. It was as if he were assessing her value like a piece of real estate.

# Chapter 9

*Emma Makes A Deal*

IN HER ROOM after dinner, Emma sat for a while by her window gazing out at the garden lit by a full moon. It was the sort of night she loved on the river with the moonlight turning the water and trees into a magical land where one could almost believe in the existence of the mythical Bunyip.

She should write up her notes on the day's events instead of daydreaming but decided she was too tired from all the walking she had done. It would wait until morning. What was more urgent was figuring out a way to get the *Mary B* back on the water.

Daniel had said George Knowles was amenable to a payment 'under the table.' She didn't have any money of her own, except the small legacy from her grandfather from which she received some income but without access to the principal. All else she had was her share in the *Mary B*. Could she offer him part of that?

The very thought made her catch her breath. Dare she? Daniel would never agree to it she was sure, but it was her share to do with as she saw fit and he would still have the controlling half share. That was all that really mattered, wasn't it? Knowles wouldn't control anything, and she could buy him out again later. If that didn't work, well he would still only own what five, ten, percent?

She realized she didn't know the real value of the *Mary B*. She would have to find out before she spoke to Knowles. She had to be able to speak to him from a position of knowledge or he would have the advantage, and he would use it if she'd judged him aright. How was she to find out? Daniel would know of course, but apart from doing this without his knowledge he wasn't around to ask.

She slept eventually and woke early, her thoughts still unresolved. She heard Janet knock on a bedroom door with a wakeup call and popped her head out to ask for some hot water.

"You're an early riser," Janet said with some surprise. "Most ladies don't get up 'afore eight."

"I have a great deal to do today," Emma replied, feeling compelled to explain even ladies rose early when the need required. Her tone must have sounded a reprimand as Janet flushed and dropped her a little curtsy.

"Of course, ma'am."

As she had done since leaving home, Emma dressed all in black with a little cream lace at the throat. She was reminded of the lovely Honiton lace Clarice Thompson had been wearing only the day before. A second meeting with that young lady's uncle was another matter she had to attend to as soon as possible.

She entered the dining room as the hall clock was striking a quarter past seven and found Mr. Nat Pickles sitting over his breakfast cup of tea, a plate of toast crusts by his saucer.

"Good morning, Mrs. Berry," he said, touching his mouth quickly with his serviette and getting to his feet. "I hope you slept well."

"Indeed, thank you." She sat, allowing him to do the same. "Mr. Pickles, could you spare me a moment?" Of all people, he would know the value of a paddle steamer. She couldn't imagine why she hadn't thought of him last night.

"Well, I have to leave for work directly. Would this evening...?"

"Just one question, please?"

"Very well."

"What is the value of a steamer these days? Say, sixty feet, general working boat?" Emma asked.

"Something like the *Mary B*, perhaps?" he asked, eyeing her keenly.

"Yes, along those lines. In good working order, of course."

Mr. Pickles named a figure Emma found satisfying.

"Are you considering buying or selling?" he asked.

"Neither Mr. Pickles. I was curious to know what my investment was worth for future reference."

"For future reference, yes. Well, I hope you get it back on the river soon, Mrs. Berry, for certainly it isn't doing you any good where it is at the moment."

"No, I hope to rectify that very soon. And thank you. I greatly appreciate your taking the time and providing me with the benefit of your experience."

The austere Mr. Pickles responded with a nod and the ghost of a smile. There was no obstacle now to her speaking to Mr. Knowles.

EMMA HADN'T given any thought to how she would get to the boatyard by herself. It wasn't such a long way, but it wasn't an area she wanted to walk through alone being full of men she didn't know. What she needed was a cab. She had seen several standing somewhere in High Street. She set off east and in the next block saw two cabs waiting outside the Shamrock Hotel.

How did one approach a cab? She had never hired one of her own accord in her life. The drivers were both dozing in their seats while their horses breakfasted from their nose bags. As Emma was thinking she would be brave and approach one, a couple came out of the Hotel, bags in hand.

"The wharf, cabbie," called the gentleman, and the driver on the front cab roused himself, jumping down to remove his horse's nosebag while the gentleman helped the lady inside. Within a few moments the cab was rattling off down High Street. Well, that seemed simple enough. What had she been concerned about? She approached the remaining cab.

"Cabbie, the boatyard if you please," she said, hoping she sounded as if hiring a cab was commonplace to her.

"Which one, ma'am?"

There was more than one boatyard? Surely Daniel had mentioned a name at some time but if so, it had escaped her, and she couldn't for the moment remember the name of the street they had walked. Some detective she was.

"The one run by Mr. Knowles?"

"Aye, you want Dutch's slip."

Emma hoped she did. She settled inside and the cab continued east down High Street and turned left into what she then remembered from the street sign as Pakenham Street. A train was steaming at the station a little further down as they bounced across the railway line. It was only a matter of minutes before they were passing the sawmill. The cab stopped near the slip, which was already busy with workmen. Emma got out and opened her purse to pay the driver, having also forgotten to ask the fare.

"Would you like me to wait, ma'am?" the driver asked. Emma looked at him properly for the first time. Kind blue eyes and a white-whiskered fatherly face met her gaze. "Thruppence for the half hour," he said.

"Thank you. I would appreciate it. My business shouldn't take any longer."

The man nodded. "I'll wait."

She must look like a real country bumpkin, but she was glad to know he would be there when she came out. She couldn't resist taking a quick glance back over her shoulder. Her cab driver had settled back to doze again, his hat tipped down over his eyes and his arms folded around the reins. The horse had found some grass to nibble on. Not a job for an energetic man, then.

Emma expected Knowles would be in the small shed or working on the boat on the slip. She didn't look for him, making her way around to the *Mary B* as she and Daniel had done the day before. She had been gazing at it for only a few minutes before Knowles sauntered out.

"The Capt'n not with you today, ma'am?" he said.

"He's taken cargo down river," Emma replied, her eyes still on the *Mary B*. It was hard to credit she had lived happily on that piece of wreckage for over twelve months.

"Lot of river work this time of year," he said.

"Yes."

Emma observed from the corner of her eye as he pulled a tobacco pouch from his vest pocket, reached into it, then withdrew his fingers and returned the pouch to the pocket. He had some finer feelings then, resisting chewing a plug in her presence.

"She's a good little work boat, that," he said.

"But she's just rotting here, Mr. Knowles." She turned to look at him. "How can we get her repaired? There must be something we can do?"

Knowles shrugged. "Labour costs money, Mrs. Berry. The insurance don't consider the rising cost of labour and materials. Nails don't grow on trees, you know, though you'd think they did if you listened to those insurance fellows down in the city."

"I'm sure it's quite difficult to make ends meet, Mr. Knowles," said Emma, allowing him to lead her on though she felt more like rolling her eyes. "What would it cost us to get her on the water?"

"Well, considering the cost of everything it would have to be, let's see, somewhere around another three hundred."

"Three hundred pounds? Heavens, Mr. Knowles, she is only a small working boat, not a luxury pleasure steamer," Emma countered. "We would be better off scrapping her and taking the insurance payout at that rate." Three hundred pounds was thirty percent of her half share, according to Mr. Pickles' valuation.

"Now, now. There's no need to be hasty. I'm sure we can arrive at an agreeable figure." His hand reached toward his vest pocket, before veering slightly, the thumb hooking into the armhole instead.

"One hundred," countered Emma.

"Now a hundred is not a figure I can countenance, ma'am. The boat is worth three thousand any day."

"I have a valuation from a reliable source who says it is worth two thousand. Mr. Nathaniel Pickles from the wharf office told me so just this morning."

"Nat Pickles, eh. Well, I s'pose I can't argue with him, but he does estimate on the conservative side. A hundred won't pay for much labour and materials, especially when I have to offer top rates to get men."

"I'm not offering cash, Mr. Knowles," Emma said, hoping her voice did not betray her nervousness. "What I'm offering is a share in the *Mary B.*"

"A share, eh." Knowles rubbed his chin. "That's certainly an interesting proposition. And who would be making over this share?"

"Why, I would of course, Mr. Knowles. I am joint owner of the *Mary B.*"

"Are you now. I would need be sure of that, just for the sake of the legalities, you understand. Not that I doubt your word."

"Of course not. It always pays to be sure of the legalities in business, Mr. Knowles. I have the papers." She had put them in her reticule at the last minute before leaving Wirramilla, thinking they might be needed if she had to prove her right to negotiate for the repairs. She congratulated herself now on her foresight.

"Hmph. Well, then, let me see. If we take Nat Pickles valuation, such as it is, then one hundred pounds would be equivalent to, ah, five percent. Mmm." Emma let him think. She had never done anything like this before. Her heart hammered. Was she doing the right thing? "Ten percent," he said at last.

"Seven and a half, Mr. Knowles. And the *Mary B* to be on the river and ready to work in thirty days."

"You drive a hard bargain, Mrs. Berry."

"I think it's more than fair, considering it's in addition to what you will get from the insurance. And the returns from your share will be ongoing."

"Aye, fair enough. We'll want it in writing, of course. The legalities, you know."

"Of course, Mr. Knowles."

"Come into the office. I might have to ask you to do the scribing. My hand isn't the most legible. I'd rather hold hammer and saw than a pencil."

In a corner of the shed he cleared a space on a bench he used as a desk, judging by the papers and ledgers piled on it. Before she began, Knowles carefully perused the title to her share in the *Mary B*, duly signed over to her by Sam. Satisfied, he set a stool for Emma to sit. Paper, ink, and pen were soon put before her.

Knowles may not have been able to write legibly but Emma soon discovered he knew how to word the document, which made her wonder uneasily how often he had done this.

"Deed of Memorial, and the date," he began, and there followed the party of the first part, herself, and the party of the second part, himself, and the agreement to transfer a seven and a half percent share, unencumbered, of the steamer *Mary B* valued at two thousand pounds when sound, to the party of the second part by the party of the first part, in acceptance of which, the party of the second part agrees to complete the repairs to the said steamer, to safe and reliable working – this last phrase supplied by Emma – within thirty days of the date of the memorial.

Emma read it through twice. It seemed to be in order, so she made a good copy for herself, and she and Knowles signed both copies, their signatures witnessed by a man called in from the boat construction. Emma rolled up her copy of the memorial and tucked it into her reticule. She held out her gloved hand.

"Thank you, Mr. Knowles," she said as he shook it. "I will be back in thirty days to take possession."

"Thank you – partner."

The word jarred on Emma's nerves. She was already thinking how soon she could buy him out. At the top of the slip, she found her cab still waiting. She had all but forgotten about it in the anxiety and stress of the negotiations.

As she was driven back to the High Street, she had to admit Knowles had behaved well, far better than she had expected. It had all been surprisingly easy, in fact. The *Mary B* would be back on the river in thirty days, and she had not paid more than she was comfortable with. She patted her reticule.

How would Daniel react? He already resented the fact she had Sam's share. He wouldn't be happy at having Knowles as a part owner as well, however small a piece he held, but getting the boat back on the water was worth it in her estimation.

Emma was eager now to pay another visit to Mr. Thompson, but it was too early for a social call.

"Could you drop me at the Primrose Tea Rooms and call back for me there at half past ten?" she asked the cab driver.

"Certainly, ma'am," he replied. "If you need a cab any time, send for Tom Crowley or leave a message with the doorman at the Shamrock," he told her when she alighted. His faded blue eyes smiled down at her.

"Thank you, Mr. Crowley. I'm much obliged."

Emma entered the Primrose Tearoom and took a table by the window where she could easily observe when Mr. Crowley returned. She placed her order and gazed out the window at the passing shoppers. It wasn't a sight she saw every day. When a familiar voice announced her tea, she looked up in surprise.

"Janet? Are there two of you?"

"No, ma'am, there's just me. I help me Mum out here as well as working at the boarding house," the girl said, looking shyly pleased with herself.

"That must keep you very busy" Emma said.

Janet lowered her voice. "It does, but it beats working for just the one. Me Mum shouts a lot. Aunt Charity isn't much better, but at least it makes a change."

Families! Janet's mother must be a real tartar if her daughter found refuge in the drabness of her aunt's boarding house. The décor of the Primrose, by contrast, was fresh and bright, with red gingham tablecloths and soft blue walls, accented by floral curtains in red, blue and yellow. Was Henrietta Pickles the source of that bright blue armchair in her room? She would ask Janet if she got the chance.

# Chapter 10

## *Clarice Thompson*

CLARICE THOMPSON herself answered the door to Emma's knock. Surprise and disquiet, quickly hidden, passed across the girl's face.

"Good morning, Miss Thompson. Is your uncle in?" Emma asked, taking note that Clarice was again wearing the white cotton gloves.

"He isn't at home, Mrs. Berry. May I take a message for him?" Emma was taken aback for a moment but quickly decided that a visit with Clarice might elicit something useful, if only to learn Mr. Thompson's schedule so she could waylay him somewhere. It was likely he would avoid setting up an appointment.

"I was rather hoping I might speak with you as well," Emma said.

"Oh. Please, do come in. Can I offer you tea?" Clarice asked as she ushered Emma into the conservatory.

"Thank you, that would be most pleasant." She didn't really need it after her morning tea at the

Primrose, but people always spoke more freely over a cuppa.

Clarice reached for the bell to call the maid. "Oh," she said, her hand going to her mouth. "I will have to leave you in order to tend to it myself. I forgot I sent Susan off on errands."

"Why don't I join you in the kitchen, then," Emma said. "There's no need for us to stand on ceremony."

"Oh, well, if you are happy with that."

"Perfectly."

Clarice, looking a little unsure, led the way to the back of the house. The kitchen looked out onto a flourishing vegetable garden. Emma took one of the two chairs at the small round table by the window.

"Susan will no doubt dawdle and visit friends and not be back until late," Clarice said, busying herself with the teapot. "Do you have trouble with servants, Mrs. Berry?"

"Not personally, though some pastoral properties do, I know. We are fortunate in that regard at Wirramilla. We have a family who have been with us for more than twenty years."

"That must be so nice for you. I don't know Wirramilla. Is it near here?" Clarice absently rubbed one gloved hand on the back of the other.

"Its hundreds of miles downriver, near to Wentworth," Emma replied, trying not to stare at the girl's hands.

"And you travel by boat all that way? That must be divine. I went on the Sunday School picnic excursion upriver last spring, and our church is planning a similar event next month. There is a place with willow trees on the riverbank, and ducks and swans in a little side water." She smiled at the memory as she sat and poured the tea. "It is so delightful. I am so looking forward to it again."

"And some pleasant company to enjoy it with, perhaps, Miss Thompson?" Emma suggested gently as she helped herself to milk and sugar. Those shining eyes were reflecting on more than willow trees and swans. Clarice blushed prettily. She looked down at her hands. Her forehead wrinkled and her shoulders sagged a little.

"Miss Thompson," Emma dived in, "I couldn't help but notice. Do you have some skin irritation? On your hands? If there is a problem… I have experience in herbal remedies, or I wouldn't presume. Perhaps I might be able to help." Clarice's hands disappeared beneath the table, her silence speaking volumes. "May I?" Emma held out her hand to the girl.

Clarice hesitated and then returned one hand to the table, turning her head away as if she would disassociate herself from it. Through the cotton glove Emma could feel a soft, plump little hand suited to its plump little owner. She gently rolled back the fabric to reveal on the back of the hand an angry red rash, weeping in parts where it had been rubbed.

"I can see it must be irritating. Have you had this problem long?"

"Several months now. The chemist gives me different ointments, but nothing seems to help."

"Hmm. It could be caused by something you have been in contact with. Have you changed anything, a cleaning product, some preparation of some sort?" Clarice shook her head. "Do you help your uncle in the garden?"

"Yes, but I always have done."

"No new plantings?"

"Nothing. The chemist has already asked me these things, Mrs. Berry." She took back her hand and tugged the glove into place before tucking both hands into her lap. Was there something upsetting the girl and the rash a manifestation of that?

"He obviously knows what he's doing," Emma said, referring to the chemist, "but he may not know all the local herbal remedies. These are things my grandmother has studied all her life and taught me much of. May I see the preparations he has given you to try?"

"I suppose so."

In Clarice's bedroom, Emma examined a collection of jars and bottles with various coloured mixtures and ointments.

"I can't tell what is in all of these," she said. "The makers don't give out the secrets of their ingredients unfortunately, but I can see what mixtures the chemist has made up. There is something I could suggest that would ease the irritation. The rash can't heal if you keep rubbing and scratching at it, you know."

"Oh, it does irritate so, I feel like tearing my skin off sometimes. Can you really make it feel better, Mrs. Berry?" she asked, the hope tangible in her voice. "Even that much would be such a relief."

"I'm certain of it. Let me write down something for the chemist." Clarice found paper and pen and Emma sat on the edge of the bed and wrote her suggestion involving an infusion of mashed bark from the styptic tree *Canarium Australianum* that grew in the tropics, and some other more common ingredients. When she got back to Wirramilla she would send Clarice a bar of chamomile soap as well.

"Now come," she said, drawing the girl down beside her. "We need to find what is causing this if we're to heal it completely. Sometimes, when our body is out of humour the trouble manifests in odd ways. Tell me, has something happened to cause you worry in these past months, something you haven't been able to talk about to your uncle or a friend, perhaps?" Clarice looked at her in surprise. "I thought so. You do want this rash to be healed, don't you?" Emma urged. "Being able to take your gloves off at the Sunday School picnic?"

The girl nodded. "It's Uncle Alex," she said, tears trembling in her voice.

"What about him?" Emma prompted gently.

"He hasn't been himself for some time. He has black moods, shuts himself up in his study. Sometimes," she shuddered, "I fear he will not come out alive. And yesterday, he was so rude to you and the captain. It isn't like him at all. There is clearly something worrying him greatly. I don't know what to do."

"When did this start? Was it around the time the fire destroyed his shop?"

"The fire? No, no, it started before the fire. It happened almost overnight. One day he was the same kind, gentle man I love, and the next, he wasn't. I've thought about it a lot, trying to work out what happened, and I remembered. It was after he had come home late from the shop one evening, which was most unusual. He was always very punctual about his hours. I asked him if he was unwell, had he seen a doctor, you know? Had some bad news told him? He insisted there was nothing wrong, kept insisting until I've had to stop enquiring, but there is, Mrs. Berry. Something is very wrong, I know it," she said, her voice trailing off into a whisper.

"I don't suppose you can remember when this was, exactly? The day he came home late." It may mean nothing, but if the timing fit...

Clarice wiped a gloved hand across her eyes and went to a drawer in her dresser from which she extracted a diary. She sat back down, and Emma

116 · Irene Sauman

waited patiently as she flicked through the pages for several minutes, reading here and there.

"It was the twentieth of March, a Tuesday. The fire wasn't until the middle of July."

Emma's scalp tingled. The twentieth of March was barely four weeks before that brief night-time meeting on the riverbank. Had Major Barnaby arranged with Mr. Thompson and then gone looking for someone to act as courier, eventually finding a willing Sam?

"Does the date mean something to you, Mrs. Berry?"

"It may fit in with our inquiries, Miss Thompson."

"Your inquiries?" Clarice was immediately suspicious. "Is this something to do with the missing packet you were asking after? Uncle Alex told you he knew nothing about it."

"His reaction to our questions yesterday suggests he does know something of the matter," Emma said gently. "It was obviously a subject he found disturbing for some reason."

Clarice clutched the diary to her. "Oh. He was most agitated all evening after your visit and this morning he took the train to Melbourne. Quite suddenly. He hadn't said anything previous about making the journey."

"This is a serious matter, Miss Thompson," Emma said, forcing herself to take advantage of the girl's upset and concern. Mrs. Paschal said a detective, whether male or female, could not be too nice. "The man who sent that packet would do almost anything to retrieve it. He would not hesitate to ruin a man in the process if it would achieve his ends or cover his own actions. I speak from experience. He has already threatened me and threatened to disgrace my late husband."

"No!" Her eyes widened.

"Tell me, has your uncle had a visit recently from a Major Barnaby? A short, stout man with an air of authority." Which was a polite way of describing him.

"That was the name you mentioned yesterday, wasn't it? No, it was the first time I'd heard it, and I haven't seen anyone such as you describe." More than likely if the Major had contacted Mr. Thompson, he would have done it without witnesses. "What was in this packet that is causing so much trouble?"

"A valuable emerald necklace, Miss Thompson. An heirloom," Emma said. "We believe your uncle is involved. Finding the necklace is all we want to do. There is no need for charges or prosecutions or any unpleasantness of that kind once the necklace has been found."

"Prosecutions?" Clarice cried out in alarm, jumping up and facing Emma. "Oh, no, that would kill him. You must understand, my uncle has been kindness itself since my parents died. He is a good man. He isn't my real uncle you understand, not by marriage, but my father was a great friend. I have known him all my life. He even adopted me and gave

me his name. He doesn't deserve this. Oh dear."
Tears threatened again.

"Even good men get caught up in bad deeds sometimes," Emma said, pulling the girl back down beside
her and speaking quietly. "As for prosecution, you say
you want to help him. You can, by helping us discover
what has happened to the packet we seek. If your
uncle has had nothing to do with it, we can clear him
and look elsewhere, but we must follow the trail as it
lays itself out before us and your uncle is a major
point in the trail right now." Clarice sniffed.

"You mentioned your uncle's study," Emma went
on. "Perhaps there is something there that will help
us. Shall we have a look? You do want to clear his
name of any wrongdoing, don't you?"

There was little chance there would be anything
relevant, but Emma couldn't overlook the possibility.
She was already afraid that if the emerald necklace had
been in the house, it was now on its way to
Melbourne.

Clarice looked most unhappy at the suggestion.
Then her chin went up.

"All right," she said. "If it will prove he has done
nothing wrong."

She led Emma back along the hall to a room in the
middle of the house. The curtains were drawn, and
Clarice lit a lamp, which seemed appropriate. What
they were doing required lamplight not the bright
exposing light of day.

A large, well-polished, dark timber desk and several matching bookcases and filing cabinets were revealed. In the shadows cast by the lamp she could discern a collection of hunting prints on the panelled walls. It was the room of a man who appreciated and could afford quality.

A black leather chair sat at right angles on the other side of the desk as if recently vacated. Emma gave a little shiver. Mr. Thompson's presence seemed very real in his private room. She viewed the cabinets with some dismay. They clearly held many papers.

"He keeps his most important documents in the safe," Clarice said. "Perhaps we should look there first."

She slid back a panel low in the wainscoting to reveal the door of a large steel safe and proceeded to turn the dial. The only sound in the room was the metallic clicking as it went around. Clarice reached for the handle and hesitated, looking back at Emma who nodded encouragement, though she could barely credit what she was party to herself.

Clarice pulled on the handle. The safe opened without a sound. Emma bent down beside her to look inside but let Clarice take out the bundles of papers. Among the contents were several small bags containing jewels or precious stones, but no packet in oilskin.

"We should look at those bags," Emma said.

Clarice handed them to her without a word and watched as Emma tipped the contents of each into her hand in turn. There were tiny glittering diamonds, half a dozen rubies, and other stones of various colour, and small gold nuggets that glowed dully in the lamp light. Emma returned them to their bags.

"Not what you are looking for, then," Clarice said, a note of triumph in her voice.

Well, it would have been too much to hope she would find the necklace or a collection of emeralds as easily as that. She helped the girl spread the bundles of papers on the desk. Mr. Thompson was certainly neat about his paperwork, marking each bundle clearly with a paper tag attached to the string that tied it. Tax, customs, bundles with names, of suppliers and clients Emma supposed. There was no bundle for Major Barnaby. Hardly surprising if his association involved something underhand.

"What about this?" Emma pointed to a small bundle marked Personal. "You open it. I don't need to see anything unless it has relevance."

"Thank you."

Clarice sat behind the desk and opened the bundle. Emma pulled a chair up on the other side and waited, resting her elbows on the desk and her chin in her hands. Clarice named and put aside the documents one by one. Her uncle's birth certificate, a copy of his father's will, several faded photographs marked with equally faded names written in ink on the back, letters from relatives in England dating back several decades. From an envelope she took out several folded and yellowed newspaper cuttings which she began to open out and lay on the desk in front of her.

"Oh, no. There must be some mistake." Clarice grabbed one of the articles, her eyes darting over the paper, her hands shaking.

"What is it?"

Clarice didn't answer. Emma reached for one of the articles still lying on the desk. Clarice grabbed them up and held them against her chest, her eyes wide and frightened.

"Don't crush them," Emma whispered urgently.

"Oh, oh." Clarice looked at the papers in her hands.

"It's all right. Now please, Miss Thompson."

Tears were spilling from the girl's eyes as she slowly laid the papers back on the desk and smoothed them out. As Emma picked one up and began to read Clarice curled herself into the chair, her hand over her eyes.

"Local Jeweller Suspected of Fraud," stated the headline in the Birmingham Post of April 4th, 1848. The article claimed a young man, one Alexander Jonas Thompson, of 139a Broad Street, Birmingham, was suspected of inserting paste stones in place of real gems in a piece of jewellery with the intent of selling the gems for personal profit. Emma felt the hair on the back of her neck prickling. Paste stones. Of course.

The article claimed the piece had been left for cleaning and repair at the premises of a prominent jeweller where Thompson was employed. The replacement had been discovered before the item was returned to its owner. Two following articles indicated Thompson had fled his home and his whereabouts were not known. There was some evidence he was living above his income and was in debt to money lenders. The articles ended there.

"It doesn't prove anything," Clarice cried hotly, uncurling herself. "It only says suspected. And it was many years ago. I know he's an honest man."

Emma thought the fact he ran away to be pretty damning, but decided not to mention that, as she didn't want to cause Clarice any further grief.

"You're right," she said. "It doesn't prove he was guilty of falsifying the gems, but you know he is involved in this matter we are investigating now. You have been worried about his behaviour and now there is this upset about our visit yesterday and this sudden journey to Melbourne. It all fits in with his having dealings with Major Barnaby regarding the emerald necklace."

"I don't believe it. I won't."

"There is one explanation."

"What is that?"

"That Major Barnaby discovered your uncle's past and blackmailed him into being involved."

"Do you think so?" Clarice grabbed eagerly at the suggestion.

"It is something the Major would do, of that I'm certain. And your uncle may not have been gaining anything from it, except to not have this old matter exposed."

"Oh, poor Uncle Alex." Clarice brightened, "But the fact he has been so upset lately proves he wasn't involved willingly, doesn't it?"

"It's quite possible." This information was more than she could have hoped for. Now she had something to work with she was keen to talk to the man again as soon as possible. "When will your uncle be back from Melbourne?"

"He didn't say exactly, only that he would be away a day or two."

"It is vital I speak with him again. Will you let me know when he returns?"

Clarice's eyes widened. "You won't tell him?"

"That I was party to breaking into his private safe and going through his papers? Absolutely not, Miss Thompson. That's between us two." She told Clarice where she was staying. "Send Susan with a message when your uncle returns."

She waited while Clarice returned everything to the safe.

"Your uncle will be himself again once this matter is cleared up, Miss Thompson. You will have helped with that." There was little more she could say to soothe the girl's concerns, to which she had only added by making her an accomplice to the invasion of her uncle's privacy.

# Chapter 11

## *Emma Feels Betrayed*

IT MADE SENSE that Major Barnaby wanted the jeweller to replace the emeralds with paste and sell off the real gems. That way Lady Annabel had her necklace, and he had the funds he needed. She should have thought of that option in the first place. So why had Mr. Thompson gone to Melbourne in such a hurry? Had it been to sell the emeralds? If so, why hadn't he given the Major the paste necklace already? Had he not made it? Perhaps he was trying to cheat the Major as well. She should have kept watch and followed him. Mrs. Paschal would not have been caught out that way. Nella was right. She couldn't solve everything herself.

Emma spent the rest of the day feeling sorry for herself, but she wasn't one to give up easily. After giving herself a good talking to, she was sitting out on the back verandah at the boarding house next morning, notebook in hand, determined to work out a plan of attack as she waited for word of Mr. Thompson's return.

She had successfully played on Knowles' desire for money. She knew now what Mr. Thompson wanted. Or, more correctly, what he didn't want, which was to have people discover he had fled London under suspicion of fraud. When she spoke to him, whenever that would be, she would have to be careful not to let him suspect how she had come by the information. If he suspected Clarice of having anything to do with it, it would destroy their relationship and blight the girl's life. She couldn't be the cause of that.

If the Major knew about Mr. Thompson's past, it was plausible she could know as well. After all, Mr. Thompson wouldn't know how close she was with the Major. Her husband had been entrusted to deliver the Major's packet – something the jeweller knew after their visit, if not before. It was believable then they may have been in the Major's confidence.

She had to wait for Clarice's note. There was no telling if Mr. Thompson would be back immediately or would be held up in Melbourne for a time. Emma felt she was clinging to a thread.

She had enquired from Miss Pickles about the trains from Melbourne and was informed there were two a day, one arriving at nine o'clock in the morning and the other at nine o'clock in the evening.

"Are you expecting someone?" the landlady had asked.

"Possibly," Emma replied.

Miss Pickle's thin lips thinned even further, and Emma knew the woman was imagining an assignation. This is a respectable house, the thin grey lips seemed to say. But the voice was silent, for the moment at least, and there the matter rested.

At lunch time, Emma ate at the Primrose Tearoom. The day was overcast, and a distant rumble of thunder on her way back to the boarding house sent her in search of an umbrella. It wasn't something she had ever neded at Wirramilla.

She chose one in an oiled green fabric from a stand outside a newsagent. The carved bone handle with silver collar connecting it to the mahogany stem reminded her of the head and neck of a mallard duck. The metal ferule was long and narrow. A useful weapon, in fact, if she ever needed one.

She made it back to the boarding house without needing to raise the umbrella, but the rain was not far off, and the air was sultry.

"There's a message come for you," Janet said by way of greeting as she opened the door to her.

She handed Emma a pale blue envelope from the salver on the hall table. Emma thanked her and hurried with it up the stairs.

"I can serve you afternoon tea in the drawing room in about twenty minutes, if you'd care for it," Janet called up after her.

"I will let you know shortly," Emma replied. She didn't seem to have stopped drinking and eating since she arrived. She threw her umbrella and reticule on the bed and tore open the envelope. The note was from Clarice as she expected.

*Dear. Mrs. Berry. Uncle has telegraphed to say he is returning on the nine o'clock train this evening. I have kept my promise to tell you, but please do not come to the house or contact me again. Clarice Thompson.*

Emma sat on the edge of the bed and re-read the note. It was clear the girl was having second thoughts about her part in the previous day's events. Clarice was another casualty of the arrangement between Major Barnaby and Sam. She would do as Clarice asked. Mr. Thompson would be at the railway station at nine o'clock. She would be there as well.

Janet arranged for the young lad next door to take a message to Mr. Crowley at the Shamrock to call for Emma in time to meet the nine o'clock train. The lad arrived back with Mr. Crowley's acceptance marked at the bottom of Emma's note. He was soaked through as the rain had finally arrived, but it didn't stop him rushing back out to spend his half-penny.

Her arrangements for the evening in place, Emma went back up to her room to finally write up her notes covering the past two days. She had barely begun when she heard Mr. Nat Pickles come in from work. The sound of another male voice suggested a new guest to the boarding house, until the tone of the voice penetrated Emma's distracted mind.

Surely not. It had to be someone who sounded like him. Needing to set her mind at rest, she slipped quietly out onto the landing to peek down into the hall below.

"Joe!"

Her brother looked up, his hand arrested as he smoothed down his sandy hair, damp from the rain despite the hat he was holding in his other hand.

"G'day, Sis." His grin crinkled the corners of his eyes.

"What are you doing here?" Emma asked. He was supposed to be hundreds of miles upriver. How was she going to explain her presence in Echuca? This was followed by a second dismaying thought. How was she to go out on her own later to meet Mr. Thompson under her brother's gaze?

"You don't look terribly pleased to see me, Em," Joe said, coming up the stairs behind Janet.

"Of course, I am," Emma rallied. "You've taken me quite by surprise. You're the last person I was expecting to see"

"Ah, so you were expecting to see someone," he teased, reaching her on the landing and accepting her kiss on his cheek.

"No, of course I wasn't."

He put his arm around her shoulder and drew her along with him through a dividing door to a room at the far end of the passage.

"I shouldn't be here, Joe. This is the men's section."

"It's all right, ma'am. Mr. Haythorne is the only male guest tonight, so far anyways," Janet said, as she left them.

"I didn't expect to see you a widow the next time I met up with you, Em," Joe said. "I'm really sorry."

"Thank you, dear." Tears pricked her eyes, but they were for herself because Joe might now find out what her marriage had led them into. "Are you here for work?" she asked, striving to appear calm.

"Been across the river several days at Moama, sorting out a problem. One of the other officers has been relieved of duty, temporarily."

Emma had read in the papers about some trouble at the customs office, but it hadn't occurred to her to connect her brother with the matter.

"So, what are you doing over here?" she asked. "Surely you'd be better off staying near your office?"

Joe busied himself with his bag. "I am, Sis, but I'm here for the night." He put a clean shirt in a drawer, smoothing it down, not looking at her. "I got a telegraph from Daniel. He sent it to Albury, and it was sent back to me at Moama. He left a letter with Nat Pickles."

"Daniel left you a letter?"

He must have telegraphed Joe at the same time he sent the telegraph to Hargreaves. And a letter? Why? To come to the rescue, of course. Keep an eye on her. Emma sat down suddenly in the armchair, red this time she noticed.

"Em? Are you feeling unwell?" Joe asked.

"Daniel called you here?" Emma said, her voice hoarse.

"Well, yes," he said, his tone reasonable. "It was fortunate I was already nearby, otherwise I probably wouldn't have been able to come at all. Daniel said he had to go on with the *Lisette* and couldn't stay. As it was, I couldn't get across until now."

Fortunate? "Why did he want you here?" She was surprised by the rawness of her own voice. If it surprised Joe, he didn't show it. A cynical voice in her head suggested it was due to his job as customs officer, interrogating people without showing his own emotions.

"Don't go getting upset, Sis." So, he had noticed, just didn't care. "We're all on the same side in this."

Daniel must have told him everything. "I thought we were," she said, "until people started sending telegraphs and letters behind my back."

"I don't know anything about that, Em. Daniel suggested I should talk to the jeweller, Thompson, isn't it? And there's something about a telegraph you're waiting on from Captain Hargreaves?" Daniel had been thorough then.

Emma shook her head. "You won't get anywhere with Mr. Thompson. He'll just go on denying he knows anything about it, as he did with Daniel and I."

"Well, we'll have proof one way or the other when Hargreaves' telegraph arrives. I'm not on duty again until tomorrow evening, so I should be able to look into this in the morning."

Emma hoped the reply from Captain Hargeaves would be helpful. She suspected the jeweller might be cheating them all. Of course, if the captain confirmed he'd made the delivery Mr. Thompson would be caught out. Criminals always made a mistake, according to Mrs. Paschal.

"How did you know I was still here at the Pickles place?"

"Nat Pickles told me."

He would have asked about her at the wharf office when he collected Daniel's letter. There she was making inquiries while inquiries were being made about her. Hah! Go keep a close eye on Emma in case she does something else stupid.

Any guilt she'd felt at contracting the deal with Knowles dissipated. Serve Daniel right for going behind her back. She wanted to shout, slap her fist on the arm of the chair, show her anger and hurt. Instead, all she could do was grip her hands tightly together and keep her anger bottled up.

"I'm the one who's going to be talking to Mr. Thompson," she said.

"What?"

"I haven't been sitting here doing nothing since Daniel left. I have gathered information. I know how to deal with him."

Joe had sat down on the end of the bed. He looked tired. He must have been fielding all sorts of issues about that customs matter, as well as the ordinary course of his work.

Where once she would have been considerate, she now felt to use it to her advantage. She wasn't just fighting Major Barnaby, but the men in her family. They had left her no other option, treating her as if she were useless or nothing but trouble. She had to sort this matter herself or forever be damned for bringing Sam Berry into the family.

"What information?" Joe asked.

"Information he will accept if it comes from me, whereas you are an outsider in this matter. You have no leverage with him."

"Of course, I have leverage. I'm a customs officer. He's suspected of receiving smuggled goods."

"What? I hope you aren't planning on charging him with that offence? How will that help us?" Emma shook her head. Could this get any worse? "And it's only suspected. We don't know he has received it yet. Even more importantly, there is someone else involved. Someone completely innocent who has given me information. If Mr. Thompson suspects her part in this she will be out on the street, penniless, without a family. I won't allow that to happen, Joe."

Joe stared at her. "You won't allow it?"

"No, I won't." She lowered her voice to give her words more weight. "I won't have you barging in with your big feet and ruining what I've set up. Joe, it was my husband who got us into this, it's up to me to get us out. And I can if all goes well."

"And if it doesn't?"

"Then you can do it your way."

Joe considered for a moment, not taking his eyes off her. "What is this information you say you have?"

Emma wasn't about to give that up. It was the only bargaining tool she had at hand. And the more who knew the less power it would have and the more risk for Clarice. She shook her head.

"Em, don't be stubborn. I know you mean well, but I'm going to be talking to Thompson one way or the other, and if you don't tell me what you know I'll be talking blind. That's not going to help our cause, now, is it?"

Emma warred with herself. If she got to talk to Mr. Thompson tonight Joe wouldn't need to talk to him tomorrow, so it wouldn't matter if he knew, would it. And it might keep him satisfied for now, lull him into thinking she was being cooperative.

"Something Major Barnaby was blackmailing him with, I believe," she admitted finally, and filled him in on the details of what she had discovered.

"Phew, well done."

"You mustn't mention where the information has come from, though," she said, keeping up the pretence he would be doing the interviewing next day.

"You can rely on it. I'm used to that in my job." He nodded thoughtfully. "Yes, I can let him think it came through you from the Major."

Emma felt a small pang of guilt at deceiving him. Dear Joe. But he would stop her going out, or insist on coming along, which could be worse. All she had to do now was find a way of slipping out to meet the nine o'clock train without his knowing.

# Chapter 12

## Ambush at the Railway Station

IT DIDN'T PROVE as difficult as Emma had feared. After dinner she took Joe to the drawing room which they had to themselves as there were no other guests and plied him with questions about his wife Catherine, whom she had yet to meet, and his work in Albury. Several times she yawned, trying not to be too delicate about it and was pleased when Joe responded.

Did he remember the way they had played that game back home, seeing how long it would take before the elder members of the family began to yawn? It hadn't always worked out well, though. Sometimes they were the ones who ended up early in bed.

"You're very tired, Joe," Emma said with sisterly concern after a particularly huge yawn, "and here I am pestering you with questions after all those late nights working. I'm sure it would tire the fittest. Why don't you go up to bed? Catch up on that lost sleep."

"I am rather bushed, Em. If you wouldn't mind?"

"Of course not, dear," she said cheerfully. "We can talk tomorrow when you're feeling refreshed." Joe gave her a quick look. Had she overdone the yawning game? He said nothing. "Breakfast is from seven o'clock to eight," she said, rising and giving him a kiss on the cheek. She made a point of sifting through the magazines on the side table and choosing one as Joe unwound his long legs and stretched.

"All right. Goodnight, Em. I am pleased to see you looking so well."

Emma sat back down again and opened her magazine. She didn't relax until she heard Joe's door close on the upper floor. She yawned. Heavens, that little trick could still backfire. She didn't want to doze, or Mr. Crowley would have to knock. That could upset everything. She hoped to slip out and back again without anyone even suspecting she had left the house.

She picked up the magazine again and tried to occupy herself with it, as part of her mind listened to the sounds outside. She heard the clip clop of a horse and the shoosh of wheels on the wet road and realised Mr. Crowley would not come quietly to the house. If anyone heard him, she had to hope they would think he was calling across the street. The hall clock struck the half-hour and a few minutes later she heard footsteps in the hall and the rustle of someone taking an umbrella from the stand. The drawing room door opened.

"Oh, it's you in here is it, Mrs. Berry?" said Mr. Nat Pickles. "Would you be so good as to put out the light when you go up?"

"Certainly, Mr. Pickles," Emma responded obligingly, and he withdrew with a polite goodnight.

She heard the front door open, letting in the muted drizzle of rain on the verandah roof cut off immediately again as the door closed. She hadn't known Mr. Pickles was going out after dinner. It caused her some disquiet to think they may have met at the door. No one questioned where a man such as Mr. Pickles went if he was out of an evening. But for a woman, even a widow, her comings and goings were monitored to see she behaved with proper decorum. It added an extra level of delicacy to what she was doing but she would show both Joe and Daniel. She would solve this matter tonight.

The sound of the clock striking the quarter hour brought Emma to her feet. She pulled on her coat and hat and doused the drawing room lamp, standing in the darkened doorway. She heard the clip clop of a horse almost immediately and picked up her reticule, checking again that the front door key Janet had lent her was tucked into her glove.

She had told the girl it was a business matter she had to attend to for Captain Berry in his absence, and which was no one else's concern. It was true in its way and seemed to appeal to Janet's sense of adventure. In the hall, she lifted her green umbrella from the stand and slipped out, closing the front door quietly behind her. Mr. Crowley, large in his wet weather cape and wide brimmed hat, stopped beside the cab door as he spied her. She didn't bother to put up the umbrella, but holding her skirt in one hand, stepped quickly down the wet path.

"Thank you, Mr. Crowley. On time, as always," she said, as she seated herself.

"My pleasure, ma'am."

The cab rocked, as he climbed back to his perch, and with a twitch of the reins and a click of his tongue they turned and were soon back in High Street. Emma hoped he had checked the arrival time of the train, and they wouldn't be late. If Mr. Thompson left the station before they arrived, she wouldn't get to speak to him before Joe did. Tonight, could be her one chance.

Gas lamps blazed along the street and the light from the windows of the hotels, taverns and oyster saloons spilled bright patches beneath the overhanging verandahs. Figures moved between the patches of light, and music and the sound of voices and laughter came in waves as the cab passed by. Emma shrank back in her seat away from the window as someone shouted to Mr. Crowley. The night-time crowd was of a different ilk to those she saw during the day. Where did Mr. Nat Pickles go on a night out?

As the cab clip-clopped into the station yard Emma could see several people waiting on the platform under cover of the awning. There was a light in an upper window of the station building where the station master and his family lived.

The train had not yet arrived and the station building partly blocked Emma's view of the platform. Across the other side of the line, she could see the double-gabled goods shed, its lights still burning. Several men were working around the rail trucks on the siding that ran through the shed.

The shadowy presence of several other horse-drawn vehicles was marked by the misty glow of lanterns like the one swinging from Mr. Crowley's cab. The only sound was the soft patter of rain on the cab's canvas top and the occasional jingle of harness as a horse moved restlessly.

It wasn't long before the faint noise of an engine reached Emma with the familiar chuff-chuff she had for years associated with the riverboats passing her home. Then a light appeared and disappeared and appeared again, as the train rounded the last bend, past trees and houses, the huffing of the engine gathering volume, until the loco, with a long-drawn hoot, hissed and squealed to a halt amid clouds of steam and sparks, its nose visible past the end of the station building.

Emma stepped down from the cab and put up her umbrella. She walked to the corner of the station building where the passengers would pass as they left. A family group, the man carrying a sleeping child against his shoulder, another stumbling tiredly by the woman's side, and a group of shop girls, arms laden with parcels, passed by hunched against the light rain. Most of the passengers were men, well-dressed and some whose appearance suggested they had barely managed to find the fare for even a third-class ticket. She scanned the faces in the dim light as they passed.

"Mr. Thompson." She stepped forward. "Emma Berry. May I have a word please."

Mr. Thompson's startled aspect quickly changed to annoyance as he recognised her.

"I've said all I have to say to you, young lady." He made to step around her, but Emma took his arm.

"It's either me or the police, Mr. Thompson. Your choice." He glanced quickly around. "I have a cab waiting."

He glared at her but did not resist. She had counted on his not wanting to create a scene. As they approached the cab, Mr. Crowley was warding off an enquiry from a male passenger who had left the platform ahead of Mr. Thompson. The man gave her and her companion a long look before he approached another cab.

Emma gave Mr. Crowley the Thompson's address, which earned her another sharp look for her presumption. She stepped up into the cab with some trepidation. If Mr. Thompson were going to bolt, it would be now. She looked back at him, his hand on the door handle, hesitating, but something in the situation decided him, or perhaps he didn't want to walk home in the rain. He climbed aboard and they rattled out of the yard.

"You may have got me here young lady, but that doesn't mean I have to talk to you," he said, not looking at her.

"Then listen. We know you had an arrangement with Major Barnaby to receive the packet we are inquiring about. It contained a valuable emerald necklace. He had a particular reason for sending it to you, didn't he, Mr. Thompson? He could have sent it openly to a jeweller in Sydney to have it valued, if that were all he required as he claims. Instead, he sent it to you, secretly, risking to smuggle it to avoid customs duty. Why was that do you suppose?"

He turned and looked at her quickly and then stared forward again. In the dim light of the cab, she saw him moisten his lips. Still, he didn't speak.

"I don't want to cause you any more trouble than necessary," Emma said more gently, "but if I have to bring in the authorities your past won't remain a secret for very long, and there may be repercussions. I'm sure your neighbours and fellow businessmen would be surprised to know under what circumstances you came to be in this country."

"So, it's more blackmail, is it?" he said hoarsely.

She felt a thrill at his words. She'd been right. Barnaby had used blackmail to involve him. Her confidence boosted, she went on. "I want the necklace returned. No one needs to know anything. That is entirely up to you."

"I never received it."

"Mr. Thompson..."

"I never received it, damn you." He passed a shaky hand across his eyes. "Barnaby has already been to see me. Do you think I wouldn't have given him what he wanted if I had it? I didn't want anything to do with it in the first place, but he didn't give me any choice. And now you."

Emma sat silent for a moment. "What did Major Barnaby want you to do with the necklace, Mr. Thompson?"

"You don't know?" He was suddenly suspicious, doubting.

"You are not the only victim in this affair," Emma said quietly. "Some things I know, others are not so clear."

"He wanted me to put paste stones in place of the genuine emeralds, of course."

So that was confirmed. "Thank you. And you didn't receive the necklace?"

"No, I did not."

Emma's stomach clenched, the disappointment palpable. She had been so certain, so sure she would have sorted the whole thing out tonight. Could she believe him? He seemed to have more to lose than gain by lying. The threat of involving the police and the fear of his past being exposed should have swayed him.

"If I find someone who said he delivered it to you, what then?"

"Are you trying to make a scapegrace of me, madam? Because that person would be lying. No one delivered me any such thing."

"I have no evidence of it at the moment," Emma assured him. "And I do not intend manufacturing any if it doesn't exist, so rest assured on that."

If he hadn't received the necklace, then where was it? And what had sent him rushing off to Melbourne? She almost didn't ask in case she inadvertently implicated Clarice, but she would always wonder. She chose her words carefully.

"Did our visit the other day prompt this trip to Melbourne?"

"It isn't relevant."

"May I be the judge of that?"

He snorted. "I saw my solicitor. I wanted to make sure everything was in place for Clarice... if anything happens to me."

Emma's breath caught in her throat. She remembered what Clarice had said, her fear for him. She put a hand on his arm.

"This isn't over yet. Think of your niece and how she would feel."

He didn't answer for a moment. "What now?" he asked stiffly, as the cab pulled up outside his house.

"We will have to look elsewhere for the necklace."

"Nothing more will be said?"

"Not by me." He turned toward her, but she couldn't read his face in the dim light from the cab lamp. "My late husband was involved, Mr. Thompson. This isn't something I wish to advertise, either."

He nodded, seeming satisfied, and reached for the door handle. "How did you know I would be on that train?"

"I didn't," Emma said quickly, crossing her fingers. "I called to see you here at your home and Miss Thompson told me you had gone to Melbourne. I took a chance. If you hadn't been on the train tonight, I would have been at the station again in the morning." Emma hoped he wouldn't question Clarice too closely. "I thought it wiser to see you alone."

"Alone! With half the town to see you accost me?"

Hardly half the town, but she did think the man who had wanted her cab had shown some interest.

"Oh, I doubt it will do your reputation any harm, Mr. Thompson," she responded lightly, "not among the men folk at least. They'll probably think you've been a bit of a gay dog."

"You are something else, young lady. I wish you luck in your quest, anyway. I daresay until that necklace is found, no one will be entirely relieved of suspicion."

He slammed the cab door, and Emma heard the garden gate click and his footsteps on the path. She tapped the roof with her umbrella.

"Back to the boarding house, thank you, Mr. Crowley," she called.

She leaned back and pressed her fingers to her forehead. Where to now? She had the proof of what Major Barnaby had been planning to do with the necklace, but could she use it to stop him following through with his threats?

She paid off Mr. Crowley and waited on the front verandah until the sound of the cab had receded before inserting Janet's key into the front door lock and letting herself quietly into the hall. A single lamp softly illuminated the hall stand and grandfather clock – and Miss Pickles rising from a chair.

"Mrs. Berry," she said, icicles dripping from her voice, "I must ask you to leave this establishment first thing in the morning."

"I beg your pardon?"

She'd had one disappointment tonight. If Miss Pickles was looking for a confrontation, she had not picked a good time.

"I run a respectable house. I will not have a woman staying here who sneaks out alone late at night."

"I went out on a private business matter concerning no one but my own family, Miss Pickles," she said, stung at the accusation of sneaking. "I didn't realise I needed your permission to mind my own business."

"Business indeed! I won't have the neighbours talking."

"And what if I refuse to leave?"

Miss Pickles looked momentarily taken aback. "A proper lady would have the decency to comply with my request."

"As you clearly believe I am not a proper lady then you shouldn't be surprised at a refusal," Emma replied, with a laugh.

"Really!' Miss Pickles positively bristled. "I will speak to Mr. Pickles about this first thing in the morning. Then we will see."

"The lady will stay as long as she chooses," said a male voice from the landing above.

Miss Pickles stood as if frozen to the spot. Emma looked up to see old Mr. Pickles, one hand in the pocket of a deep-red velvet smoking jacket, pipe clenched between his teeth, and a book in his other hand, finger inserted between the pages. In the soft shadows of the upper landing, he could have been the hero of any number of romantic novels. Emma walked past Miss Pickles and ascended the stairs.

"Goodnight," she said quietly, as she passed him.

"Goodnight, madam."

As she closed her door, she heard him say: "Go to bed, Charity." His tone was not gentle.

Emma sat on her bed and tried to calm her thumping heart. Two confrontations in one night were trying on the nerves. Fancy Old Mr. Pickles speaking up for her in that way. He was taking far too much interest in her, though what that interest involved she didn't dare to imagine. Emma didn't care much for Miss Pickles, but she felt a certain sympathy, and she had probably added to the lady's woes.

She hoped she wouldn't have to stay in Echuca much longer. Despite old Mr. Pickles' orders, it would be uncomfortable to remain at the boarding house unless she could make peace with Miss Pickles, and she didn't hold out much hope of that happening.

And she had no success to tell Joe about in the morning.

# Chapter 13

*Not the News They Wanted*

EMMA WOKE suddenly in the early morning light to the sound of the grandfather clock in the hall downstairs striking six, with the immediate knowledge she had not left Janet's key out for her as promised. Where had she put it? Leaping out of bed, she scrabbled for it in her reticule, at the same time slipping her feet into her house slippers. Where in heaven was it?

She picked up her gloves and shook them. The key fell to the floor. Scooping it up, she pulled on her wrapper and with her hair still tucked under her mob cap, stepped out into the passage. At the top of the stairs, she paused.

The clatter of breakfast preparations could be heard from the kitchen. She ran lightly down the stairs and into the hall. Pulling the front door open, she startled a distressed Janet with the doormat in her hand. She dropped the key at the girl's feet, closed the door in her face, and turning, walked briskly down the hall in the direction of the rear door and the privy, just as Miss Pickles emerged from the kitchen. Emma pulled her wrapper more tightly around her.

"Good morning," she said, hearing Janet's key in the door as she sailed past the woman.

"Morning Aunt," Janet's voice came brightly from behind her.

Emma drew a long breath as she crossed the yard and berated herself for coming so close to causing trouble for the girl. She really must be more careful. On her way back inside, she looked in at the kitchen.

"I do apologise for not letting you know last night, Miss Pickles, but could I please have toast and tea in my room this morning?"

Miss Pickles couldn't un-purse her lips sufficiently to reply and banged the kettle down on the hob. Janet gave her aunt a startled look and then looked at Emma, who ignored the girl for her own well-being. Back in her room, she got out her notebook and climbed back into bed, intent on bringing her notes up to date. She wanted it done before she saw Joe. She had hardly started when a tap on her bedroom door announced Janet bearing a kettle of hot water.

"Why didn't you leave the key under the mat as you'd said, ma'am," she burst out in an undertone. "I was dead afraid I was going to have to knock and tell Aunt I'd forgotten it. She gets right annoyed about things like that. Says I'm irresponsible. Didn't you go out after all?"

"I am truly sorry, Janet. I forgot all about the key until I heard the clock strike this morning."

"You would have put me in a right spot with her."

"I'm afraid she may already suspect it was your key I had." Unless Miss Pickles thought her father had given it to Emma. Now, that was a thought not worth going into.

"What do you mean? What happened?" Janet asked, turning from putting fresh hot water in Emma's bowl on the washstand.

Emma told her briefly what had transpired.

"Grandfather spoke up for you?" Janet said amazement in her voice, her aunt's behaviour seeming not to draw any surprise. "Well, that is a wonder, ma'am. That is indeed. I've never known him go out of his way to be nice to any of our guests. He even ignores me unless he wants something." She looked slyly at Emma. "You don't suppose...?"

"No, I don't suppose. And I've done nothing to encourage him to suppose. Now, what about my breakfast, miss?"

"What about Aunt and the key?" Janet countered.

"Act as if it never happened. She can't prove anything."

"That's never stopped her before," Janet grumbled and left.

Fifteen minutes later she was back with Emma's tea and toast. Emma was sitting in bed drinking her second cup when Joe knocked on her door.

"You up, Sis?"

"Come in, Joe. You're looking better for a good night's sleep."

"Feeling a bit brighter too. Any brew left in the pot?" he asked, picking up the teapot and giving it a shake.

"Sorry. Miss Pickles counts out the tea leaves and measures the water to the drop for two cups only." He put the teapot back on the tray.

"Not your favourite person, then?"

"No, 'fraid not. She ordered me out of the house last night."

"She what? What have you been up to?"

"Thank you for the vote of confidence. She had her reasons, in a manner of speaking."

"And what might they be?"

"Sit down and I'll tell you."

"This is a mighty dry conversation."

"Take the teapot down to the kitchen then and see if you can get it refilled. And don't forget an extra cup. And some more toast. Use your considerable charm."

Joe left with Emma's tray and the empty teapot and toast rack and was soon back with a fresh pot and a cup for himself.

"Toast will be along shortly. You have upset the old hen, haven't you," he said, as he refilled Emma's cup and poured one for himself, heavily lacing it with sugar. He plopped himself down on the foot of her bed. "I thought she would have a fit at the mention of your name."

"She considers me a lost woman," Emma said with a short laugh. Joe raised his eyebrows. "Here," Emma handed him her notebook. "You may as well have the full story from the beginning."

Joe read quickly, washing the words down with gulps of tea. "You're not trying your hand at one of those penny dreadfuls, are you?" he asked tossing the notebook onto the bed when he had finished.

"No, unfortunately. This is very real."

"Hmm. Not a good situation, is it? Barnaby's behaviour doesn't surprise me," he said. "This idea of a colonial gentry, like that in England, is making people of his type think the laws don't apply to them, unless they're laws of their own making. Are you certain Thompson was telling the truth last night?"

"As positive as I can be," Emma replied. "He has more to lose by his involvement now the necklace has disappeared. He can't be sure that either the Major or I won't reveal his past as the search continues, and he must know he's still under suspicion of receiving it. There is one good thing," she added. "We have proof now of what Major Barnaby was about and can use that knowledge to keep him quiet."

"Huh."

"What? You don't think so?"

"It isn't in Thompson's interest to speak out about it, is it, if push comes to shove. Unless you think he could stand up against Barnaby's bullying?"

Emma didn't need to consider her answer. "I'm not sure he could." She didn't want to push him either. She was afraid any hint of his past becoming widely known would be more than he could live with.

Joe nodded. He looked at her keenly. "Why didn't you tell me you were going out to see him last night, Em?"

"What would you have said if I had?"

"This isn't like back home where everyone treats you with respect because you're the boss's daughter. It's dangerous out there, especially at night."

"I wasn't by myself at any time, Joe. Mr. Crowley was always there."

"The cab driver? You've known him, what, two days?"

"I trust him, Joe," and realised she did. A cab man had to be trustworthy, else he couldn't stay in business.

Joe groaned and rubbed his hand through his hair. "No wonder Daniel wanted me here."

"Don't you start, Joe. I am not useless, nor stupid. I'm fit and capable of taking care of myself. I won't be stopped from doing what I need to do because people think it isn't something a woman should do. We do have a queen, remember. You can be certain no one tells her she can't do something because she's a woman."

"All right." Joe held up his hand. "Don't start preaching now. I'm just reminding you of where you are and that you need to be careful."

"I am, Joe." Just not careful enough to escape the ire of Miss Pickles and almost get Janet into trouble. The girl came in at that moment with a fresh stack of toast and a pot of marmalade.

"How long is it since Hargreaves left for the Bidgee?" Joe asked when Janet had left. He wiped marmalade off the knife blade and licked his finger before dropping the knife onto the tray resting on the bed between them. When he reached for Emma's notebook again, she pulled it back out of reach.

"You'll get it sticky. I don't know exactly, but he'd made the junction before we reached it on the way up and that was four days ago."

"We'll check in at the wharf office about midmorning."

"All right. Let's go for a walk when we've finished breakfast. I feel the need for some exercise." And the need to keep out of the way of Miss Pickles and her father.

The rain had cleared, and the air smelt fresh and clean, but the mud in the streets was deeper than before. Emma walked beside Joe along High Street, clinging as close as possible to the shop fronts where the ground was driest, her stride matching his, his hand in his pocket, hers tucked under his arm.

"When is the *Mary B* going to be back on the river?" Joe asked. "It is being rebuilt?"

"Yes, at this very moment." Emma was delighted to tell him. "Let's walk to the boat yard and see her. It's by Dutch's slip."

"Goodo."

They walked in silence for a few minutes.

"I don't want to see the old place lost to us, Em," Joe said as if out of nowhere, surprising Emma who had been looking in the shop windows and checking what other women were wearing. "Where would Mother and Father go, and Lucy and Nella? Thirty years is a long time to live somewhere, expecting it to last forever."

Emma had been avoiding those very thoughts. She didn't think Lucy, or Nella and Jeff, or any of the Wirras for that matter would have difficulty finding employment elsewhere, but her parents were another matter. Father would be devastated if he lost Wirramilla. Thirty years was a long time, as Joe said.

"Are you afraid you will end up supporting them?" Emma asked now.

"You think I wouldn't?" Joe replied, a challenge in his voice.

"That's not what I meant. I wouldn't want to be Catherine with Mother in the house. She's put up with Grandmama all these years. Having the chance to rule over her own daughter-in-law might be too much of a temptation. And you'd have Grandmama there as well." Without her stillroom and herbal garden to keep her occupied.

"Catherine isn't like any of you Haythorne women. She'd be fine."

Emma shook her head. She didn't know which of them to feel most sorry for; Catherine because of Mother, or Joe because he would bear the brunt of Catherine's unhappiness. She didn't ask what he meant about the Haythorne women. He might tell her.

"Well," she said taking a light tone in the face of such dire consequences, "if we do lose Wirramilla, at least Mother won't be able to nag at you any more about coming back to run the place."

"I've never seen that as a problem. I'd put Jeff in as manager when the time comes. He's perfectly capable."

"Perhaps it'd be better if we did lose the place then," Emma said with a small laugh. "Mother would never survive Nella taking her place in the homestead." A wave of regret washed over her at the way she and Nella had parted.

"Are we going to lose it, Em?"

She squeezed his arm. "Not if I can help it," she said quietly, not sure if either of them believed it.

◇◇◇

THERE WERE a handful of men working on the *Mary B.* The boat was upright now, supported on block work. The timbers on the near side had been cut away around the shattered portion and trimmed, creating a neat hole that was already being filled with new timbers. Inside the hull someone was hammering, and under the sound, a bass voice was singing in breathy snatches in a language Emma didn't recognise. A large part of the upper deck had been stripped out. That section would not be rebuilt until the steamer was floated, but Emma was surprised at the extent of what would have to be done.

"Mrs. Berry." Knowles dropped down from the steamer. "This is an unexpected pleasure." His voice was oily. She hoped he wouldn't say anything which might require an explanation to Joe. She was as reluctant to tell him about transferring a share of the steamer to Knowles as she was Daniel.

"My brother Joseph Haythorne, Mr. Knowles," she introduced them.

Knowles put his hand out to Joe. "George Knowles," he said as they shook.

"Mr. Knowles, why have you stripped the upper deck?" Emma asked. "That wasn't necessary surely?"

Knowles looked to Joe with a quick lift of the eyebrows as if to say 'women!' Emma couldn't see Joe's response, but she immediately felt annoyed at the attempted collusion.

"The upper deck was badly water damaged ma'am, and I have plans for enlarging the accommodation. I did hope to surprise you with it."

"You have certainly surprised me, Mr. Knowles. I didn't realise you would be taking liberties with the repairs without speaking to us about it."

"This is a good opportunity to increase her earning capacity. See here," he turned to Joe, "by putting a flying extension over the rear cargo deck we get extra floor space up above for two more passenger cabins as well as providing weather cover to the lower deck."

"Seems like an excellent idea. Can you do it within the insurance payment?"

"Oh, no trouble with that. No, no. I've got hold of some salvaged timbers at little cost. And I do the job right, Haythorne. No half measures."

"I'm pleased to hear it," Joe said, his tone giving no indication as to his thoughts on the matter.

Emma walked around the far side of the steamer. Knowles followed close behind, pointing out the work he was doing to Joe. She had to admit what he proposed would be an improvement, even if he were doing it to increase his own take from the boat's operation.

She had seen boats being repaired on the riverbank where they had been hauled up. Only work that was strictly necessary was done under those conditions. It might after all have been to the good the *Mary B* had been floated back to Echuca and left waiting for repairs. Perhaps giving Knowles a share in the steamer would turn out to be of benefit to them all. Wait until Daniel saw the result. He couldn't complain then.

Knowles shook Joe's hand and gave Emma a salute before going back to his work.

"Interesting," Joe said, as they left. "Seems to be taking a very personal interest in the *Mary B.*"

"He has a good reputation," Emma said. "I can see why now. Is it too early to check in at the wharf office?" she asked, changing the subject.

Joe pulled out his pocket watch. "Past morning teatime, anyway. We'll go see if a telegraph has come in."

At the wharf, the loading of cargo onto the riverboats and back loading of wool bales into the railway trucks was still going on as if there had been no cessation during the intervening hours since she was there. Indeed, there had probably been only a few early morning hours of quiet. The office was a hum of activity.

Joe breasted his way to the counter and soon returned clutching a pale-yellow envelope. They moved into a corner of the room out of the way, and he opened it, pulling out the folded sheet and holding it so they could both read it.

*All items on person of Captain Sam Berry left
with Andersons at Merrim for Mrs. Berry.
Hargreaves.*

"No," Emma whispered. "No, no, no." All she'd
received was his watch and a penknife, a few coins,
and his captain's papers. The packet with the necklace
was still unaccounted for. This didn't help them at all.

# Chapter 14

## *A Message from the Grave*

"I KNOW YOU told me you weren't hungry," Mrs. Lockwood said, putting the tray down on the side table near where Emma was sitting in their cabin, "but I had the cook make up a small plate for you in any case, and a nice fresh brew. You'll feel better if you eat something, my dear."

Emma hadn't eaten since the previous afternoon, when she and Joe had taken leave of one another, he to return to his work at Moama and she to board the P.S. *Sapphire* for home. Her mind had kept returning again and again to the news she was taking back to Wirramilla, until she felt ill and exhausted.

"It's very thoughtful of you," she said now, "but I really don't..."

"Try a mouthful or two. Nothing seems so bad when you are well fed, my dear. Take it from someone who knows."

Emma had no doubt Mrs. Lockwood knew. She was one of the most well-fed ladies she had ever seen. Now she pulled the side table closer to Emma's chair.

"There," she said. "Have a pick at it, dear. Come along now, humour me." She sat herself down on the edge of her bed, which creaked ominously.

Emma looked at the plate. Braised mutton in a thick, rich gravy with mashed potato and some greens. Beside it was a small bowl with apple crumble. It did look inviting, even if her stomach wasn't agreeing with her eyes.

"Eat," Mrs. Lockwood ordered, and Emma obediently did, first taking a tentative mouthful and then realising she was indeed hungry. She cleaned the plate and drank the tea, feeling better as promised.

"There now," said the older lady, satisfied. "Why don't you take the tray back to the galley and get yourself some fresh air."

"Thank you," Emma said, giving Mrs. Lockwood a kiss on the cheek.

"Go on with you. Everyone needs a little mothering sometimes," Mrs. Lockwood said, looking pink and pleased.

Emma wished mothering were all she needed. Daniel would receive Hargreaves telegraph at Euston and know that all was lost. Mr. Thompson would not be able to withstand Major Barnaby's threats to expose him and could provide no insurance against the man. They still needed the necklace to satisfy the Major, and she had no idea where to find it.

Could her father cover the cost and allow her and Daniel to repay it? She couldn't be sure. It was a daunting amount and could cripple Wirramilla if it coincided with a poor season or two.

A willy-wagtail landed on the railing where she stood and cheekily hopped back and forth, puffing out his white chest, his black tailcoat bobbing and fluttering. Lucy believed wagtails were gossips who brought trouble and she always chased them off. They were certainly cheeky little fellows.

"You're not helping," Emma told him. "It can't possibly get any worse."

The bird cheeped his 'pretty little creature' call and flew away. There had been a willy-wagtail sitting on the railing in the Merrim graveyard that last day before she'd returned to Wirramilla. It was a memory Emma hadn't even realised she had.

The *Sapphire* was scheduled to call at various pastoral stations along the way to deliver cargo and Merrim had been one of the places mentioned. She would take the opportunity to visit the Andersons, and the grave of Sam and their tiny son. Who knew when she would be back that way again?

The swampy, low-lying lands that marked the miles downriver of Swan Hill eventually gave way to heavily timbered countryside as they approached Merrim station later next day. Mrs. Lockwood elected to accompany Emma to the homestead. She was full of energy for such a large lady and clearly enjoyed meeting people. Emma was glad of the company.

Halfway up to the homestead they met a servant girl coming down to the *Sapphire*, drawing a small flatbed cart behind her, clearly intent on collecting some stores from the riverboat.

"Hello. It's Deelie, isn't it?" Emma said, recognising the Irish girl.

"And Mrs. Berry, it is. Glad I am to see you looking so fine." Emma told the girl she was hoping to see Mrs. Anderson. "The Andersons have gone," Deelie said. "Mr. Fraser is the manager now."

Emma was surprised. The Andersons had seemed very settled and content when she had been here before, and she was disappointed not to see them.

"Would it be all right if we visit the graveyard?" she asked.

"Mr. Fraser wouldn't object to that, for sure," Deelie said, and went on down to the landing.

Emma and Mrs. Lockwood continued up the rise and then picked their way across a roughly ploughed paddock. Their destination was a stand of eucalypts protecting the graveyard in the middle of the ploughed area.

They were not alone. A young man was sitting beside a simple wooden cross, brushing twigs off a grave mound. He had the dark hair and fine, pale-skinned features typical of the Irish. A child of about a year old, unsteady on his feet, clutched the man's shirt. He stood as they approached, and the child sat down abruptly and let out a wail.

"Wheest, now," the man said softly, and gently touched the child's head. The wail ceased.

"Please, don't let us disturb you," said Emma.

"You are visitin' someone?" he said, his lilting accent confirming Emma's original assessment.

"My husband, Sam Berry."

"Ah, now!" He stepped aside to reveal a little way behind him the gravestone Daniel had erected on Sam's grave. "Very sad that, all right."

Emma walked around to the grave, noticing for the first time the posy of wildflowers on the grave the young man was tending.

"Your wife?" she asked softly.

He nodded. "My Bridget. She left us six months now, but she left me this one, my little fellow."

"What's his name?"

"Liam." The little boy looked up at his father at the mention of his name, a smile lighting his face. Emma felt the familiar tug at her heart at the sight. Would it ever ease?

"And who looks after him while you work," asked the ever-practical Mrs. Lockwood, who had seated herself on a log in the shade of the trees.

"Myself for the most. I look after the horses and the stable. The Missus, she helped with him. Deelie, herself at the house helps out now when she can."

Emma couldn't imagine a much more dangerous place for a small child than a stable. One kick was all it would take if he wandered into the wrong place.

Mrs. Lockwood must have been thinking along similar lines.

"If you need to find another place, I can offer you one up on the Darling," she said. "That bonny lad would fit in with my grandchildren a treat."

"He would?"

"Oh, yes. I've a tribe of them and more to come most likely. And there's always a need for an extra hand."

"Thank ye, I'll think on it alright."

Emma turned her attention to Sam's grave. Daniel had done him proud with the marble headstone.

Captain Samuel Earle Berry,
drowned at the sinking of the Mary B
20 May 1875 and infant son stillborn, 21 May.
Erected by his grieving brother Daniel.

A father and a stillborn babe and no mention of wife or mother. Well, Daniel had paid for the stone, after all. The wording was his choice. It was as if she hadn't existed. She may carry Sam's name, but she was not really a part of the Berry family, not any more anyway. And certainly not if Daniel had anything to do with it. She was a relic, rail against it as much as she liked.

But where was the necklace? What did you do with it, Sam? A line from a Henry Kendall poem sprang to mind.

*Or who knows but that some secret lies beneath
yon dismal mound?
Ha! a dreary, dreadful secret must be buried un-
derground!*

If only he could answer. The sound of the conversation between the Irishman and Mrs. Lockwood
encroached on her thoughts.

"It was my gift to Bridget for the boy," the young
Irishman was saying. Emma looked around. He had a
pocket watch in his hand and was displaying a locket
that hung off the winder.

"I thought to bury it with herself," he was saying,
"but then I would have nothing to show the boy
about his mother."

"What delicate little portraits," said Mrs.
Lockwood, taking it from him. "Look at these, my
dear," she said, seeing Emma was watching. "Aren't
these the most delightful little paintings? How do they
make such lovely likenesses so tiny?"

"They are lovely," said Emma coming to look at
them. The images were delicate though a little naive,
done probably by an amateur artist passing through,
but he had caught the likeness of the young Irishman,
so probably of the girl as well. "Your Bridget was very
pretty."

"She was, that," he said, as Mrs. Lockwood handed
him back the watch and locket. "The captain had a
gift for you too, I saw," he went on, speaking to

Emma. "I couldn't help but notice it you see, knowing you were soon to have a child and me having
given such a gift to my Bridget and them both gone,
just like that."

"A gift?"

A prickling sensation manifested itself in Emma's
scalp.

"That thin box wrapped in oilskin? For sure it was
some trinket. Not a time to forget, so," he went on
quietly. "Jack and me it was dug the hole, and we
stood by next morning showing our respect when
your man was laid to rest. It was after closing it up we
had to open it again for the wee mite. The Missus, she
wrapped him up well in a piece of stuff such a tiny
wee packet he was. She was a good lady. Liam misses
her." He looked at the boy who was pulling apart the
flowers on his mother's grave. "A boy needs a
mother."

"You saw a box wrapped in oilskin?" Emma
repeated, the rest of what he said washing over her.
She felt as tightly wound as a spring.

"I did." He looked at her and frowned. "Captain
Hargreaves, it was, off the *Invincible*. He went through
the pockets and brought everything to the Missus. He
was particular we all see."

"What was in my husband's pockets, exactly, do
you remember?"

"Ah, well, a pocket watch, some papers in an oilskin pouch, some small coins I recall, how much I

don't know." He shrugged. "And the little box, wrapped in oilskin."

"And they were given to Mrs. Anderson? All of them?"

"They were."

Emma let out her breath in a long sigh. He had seen the packet. It had been here, in Sam's possession. It had to have been the necklace. It was the first tangible clue to its existence.

What had happened to it once it had been put in the care of the Andersons? Had they opened the packet, found riches beyond their imagining, taken it, and run? Emma found that difficult to equate with the people she had known, however briefly. Perhaps the temptation had been too much.

"Are you all right, my dear?" asked Mrs. Lockwood.

"Yes, yes." She turned to the young man. "Do you know...? I don't even know your name," she said, belatedly remembering her manners.

"Brendan O'Neill."

"Mr. O'Neill, do you know where the Anderson's went after leaving here?"

He shook his head. "Deelie, herself up at the house, could know."

"I will ask her. You have no idea how important it is to me, what you have told me. That packet has disappeared," she said, feeling she owed some sort of explanation. "I would dearly like to find it."

"It's from himself," Brendan said simply.

Emma looked back at Sam's headstone.

"Yes." Just not the way he imagined.

They left Brendan O'Neill and his son at the grave-yard and walked back to the homestead. Deelie, when questioned, remembered Mrs. Anderson had talked of a sister at some place at the Bendigo goldfields. She was sure they were going there, at least to begin with. Emma's heart sank. How was she going to track them down there? They could be anywhere.

"She wrote something down," Deelie said, going to a drawer in the kitchen dresser and showing Emma a piece of writing paper. It was inscribed in pencil "Mrs. Peggy Anderson, C/O Post Office, Eaglehawk."

"Why did they leave?" Emma asked.

Deelie shrugged. "She said it was because of Danny. You remember, the poor little one not right in his head." Deelie looked as if she had more to say but the *Sapphire*'s whistle sounded at that moment, summoning them back.

Emma was in a quandary. She wanted to travel to Eaglehawk to search for the Andersons with the one small clue Deelie had given her, but the *Sapphire* was heading in the wrong direction. It would be a waste of valuable time to travel on to Wirramilla and then get another boat back to Echuca. Besides, she couldn't return home and then leave again without

172 · Irene Sauman

explanation, and the thought of giving that filled her with dread.

These thoughts occupied her mind as she and Mrs. Lockwood made their way back down to the river. As soon as they were on board, Emma rushed up to the wheelhouse to ask Captain Bennett to delay for a few minutes, because she was leaving the boat.

"One day, my dear, you must tell me what this is really all about," Mrs. Lockwood said. "I sense an interesting story."

"Perhaps I may," Emma replied, with no intention of doing so.

Mrs. Lockwood waved to her from the upper deck as, with a final blast of the whistle, the *Sapphire* steamed into the centre of the river and on its way. Emma squared her shoulders and walked back up to the homestead. She hoped the new manager believed in the hospitality of the bush.

# Chapter 15

## *Finding Mrs. Anderson*

"YOU ARE BACK with us again, Mrs. Berry," said Mr. Nat Pickles, his tone a trifle querulous when Emma presented herself at the counter of the Echuca wharf office. The three days on the PS *Daphne* as she returned upriver had been long and tedious, impatient as she was to get on and find Peggy Anderson.

"Just passing through today, Mr. Pickles," Emma replied. "I wish to leave this letter for Captain Berry to collect when he returns from downriver. It's most important. You will see he gets it, won't you?"

"Of course," came the slightly stiff response, as if his efficiency were being called into question.

Emma stifled a sigh. Was it her manner that upset some members of the Pickles family, or were they overly sensitive? Perhaps Mr. Pickles had been subjected to a litany of complaint about her from his sister. She thanked him pleasantly and turned to leave.

"I hope you have made a hotel booking for tonight, Mrs. Berry," he said. "Because every decent room is full for the latest excursion from Melbourne, and whatever was left has been taken by those coming in from outlying places for the concert and the ball tonight."

Emma was dismayed. She had been planning on staying at a hotel for the night, having no intention of begging Miss Charity Pickles for a bed or of meeting old Mr. Pickles again.

"I had best see if I can stay on the *Daphne* for to-night, then," she said thinking quickly.

"It would seem like the best move."

"Thank you for the warning, Mr. Pickles. I do appreciate it."

Emma quickly went back on board the *Daphne* and secured her cabin for one more night, then went in search of Mr. Crowley's cab. The streets were crowded, groups of men and women spreading across the footpath, standing around, making progress difficult. When she finally reached the Shamrock Hotel, Mr. Crowley's cab was nowhere to be seen.

She had planned on a visit to the boat yard to see how work on the *Mary B* was progressing, but more important was to book Mr. Crowley for the morning to catch her train. She looked up and down the street, uncertain of her next move. The Shamrock's door-man appeared at her elbow.

"Are you wanting a cab, ma'am?"

"I was hoping to catch Mr. Crowley. I need to book him for tomorrow morning to catch the train."

"I can do that for you, ma'am. What name shall I give, and where shall I tell him to collect you?"

Emma told him and was glad when he wrote it down in a little notebook. She would not have felt confident had he relied on his memory.

"Very well. I will make sure he is informed."

With her cab arranged, Emma wondered if she could walk to the boat yard. There were so many ordinary people out and about it felt quite safe. At the top of Pakenham Street, she saw a group a little ahead wandering down past the railway station towards the slip, and another lot strolling back. She went on. The group ahead paused to examine the half-built boat on the slip and Emma could see past them on the river the *Mary B* floating. The boat's hull was repaired and caulked, and the framework of the upper structure rose impressively, partly clad.

There was no activity in the boatyard, the men obviously having finished for the day. The door to the shed was closed and a shutter drawn across the window opening. Emma would have liked to look over the boat, but the plank to the deck had been removed for the night. She had to be satisfied with the progress she could see from the bank. It cheered her heart to see the *Mary B* back on the water.

She began to follow the sightseeing group back up to High Street. As she did so, three men passed them, coming down. For a moment, she thought she was seeing things, but no. One of the men was Major

Barnaby. Her step faltered. He was talking to the other two, who were clearly gentlemen by their dress, and didn't appear to have noticed her yet, but she was going to walk right by him. What was he doing here? Was he checking up on her? Had he told anyone his story about the theft of Lady Annabel's emerald necklace?

Her heart in her mouth, Emma walked on the distance between them closing with every step. If the sun had been shining or it had been raining, she could have hidden behind her umbrella, but it would look odd to raise it in the growing dusk. She kept her eyes straight ahead, as if lost in thought. One of the men raised his hat as they passed. The other man was busy speaking and didn't take any notice of her, but the Major slid a sharp sideways glare her way letting her know he had recognized her.

Emma's mind froze while her body kept moving as of its own accord. A little further on she forced herself to step to the side of the road and pulled out her handkerchief, dabbing at her nose, while she looked back down toward the river. The men were standing in front of the *Mary B*. Was the Major telling his companions he was about to acquire the Berry's boat? What other reason would he have for being here?

She crushed her handkerchief in her hand, her mind in turmoil, and hurried on before the Major turned back and saw her standing there. She reached

High Street and saw a banner across a shop front announcing a concert and ball that night.

Hadn't Mr. Nat Pickles said something about people coming into town for such an event? Could that be why Major Barnaby was at Echuca? It could be so. She wanted to believe it. Still feeling shaken, and seeking some comfort, she took herself to the Primrose for an early supper and several cups of well-sugared tea, before hiding herself in her cabin on the *Daphne*.

THE DOORMAN at Cooper's Family Hotel whistled up a cab. "Eaglehawk Post Office, Ted," he said to the driver as he closed the cab door behind Emma.

She had arrived safely in Bendigo without any further sighting of Major Barnaby and was now on her way to track down Peggy Anderson. The cab rattled through town before turning into a sparsely settled residential area, dotted with modest weatherboard houses and shacks and mullock heaps. The roads were busy with wagons and various carriages and buggies. Fifteen minutes on they entered an imposing commercial area lined with two-storey brick buildings with parapeted facades. Emma noted several banks, including the Oriental, and several churches, as well as hotels and numerous small shops.

At the end of the strip the cab pulled up beside a triangular-shaped public area nestled between Sailor's

Gully Road and Peg Leg Road. Set back at the blunt end of the triangle was a very new two-storey, red brick Post Office, and a single-storey town hall and courthouse. Emma alighted and handed up her sixpence.

A dozen or so men were on the verandah of the Post Office, leaning on the wall and the railing. Gaunt faces with cigarettes dangling through unkempt beards, moleskins held up with twine or belts pulled in several notches, shirts roughly darned but clean.

She had read that the gold mining industry was in a downturn, mines played out and jobs hard to find. Many who had been employed by the big mines were now out prospecting for themselves and not doing well. She went up the steps to the verandah, the men silent as she passed to the door. Tomorrow, they might strike it rich. There was nothing a herbalist could offer to treat gold fever. Inside, behind the counter, several clerks were handing out letters and parcels from the pigeon-holes behind them. The dejected faces of those who left empty-handed resonated with Emma as she waited her turn.

"May I help you, ma'am?"

"I do hope so," Emma said. "I'm trying to locate a friend who has moved here from the country. She has given her address as care of this Post Office."

"A great many people do until they have an address, ma'am. Have you tried writing to her?"

"Well, no, I was coming to Bendigo so thought I would see her myself." She couldn't write and announce herself. If the Andersons had stolen the necklace a letter would only warn them.

The clerk, a young man with dark oiled hair neatly smoothed back from his face, looked at her for a moment. Emma knew he was thinking she must be a little stupid.

"What is your friend's name?"

"Anderson. Mrs. Peggy Anderson."

He stepped along the row of pigeon-holes to the 'A' and rifled through the letters there.

"There's letters for a B. Anderson and an M. R. Anderson."

M – for Margaret, Meg, Peggy? The clerk returned the letters to their pigeonhole and came back down the counter to Emma.

"Why don't you leave a note for her so she can contact you?" he said.

"I may do that. Thank you very much for your trouble. I do appreciate it."

"My pleasure, ma'am."

On the other side of Peg Leg Road Emma saw Meckling's bakery, with tables and chairs visible inside through the large window. She waited for a cart to go by and crossed, raising her handkerchief to her nose as she passed a man working his way casually along the road with a shovel, and a barrow redolent with horse droppings. The bell above the door tinkled as she entered the bakery.

She chose a seat facing the window where she had a clear view of the Post Office. There was a chance Mrs. Anderson would call to check for mail while she sat there. One could only hope.

The waitress placed a menu before her and Emma realised it was time for lunch. She ordered a ham and tomato sandwich and a pot of strong tea. She was thinking more clearly by the time the sandwich plate was empty, and she had finished her second cup.

She couldn't sit there all afternoon on the chance Mrs. Anderson would choose to call at the Post Office. It might work for Mrs. Paschal when she was staking out a place, but what worked in detective fiction wasn't always practicable in real life.

Whenever a cart or carriage passed down the street it obscured her view of the Post Office, and a cab had stopped right outside her window for the past few minutes. Added to that, the tea had given rise to a call of nature, which meant abandoning her post for five minutes while she sought out the backyard privy.

A letter was the only method available of contacting Peggy Anderson. So how could she word it to ensure the lady wasn't frightened off? Emma had the fleeting thought of writing one of those, 'Would so and so contact such and such to learn something to their advantage,' but it seemed overly dramatic and, anyway, there wasn't anything of advantage on offer.

It was Saturday and the Post Office would be closed tomorrow. She also had to give Mrs. Anderson time to collect the message. Finally, after several false starts and crossings-out, she wrote in her notebook:

*My dear Mrs. Anderson. I am in town for a few days. I will be at Meckling's bakery opposite the Eaglehawk Post Office Tuesday at 3 o'clock. I hope you are free to come. I look forward very much to seeing you again. E.*

That should pique some curiosity. She paid for her lunch and went back to the Post Office. The clerk she had spoken to wasn't in the public area, which was as well. If Mrs. Anderson made enquiries as to who had left the letter he might remember and be able to describe her well enough to recognise.

After acquiring notepaper and envelope, she copied out her invitation, sealed and addressed it to Mrs. Peggy Anderson, C/O Post Office Eaglehawk, and watched the clerk slip it into the pigeon-hole for 'A'. She would check at the Post Office on Tuesday to see if the letter had been collected. There would be no point waiting at the bakery for someone who was not going to show up.

Emma now had two whole days to fill in before the appointed time. On Sunday, the town was closed and quiet and she spent the morning in the hotel lounge, reading and watching the other guests, and partaking of a pleasant lunch in the dining room.

Monday proved brighter. Emma window-shopped along High Street. It seemed every town had the same name for their main thoroughfare. She took lunch in a little cafe next to the Beehive Stores overlooking the town square with its noise and bustle and thoroughly played the tourist. It would be something to remember when she returned to the relative peace of the country.

Next day, around half past two, she left for Eaglehawk and a little before three o'clock was paying off her cab outside the Eaglehawk Post Office. The public space presented a different scene to the one she had seen two days before. A speaker on a soap box addressed a crowd of workers on the dangers of cheap Chinese labour. He was receiving a good hearing, if the cheers and shouts of encouragement were anything to go by.

Emma had trouble understanding the threat so many seemed to feel from people of a different culture but wondered if she would think differently if she felt her own livelihood was threatened. Several constables were standing about the square keeping a watch on proceedings. If it weren't for the police presence, she might not be feeling so secure either. With that sobering thought she entered the Post Office, which was quieter today, perhaps because of the entertainment outside.

"Is there any mail for Mrs. Peggy Anderson?" she asked the clerk.

It was the same clerk she had spoken to on Saturday. He gave her a look as if wondering if he knew her. He riffled through the envelopes from the 'A' slot.

"There's an E. Anderson." Emma shook her head. "No, nothing, ma'am." He deftly slipped the mail back into its place. "Is there any other way I may assist?"

"No, thank you."

That her letter was no longer in the pigeon-hole meant Peggy Anderson had collected it. Now she had to wait and hope the lady kept the appointment. Outside, the crowd around the soapbox speaker was growing. She was about to cross the street to Meckling's bakery when she saw Mrs. Anderson approach the bakery window and peer in. Emma hastened her step.

"Mrs. Anderson." The woman turned sharply and frowned at her. "Emma Berry, do you remember? At Merrim Station some months back, you were exceedingly kind taking me in and caring for me."

"Mrs. Berry, Emma, my dear. For goodness' sake, of course, I remember you. I wasn't expecting... You did take me by surprise."

A roar went up from the crowd in front of the Post Office.

"Oh dear, I fear there's going to be trouble." Mrs. Anderson pulled her shawl more firmly around her comfortable frame, as if the knitted fabric would offer some protection from an angry mob.

"Shall we go in?" Emma moved to the shop entrance. "It would be safer inside."

"I would love to chat, my dear, but I'm supposed to be meeting someone here," Mrs. Anderson replied, peering back at the window.

"It is I you are meeting, Mrs. Anderson. I sent you the letter."

"You did? What an odd thing, signing yourself in that way." She sounded disgruntled. "I couldn't make head nor heel out of who it might be. Had me right puzzled, I must say."

"I will explain," Emma said holding the door open for her, at the same time feeling embarrassed at the subterfuge now she was face to face with the lady.

# Chapter 16

## *A Plea for Help*

MRS. ANDERSON gave Emma a quizzical look but entered the bakery. They took their seats at a table away from the window and the disturbance outside. An older couple were the only other occupants of the place.

"I was surprised not to find you at Merrim Station when I called there," Emma said after they had placed their order, and before Mrs. Anderson could question her.

"Oh, I had to leave. Danny went and got his-self lost," Mrs. Anderson said.

"Oh, my goodness." Deelie had mentioned something about Danny.

"Lost or taken, we don't know," Mrs. Anderson went on. "We searched for a week. There weren't a piece of ground in the place we didn't go over again and again. I couldn't sleep for the thought of him lost and frightened out there, his little body failing." She wiped a tear from her eye with the corner of her handkerchief. "I'd given up all hope, resigned m'self to never see him again, when late one afternoon up rides Mr. Jack Bishop, from Lirriup Station upriver, with Danny on his saddle. He'd found him with the blacks what were passing through."

"Good heavens. He was all right?"

"Looked like a little black himself, he did. And smell. They'd coated him with that goanna fat they put on themselves to keep off the biting things and the ticks and all. My, did he yell with all the scrubbing I had to give him. Did my heart good to hear him, it did."

"And you don't know how he came to be with them?"

"Well, he can't tell us, poor lamb. We'll never know, but likely he followed them, 'specially if they give him something to eat, and then he wouldn't know how to get home. I couldn't stay. I'd have had to tie him up for fear we wouldn't be so lucky next time."

Emma shuddered. She had heard stories of children lost in the bush. And then there was her brother Michael, who hadn't been found for several days after his fall from his horse.

"What is Mr. Anderson doing now?" she asked.

"He's on the railway. He's a fettler, one of them what takes care of the track. That were what he did years back before we went up-country."

"And you are living here in Eaglehawk?"

"Oh, we are. We'd never fit in one of them little two-room railway cottages they'd give us. No, we're staying with my sister. It's a bit cramped still, what with our five and her four but she's on her own since her husband up and left and we can help her out, like, so it suits us both."

"And how are the other children? Is everyone well?"

"They are indeed, thank you kindly for asking."

Mrs. Anderson launched into an account of how the two older boys had found employment at Arblaster's Powder Factory, with good money they brought home to the family each week, and seventeen-year-old Mary was walking out with one of the clerks from the courthouse.

"Good luck to them," Emma said.

There was no evidence among all that of suddenly acquired wealth. Their tea and scones arrived, and the interruption gave Mrs. Anderson a chance to think about how she came to be where she was.

"I have to say, happy as I am to see you looking well, I am a bit put out at being messed about like this," Mrs. Anderson began, as she generously spread fig jam and cream onto a hot scone while Emma poured the tea. "But then, I suppose losing your dear husband and child in a matter of hours is enough to turn anyone's mind a bit. Thank you, dear," she said accepting the cup of tea and adding cream and sugar.

Emma thought it prudent to ignore the inference she was somehow unhinged by her grief. "I need your help, Mrs. Anderson," she began, stirring her tea and leaving the scones to her companion. "I understand some items my husband was carrying at the time he died were left in your care by Captain Hargreaves. You remember him?" Mrs. Anderson, her mouth full of scone, nodded. "Among those items was a small packet sealed with wax," Emma went on. "It contained a valuable piece of jewellery and I'm afraid – there is no easy way to say this – it went missing while it was in your home. It wasn't among the items I collected when I left. I must find it, Mrs. Anderson. It's especially important."

Mrs. Anderson stopped with a piece of scone half-way to her mouth. Emma could almost see the cogs turning in her mind. She might be uneducated, but Emma knew she wasn't a stupid woman.

"And that's why you didn't put your name on the letter, is it? You thought if we'd stolen your precious packet, I wouldn't meet you." She leaned toward Emma across the table. "After all the care I give you at the time you lost your poor bairn and you thinking we're naught but thieves. I can't believe..."

Emma had no way of excusing or explaining that suspicion. It existed, but if Mrs. Anderson had acquired thousands of pounds' worth of jewellery she was hiding it well.

"I need your help again," Emma interrupted, leaning forward, taking Mrs. Anderson's free hand in both hers. "That packet contains a valuable necklace my husband was delivering for someone. The man who owns it wants it returned or paid for. If I don't find it, the cost could ruin my family."

That sounded even to Emma's ears like a story from a penny dreadful, as Daniel claimed, but she went on as Mrs. Anderson's eyes widened.

"My husband made poor judgement in getting involved and now my family is in danger of losing everything. I married him and brought this on us, so I must find this piece of jewellery and restore it to its owner and make everything right. Dear Mrs. Anderson, won't you help me?"

"Really? My goodness. This is real, is it?"

"I'm afraid so."

"And these jewels, they're valuable?"

"Very."

"Well, well, indeed. What a tale. I can't say I remember the packet you're speaking of, my dear. It's some time ago now, and a lot has happened. I don't know how I can help."

"Perhaps someone else in the house might remember it. Might have seen something?" Emma said, trying to hide her despair at Mrs. Anderson's words. "There was a lot of confusion, people in and out."

Mrs. Anderson nodded. "There was. I remember that well enough." She paused. "I suppose you want to ask the children about it."

"If I could, please? Children notice things without understanding their importance."

Mrs. Anderson nodded again, but there was a reluctance Emma could well understand.

"Have some more tea," Emma said, taking up the teapot.

"Thank you, dear. I don't mind if I do."

By the time the teapot was empty, and the plate of scones held nothing but crumbs, Mrs. Anderson had resigned herself to taking Emma home with her. Once outside, they found the crowd had grown and become unruly. A scuffle had broken out on the outskirts.

"We live further up off Sailor's Gully Road," Mrs. Anderson said. "We need to go round the square, else it's a walk through that bush they call a park." She indicated the area of bush on the opposite side of the junction.

"It should be safe enough," Emma said.

They were in the middle of Sailor's Gully Road and almost past the gathering when a group of mounted constables galloped in. The crowd scattered. Men ran in all directions, shouting and cursing as the horses plunged in amongst them, the constables wielding their batons indiscriminately, the officers on foot joining their mounted colleagues. In a moment,

Emma and Mrs. Anderson found themselves caught in the middle as the melee spilled across the street. It was like a cattle stampede but without the horns.

"Stand close and stay still," Emma cried.

"Don't worry about me, dear. I've got me hat pin," Mrs. Anderson responded.

Emma shifted her grip on her umbrella and held it ready to fend off anyone who came too close. Dust rose and swirled around them like the smoke of battle, stirred up by the many feet of men and horses. Several men dodged past them with startled looks, but a third fell at Emma's feet, stunned by a blow from the mounted constable chasing him.

The officer raised his baton to strike again at the fallen man. Instinctively, Emma thrust out her umbrella to parry the blow, at the same time putting up her free hand toward the horse's head. The constable looked up, seemingly startled at the sudden appearance of a green umbrella in a woman's hand and met Emma's eyes.

"What the devil..." He pulled his horse sideways to them and the man on the ground took the opportunity to scramble away. "This is no place for women," the officer shouted. "What do ye think ye doing?"

"Trying to cross the street," Emma responded in the same spirit. "Did you look to see who was around before you galloped in?"

"You tell him," Mrs. Anderson said, her hat now askew without its pin. "Putting innocent people in danger of getting their selves killed like that."

"I could arrest you for interfering with police business," he blustered, his face red.

"Harassing innocent people going about their own business, more like," said Mrs. Anderson, restoring her hat to its proper place.

"Perhaps you could escort us to safety, officer," Emma suggested.

The dust was beginning to settle, revealing several men on the ground and another, who Emma recognised as the speaker, in the hands of the constables. A mounted policeman reappeared from a side street. Emma hoped he hadn't left any wounded behind. The rest of the crowd had disappeared as if it had never been.

"The danger is past," the constable replied and wheeled his horse away.

"Well, that were a bit of fun, eh?" Mrs. Anderson said, as they reached the far side of the street. She coughed. "I could do with another cuppa though," she said. "That dust does dry out the throat."

Nor was Emma sorry to sit down in the kitchen when they reached the home of Mrs. Anderson's sister. One always felt a little shaky after a confrontation. It was a good idea to let the mind as well as the body settle. Mrs. Anderson regaled her family with their adventure as a pound cake was produced, and tea brewed.

"You could have been killed, Peggy," Maureen Miller said aghast, to her sister. Mrs. Miller looked like Peggy Anderson, but without the spirit. Life had ground her down.

"It weren't so dangerous, pet, don't fret."

"You'd best not tell Da," Mary warned from her place by the kitchen fire. "He'd want us to get out of town."

"No, best not. You hear that, our Katy," she said addressing her younger daughter who was watching Danny and the littlest two Miller children, as they played with coloured wooden blocks on the kitchen floor. "Not a word about my adventure to your Da, right."

"Yes, Mam," replied Katy.

"What's a venture?" asked one of the Miller children, but he did not receive an answer as Katy was busy preventing his brother from swallowing a block whole.

"Now then, my lot," said Mrs. Anderson, licking crumbs of pound cake from her fingers. "Mrs. Berry has some questions for you."

# Chapter 17

## *A Letter from Father*

"WHAT DID THIS packet look like, again?" Mary asked, as Emma explained about the items found in Sam's pockets and left for her on the hall table at Merrim station.

She had been careful not to sound as if she blamed anyone for taking it, but Mary seemed to immediately think she was doing just that by the tone of her voice.

"I don't remember seeing anything."

"I haven't seen it myself," Emma explained. "It was described as small and thin, wrapped in oilskin with a red wax seal." Emma heard a small intake of breath from Mrs. Anderson. "Do you remember it, now, Mrs. Anderson?"

"No, no. I don't recall ever seeing anything like you describe." Emma thought Mrs. Anderson spoke a little too quickly. She looked at Mary. The girl was staring at the children playing on the floor. Emma's gaze followed hers and met Katy Anderson, staring unblinkingly back at her.

"You've thought of something, haven't you," Emma said her voice soft and hopeful. "Please, what is it?" No one spoke for a moment.

"He wouldn't have meant to. He just likes them sunshiny colours," Katy blurted out.

"Who does?"

Katy looked at her brother. Emma noticed for the first time all the blocks Danny was stacking were red and yellow.

"You mean Danny?" She'd had little contact with the boy when she was at Merrim and had little knowledge of his affliction except that he didn't speak or interact with anyone and seemed to live in his own world.

"He does like them bright colours," Mrs. Anderson admitted. "I suppose the red wax might have took his eye. It's possible, I suppose. Oh, dear."

"You think Danny may have taken, picked up," Emma corrected quickly, "the packet because of the red seal?" Her heart quailed. Thousands of pounds' worth of heirloom jewellery as a child's plaything. "What would he have done with it?"

"He carries things round, leaves them places," Katy said.

"Oh dear. If he's lost that...," Mrs. Anderson said, her voice quavering.

"We don't know he took it, Mam," said Mary stoutly.

"And we can't ask him," said her mother. "Poor simple lamb."

"You need to talk to the boys, too," Mary said looking at Emma. "To make sure and certain its none of us took it."

"There's no need for that voice, girl," Mrs. Anderson chided.

"Well, she comes here accusing us of losing these jewels we've none of us set eyes on..."

"I'm not accusing anyone," Emma interrupted, struggling to control her voice. She was having trouble crediting that a child may have been the cause of the packet disappearing. Had Captain Hargreaves really left it at Merrim?

"I just need to find it if it's at all possible. The last we know it was left for me at Merrim homestead after my husband was buried, so I have to start there." She seemed to have been starting in a lot of places. Mary flushed and looked away.

"Go fill the wood basket, pet," said her mother. "The boys will be home wanting their supper soon. I apologise for her, Emma," she went on when Mary had gone out. "She's had the irrits all day."

Emma shook her head. She understood. It was not comfortable for any of them. "It's no matter. You say Danny hides these bright-coloured things, Katy?"

"Well, he leaves them all about the place. They turn up here and there most times." Here and there, on a 20,000-acre sheep station. The possibilities were endless.

"Danny wouldn't have wandered all over the property, though, would he?" she asked.

"Oh, no," Mrs. Anderson interposed. "He never went far from the house. Which is why I never worried about him before he got lost this last time. He likes to be by people, though he don't talk or anything. Katy keeps an eye on him most of the time. He has no sense of keeping his self safe."

Emma looked again at the boy, absorbed in his own world, stacking and re-stacking his blocks. "So, the packet could be around the homestead, the farm buildings, somewhere like that? Is that what you are saying?"

Mrs. Anderson nodded. "I guess that would be right."

"Da took him out with him on his horse, sometimes," offered Katy.

Emma sighed. What hope did she have of finding it if Danny had indeed hidden it, or left it lying around? Mary came back in with the wood and fed the stove. The older Anderson boys, Alec and Dick, arrived home from work, coming into the kitchen in their stockinged feet, their boots left in the scullery, two short wiry lads, replicas of their father. The story was gone over again for their benefit.

"I 'member that small box," Alec Anderson said, after a moment's thought.

"You saw it?" Emma's heart leapt, and she mentally begged forgiveness of Captain Hargreaves for doubting his honesty.

"Aye, I did. I wondered what was in it, but I never imagined it were expensive jewellery." He pondered on that for a moment. "It were on the hall table, by a nice pocket watch. I was thinking I'd get one like it meself one day. Da has a silver watch he buttons into his vest pocket, but I fancy having one with a chain."

"Giving yourself airs now, are you?" said Mary.

"I don't see why I shouldn't have it, if'n I work hard enough," Alec fired back.

"Course you can," his brother agreed. "I don't remember no little box, meself. Don't remember anything about those things at all."

"You walk around with your eyes closed, you do," Alec chided him. "Fall over your own feet, you do."

"What do you think might have happened to it?" Emma asked, wondering at the same time if someone who fell over his own feet should be working in an explosive powder factory.

Alec shook his head. "Don't know. I just remember it being there."

"Was there anything written on it, an address perhaps?"

"Nah, don't think so." He turned his attention to the bowl of stew and slice of bread Mary placed in front of him.

"Hey, perhaps Danny picked it up and put it somewheres," Dick said. "Like a magpie he is." He didn't seem concerned about placing suspicion on his younger brother. Perhaps he thought it wouldn't matter, given the lad's mental condition.

"You could go on a real treasure hunt." He laughed, spraying breadcrumbs.

"Don't speak with your mouth full," scolded Mary, taking a swipe at his head with her dishcloth. "You've lost all your manners since you been working at that place."

"What's with you, Mary? Jimmy not speaking to you?" Dick jeered, grabbing the cloth.

"Stop your grating now," ordered Mrs. Anderson. "I can find plenty of chores for you all if you've so much energy."

Mary whisked her cloth away and retreated sulkily to the side of the fire. Dick grinned at her and turned his attention to his supper.

"Where would I look?" Emma asked.

"Our Katy would know," said Mrs. Anderson.

Katy shrugged. "In and round the sheds, under the tank stands, um, around the sheep wash."

"That's where he put the geraniums, weren't it? He decorated the stones in the sheep wash wall," said Mrs. Anderson. "I never could keep any flowers on those plants."

"He plucked all the petals off my red roses, too. Scattered them over the path," Mrs. Miller, who had been sitting silently until then, spoke in an aggrieved tone.

Mrs. Anderson frowned. "You know he don't mean anything by it, pet," she said. Her sister subsided.

"Anywhere else, Katy?" Emma asked.

"I found a yellow tobacco tin once in a hollow in one of the trees along the creek, and sometimes he went up to the graves, but he was always poking about somewhere." Katy began to look upset. "I don't know any more, Mam."

"There, there, pet. You done your best. You couldn't ask more of her, could you Mrs. Berry?"

"Not at all," Emma told her, smiling at the girl.

It was enough to suggest a search of the place would need to cover a wide area. If Danny had anything to do with it. The packet could have been picked up by someone else who had come into the homestead. Or someone who found it where Danny had left it. Anyone, in fact. She had been two weeks at Merrim after the birth. The items left for her would have been sitting on the table in the hall all that time.

"I'm terribly sorry, my dear. I do feel responsible," Mrs. Anderson was saying. "It never occurred to me to put those things away somewhere. I was afraid I'd forget them if they weren't left out in sight. If'n it was Danny what took it..."

"It may not have been. Don't upset yourself about it, Mrs. Anderson. You aren't responsible for this problem," Emma said, trying to assuage any feeling of guilt they may have, and her own for placing them in this position. It hadn't been of their choosing that the *Invincible* had deposited a body and a woman going into labour on their doorstep that night.

The clock on the mantelpiece chimed the quarter-hour. It was after five. She had taken up enough of the Anderson's time and goodwill. Despite her words of assurance, she was aware of the unease among the family that suspicion had fallen on them. Mary hadn't looked her way since coming back in with the wood for the fire and the girl's upset was apparent in the way she held herself. Emma had brought an uncomfortable atmosphere into the Anderson's house which would linger.

She took a slightly strained leave of Mrs. Anderson, promising to write and let her know of her success or otherwise and to keep in touch. Alec was conscripted to walk back with her to the Post Office, where she caught a cab. She sank into the seat, wrung out with the events of the afternoon.

What had she been hoping for? Had she expected Mrs. Anderson to say, 'here you are', and hand over the necklace? Well, that would have been nice. Now she would have to return to Merrim and question everyone, transferring more guilt on the way and if no one could tell her anything, search the place. If the manager Mr. Fraser allowed. Dick Anderson had called it a treasure hunt. Pity she didn't have a map marked with an X to go on with.

On the way back to her hotel, Emma had her cabbie take her to the railway station and wait while she bought a ticket for the morning train to Echuca.

"I also need a connecting booking on a paddle steamer going down river," she told the ticket clerk.

He checked the day's newspaper notices. "The *River Princess* is accepting passengers," he told her. "She is scheduled to leave Echuca at half past nine tomorrow morning. Shall I telegraph a booking for you, ma'am?"

"Yes, please. As far as Merrim Station." She gave her name for the boat booking and paid for her train ticket.

EMMA SPENT part of the train journey writing letters to Joe and Daniel, letting them know the packet had been seen at Merrim and her planned visit to search for it there. She was quickly off the train when it arrived at Echuca and managed to secure Mr. Crowley's cab among the several waiting outside the station.

On the way to the wharf the sight of a short corpulent man walking along the street caused Emma's heart to leap. As they passed him, she saw with relief it was a stranger. She leaned back in her seat wondering if she would ever be able to see such a figure again without flinching.

She left both the letters she had written at the wharf office and was surprised to find a letter waiting for her. It was from her father. She popped it into her reticule to read later. When she inquired as to when the *Lisette* was expected back, she was informed the boat had left Swan Hill early the day before and was due in Echuca late next day.

She would miss Daniel by a little more than twenty-four hours. She pondered the wisdom of waiting for him, but it could be several days before he sailed again. There didn't seem to be anything to gain, and she was eager to get to Merrim. With any luck, Daniel would be able to collect her on his way back downriver with Lady Annabel's necklace safely in her hands. She could only hope.

She boarded the *River Princess* and once settled in her cabin, opened her father's letter, unsure of what she would find.

The letter began with one word: *Daughter*. Emma flinched. Not 'Dear Daughter'? She took a deep breath and read on.

> *I hope this letter finds you well. The news I have received this day has greatly unsettled me and your continued absence only adds to my concerns. Barnaby paid another visit to Wirramilla today with a tale of smuggled goods and missing*

*jewellery. I can scarcely credit it. Whatever was Sam Berry thinking? And it appears you know all about it.*

*Why did you not speak to me about this instead of scurrying off in secret? To say I am disappointed is an understatement. Daniel also said nothing when he called in on his way past last week and seemed unclear about why you were still in Echuca. Then he did not stop in on his way back upriver. Avoidance? I must surmise so. I suspect he has not been entirely honest with me either.*

*I made it clear to Barnaby I would not be held responsible for your husband's actions. More fool him to have trusted Sam Berry with such a mission. At that, he threatened to claim Sam had been a party to stealing the Montague necklace and that you were also involved. You have fled with the proceeds, he tells me. You can imagine my feelings on that score.*

*Whatever tales Barnaby tells there is clearly something underhand about the whole matter. I expect your presence here immediately on receiving this letter with a full explanation.*

*God speed.*

*Father*

Emma exhaled a long breath, her body slumping. Could it get any worse? Her father was clearly furious. And worried. Even if she found the necklace now her family would always know what Sam had done, what she had let them in for.

Just on dark that evening the *River Princess* steamed past the *Lisette,* heading up-river, both vessels bearing full lights, a blast from the *River Princess'* horn acknowledged in turn by the *Lisette.* The old saying of ships passing in the night took on a new meaning for Emma, as she felt a pang of loneliness at Daniel's near presence without his even knowing she was nearby.

# Chapter 18

## Merrim Station

NO ONE WAS in sight as Emma walked up from the river three days later. A light mist, already starting to dissipate in the early morning air, hung over the water, but the sunlight catching the iron roof of the Merrim homestead, perched on the rise, promised a warm day. She took herself around to the kitchen and surprised Deelie as she was drawing water from the tank at the corner of the slab and iron building.

"I'm parched for a cup of your good tea, Deelie," she said, by way of greeting.

Deelie laughed as Emma followed her into the kitchen. "I'll make us a pot soon as I take some hot water in for him."

She swung one of the two large black kettles away from the fire and poured hot water into the tin bucket on the hearth. The smell of bread baking filled the kitchen.

Emma located the teapot and made up a brew, setting out the cups on the scrubbed pine table. When Deelie returned, she pulled three loaves of bread from the oven fitted into one half of the fireplace. She set two in the open window and cut off the heel of the other, spreading it thickly with yellow butter and cutting it in two, putting one half on a plate for Emma. They devoured the hot bread in silence and washed it down with their first cup of tea.

"So, did you find Mrs. Anderson down at that Bendigo, then?" Deelie asked.

"I did. She sends her regards. Mary is courting, he's a clerk at the courthouse called Jimmy, and the boys are working at the powder factory."

"Ah, and Danny and young Katy, they are all right then?"

"They seem so."

"Fine, fine. I do miss them."

"Top of the morning to ye, sweetheart," said a male voice. Brendan O'Neill's face was at the window, smiling at Deelie as he reached for the loaves. He started at the sight of Emma and coloured. "Ah, and good morning to you. I'll just be taking these for the boys." He was gone before either woman could do more than smile in response.

Emma looked at Deelie with eyebrows raised in question. Deelie blushed. She got up from the table and busied herself putting thick rashers of bacon in a pan on the grating.

"He seems a nice fellow," Emma said.

"Aye, he is that."

Emma had the feeling matters weren't all rosy from Deelie's tone of voice.

"Is there a problem?" Emma said

Deelie banged the fork against the pan. "Bren's afraid he's going to be let go any day. Mr. Fraser says he can't do his work if he's looking after Liam as well, and he isn't paying him to be a nursemaid."

"And you don't want to look after Liam? I can understand that. A child is a big responsibility. Or isn't that an option?"

"It is not. He doesn't want me doing it either, though I do whenever I can," Deelie assured her. "But I don't like it here anymore, not since the Andersons left. I've no one to talk with all day, except for Bren. I wouldn't have come if it had been only men here. And I don't want to stay now."

Emma had to admit it wasn't an ideal situation for a young woman. She had been the only woman on the *Mary B*, but her position there had been quite different to Deelie's, and she got to talk to any number of women on her travels.

"You must find it lonely. Is there a reason you can't look for another place?" Emma asked.

She remembered Mrs. Lockwood's offer to Brendan when she was at Merrim previously. Had Brendan followed up on it? She didn't like to ask in case he hadn't told Deelie. Perhaps he had his own reasons for not wanting to move, reasons that didn't include her. From the little Emma had seen he was still attached to the memory of his dead wife.

Deelie looked at her despairingly. "We can neither of us read or write," she blurted out and got up again to tend to the bacon and add some eggs to the pan.

That did present a problem. No matter the advances in communication, it still required people to be literate.

"Isn't there anyone here who could help?"

"Bren asked Mr. Fraser but he wouldn't do it. He says it isn't his problem to find new places for people who want to leave. And Mort just laughed at Bren when he asked him."

"Who is Mort?"

"A miserable old lump who likes to see others just as miserable," Deelie said savagely. "Always pouring poison in Mr. Fraser's ear, he is. He looks after the veggie garden and the orchard." She put bacon, eggs, and bread onto a plate, and set up a tray, adding a teapot, mug, and milk. "Bren might go and find us something and then send for me, but it's hard to manage with Liam." She left to serve Mr. Fraser his breakfast.

Emma poured herself another cup of tea. If ever she complained about her lot again, she would remind herself of Deelie and be thankful. She still thought the pair of them could take themselves and young Liam off on a boat and find a better place to work, but she had no idea of their resources, how long they could survive between jobs or their commitment to one another for all that. The world could look big and frightening sometimes, especially if you didn't feel confident of negotiating it because of your lack of education. Not being able to read or write must be a little like being blind and staying where you were the safer option.

This Mort person Deelie had mentioned didn't sound very pleasant. Was he the type who would chance his hand and pick up an item left out in full view? She had a vague memory of seeing someone tending the vegetable garden down by the river when she was here those few months back, but she hadn't met the man.

When Deelie returned with the empty tray, Emma had come to a decision.

"How would it be if I write and make enquiries about positions for you and Mr. O'Neil?" she offered. "Would that work for you?"

"Would you?" Deelie's face brightened, then clouded again. "You'd have to read the answers for us as well. How would you do that when you're not here?"

"I'm sure we could find a way." She hadn't yet explained her reason for returning to Merrim, but the opportunity of helping Deelie and Brendan could ensure their help in her own search. If Brendan considered it help. She wasn't so sure of that yet.

"We'll do anything we can if you help us get out of here, Mrs. Berry."

"I'll do my best. We'll go over to the stable and speak to Mr. O'Neill once I've spoken with Mr. Fraser, and I'll explain what I'm doing here. I think we can help each other, Deelie, which is even better. And please, call me Emma."

"I will, thank ye."

Emma knew there were always positions advertised in the newspapers and she still had Mrs. Lockwood's offer in mind. And then there was Nettifield. A housekeeper like Deelie was just what they needed to free Bea to marry her Thomas. Unless Matty had made up with Dotty. She wondered how the girl had felt about Matty not seeing her for several months. She doubted George Macdonald would agree to hiring a housekeeper, and Liam was a handicap no matter how you looked at it. Best not complicate matters there more than necessary.

Emma waited until Mr. Fraser had finished his breakfast before searching him out. She caught him on his way to the stables. He remembered her from her visit ten days before and she remembered his dour, grumbling manner. Nothing had changed in that regard.

"Sounds like a will-o'-the-wisp," he said, his Scots brogue thick with ill humour after she'd given him an explanation of sorts as to her mission. "It's your time to waste."

"I would be most willing to pay for my board, Mr. Fraser. I may need to stay for several days. And I hope you won't mind my talking to your men. I believe most of them were here under the Andersons?"

"Aye. Not much has changed. Sassenachs the lot, more's the pity," he grumbled. "I'd like to turn the whole lot over. Bed and meals'll cost ye three shilling a day," he added, as he walked away.

Emma stared after him. Miserable old goat. He'd be lucky if he kept the men he had with that attitude. Sassenachs indeed. She would keep out of Mr. Fraser's way, and he could keep his grumbles and lack of manners to himself. Her shillings were all he would get.

Deelie was peeling potatoes with a cup of tea at her elbow when Emma returned to the kitchen. A cabbage and several turnips waited attention.

"Irish stew?" Emma asked.

"Ah, no, taties and mutton with the others on the side with butter and pepper. That's the Irish way, for sure."

"I look forward to it. I'll eat in here when you do Deelie if you don't mind my company."

"I would hope to be more pleasant company than that dour man, anyway," Deelie said, with a knowing look.

"Much more pleasant."

To speed up their visit to the stable to talk with Brendan O'Neill, Emma helped Deelie with her chores, cleaning out the fireplaces and resetting the fires in Mr. Fraser's bedroom and dining room, which also served as the parlour. Then they dusted the rooms, swept the floors, and restocked the kitchen wood bin.

"You shouldn't be doing this," Deelie protested.

"Nonsense. I had to do my share of work when I was growing up." Not to mention what she did on the *Mary B*. The thought brought a sudden wave of regret for lost dreams. Deelie herself was a reminder of the time at Merrim after Sam died.

Back in the kitchen, Deelie made up tea in a tin billy. "I take morning tea to Bren and Liam when I can," she said by way of explanation, "when Mr. Fraser is away from the house."

Emma suspected they probably got a lot more than morning tea. Deelie wrapped some biscuits in a cloth and put them in a basket with a jug of milk and an extra mug.

"Right then," she said handing the basket to Emma, "don't spill the milk."

Brendan was forking hay into the feed bins when they arrived at the stable. Liam was playing in a pile of straw, wearing a little harness fastened with rope to the corner post of an empty stall. Both father and son brightened as Deelie and Emma came in, though Emma had no doubt their pleasure had nothing to do with her. Liam cried out to Deelie, holding up his arms. She handed the tea-billy to Brendan and unhitched the boy.

"You're gettin' almost too big for me to carry, m'lad," she said, giving him a big hug. She led the way into a room at the end of the stable, Liam on her hip. The dirt-floored room held a small deal table and two wooden chairs. A curtain partly hid a bed against the opposite wall. Deelie put Liam down on a multi-coloured plaited rug that filled the small space between the furniture, where he promptly set up a wail.

"Wheest, now. You'll not get a biscuit if you keep up that fearsome noise, m'lad," she told him, but he continued to whimper until the biscuit was provided. Brendan produced a tub for himself to sit on as Deelie set out the mugs.

"Emma has kindly offered to help us with letters to get a place together," she said as she carefully poured tea from the billy into three of the mugs.

"That's mighty good of you," Brendan said, not looking at Emma.

Deelie poured milk into a fourth mug and Brendan took it, kneeling and holding it for Liam to drink.

"Do you remember the lady I was with when I called in before?" Emma asked, hoping she wasn't about to create dissension if Brendan hadn't mentioned Mrs. Lockwood's offer. "She was concerned about Liam being in the stables here. She thought she might have a place for Mr. O'Neill."

"What's this?" Deelie asked.

"She just said Liam would fit in with her grand-children, is all. She was just being polite," Brendan replied, his attention still on his son.

"True," Emma agreed, "but she might know if anything was available around Wentworth. I could write and ask her for a start. Just in a general way, if you would like me to do that. You would be closer to a town there too."

"Bren?"

He sat back down at the table and picked up his mug of tea. "Sure. That'll be fine." He didn't sound particularly enthused at the idea.

"Thank you," Deelie said to Emma, with a small frown in Brendan's direction.

Was he embarrassed at not being able to read or write? Or did he simply not want to take Deelie with him? She didn't want to arrange for a new position for them and then have them not take it, but in the end, it would be up to them. Right now, she had more urgent business.

# Chapter 19

*Stepping Lightly*

"THERE IS SOMETHING I need your help with, both of you," Emma said. "The reason I've come back. Do you remember, Mr. O'Neill, that little oilskin packet you mentioned to me as being among the possessions my husband was carrying when he died? The items Captain Hargreaves left with the Andersons?"

"I recall it, alright."

"He told me about that," agreed Deelie. "That's why you went to find Mrs. Anderson, wasn't it?"

"Yes. Well, that little packet did contain jewellery, as you supposed, but it wasn't meant for me."

Emma told them about the Montague emeralds. There were some people she had to trust with the true story, or at least as much as they needed to know if she was to have their help. Calling it a sentimental trinket didn't support the urgency she felt now. As with Mrs. Anderson, she didn't mention names and this time she didn't mention any threats either. It was simply a lost piece of expensive jewellery her husband was asked to deliver. Deelie's eyes grew wide as she listened.

"He did do that, young Danny," she said, as Emma related what the Andersons had told her about the little boy's habit of picking up brightly coloured objects.

"Do you think that's what happened to it?" Brendan asked.

Emma shrugged. "I really don't know. I'm trying to check other possibilities as well, like who might have come to the house in those few days and perhaps seen the packet on the hall table. Could one of the men working here have seen it?"

"No," Deelie said. "They never come to the house unless for something urgent and then they come to the kitchen or the back door. Mr. Anderson, he always went over to give their orders."

"That's true for sure," Brendan agreed. "Always I would bring Liam to the kitchen and Deelie would take him in."

"Do you remember any strangers calling in during those days I was here?"

Deelie and Brendan looked at one another and both shook their heads. "Men often pass through here," Brendan said. "There may have been someone, there may not. It's a long time ago now, like."

"Mr. Fraser said none of the men have left since the Andersons were here."

"Nothing's changed except the manager," Brendan assured her.

"How many are employed here, now?"

"There's six living in the quarters, and three shepherds who stay out with the flocks," Brendan said. "They haven't put in much fencing yet. And Mort in the shack. You'll see him around."

"I'll speak to him. Is it Mr. Mort?"

"Mortimer is his name, but everyone calls him Mort," Brendan said.

"It'll be most likely Danny took it, I'm thinking," Deelie said. "That red wax seal you said? He was right taken with red, wasn't he, Bren."

"He was."

"You'll be wanting our help to search the place, then?" Deelie went on.

"Would it be possible to search without anyone else noticing what we were doing?" Emma asked. "Or at least, not letting them know it was something valuable."

"Why? Oh, they might go searching for it and not tell if they found it?" said Deelie. "We wouldn't do that, Emma. Not me and Bren. We wouldn't know what to do with a valuable piece of jewellery, anyway, and that's the right of it."

"I wouldn't have taken you into my confidence if I'd thought you would," Emma assured them, but there was a risk, though small enough, she hoped.

"Mr. Fraser wouldn't be too pleased if everyone went off on a treasure hunt, anyway. He'd be right annoyed," said Deelie, picking Liam up onto her lap as he began to fret.

Emma hoped it might keep Mr. Fraser from mentioning her quest to the men himself.

"We could spin a tale or two if asked," Brendan said, with a grin. "Liam could have lost a ball under the woolshed, such like, if anyone sees me searching about."

"And I could be looking for wild herbs, or some eggs from the hens that got out of their yard," Deelie added.

Emma laughed. "All right. I see I can leave that to your fertile imaginations. It's best if as few people as possible know something valuable has been lost. And thank you both so much for offering to help."

"Where else do we search?" Brendan asked.

"Everywhere, I would say," Deelie said, her enthusiasm for the task obvious. "Under every bush and tree and rock and log and building. Wherever Danny went. At least he didn't wander far, 'cept that once." She frowned. "Ooh, you don't think he would have taken it with him when he went off with the blacks?"

"Heavens, I hope not," Emma said, wishing Deelie's imagination was a little less active. She didn't want to think about other possibilities, or she would be beaten before she started. "It will take several days to search the place, given you both have your work to do, and we need to make sure we don't cover places we've already done, or miss any," she said. "What we need is a map."

"A treasure map." Deelie clapped her hands.

"I could draw that," Brendan offered.

"Could you? That would be most helpful. Do either of you have paper? It will need to be larger than my notebook page."

"I don't think... Oh, I've got some brown paper put away that came around a parcel," Deelie said.

"That would do."

They collected up the tea things and the three of them, with Liam, returned to the kitchen where Deelie produced the brown wrapping paper from the back of a cupboard. It was too creased for drawing on, so she put a flat iron on the fire to heat and soon had it smoothed out, ready for drawing on.

Brendan set to work at the kitchen table with a pencil supplied by Emma, Deelie hanging over his shoulder adding her 'penneth worth. Emma made sure the hiding places Katy had told her of were included while she kept Liam occupied with a supply of Deelie's oat biscuits.

The homestead, gardens, farm buildings, water tanks, stockyard, trees, river, creek, sheep wash, and graveyard appeared under Brendan's skillful fingers. Pictures of woolly sheep identified the woolshed, horses marked the stable, and human figures denoted the domestic buildings. Emma was impressed with the finished result and said so. His pale face took on a pink tinge at her praise.

"We need to divide the place between us," Emma said, looking over the map. "There will be some places you can search more easily than Deelie or I, Mr. O'Neill. Put a circle around the places you think you could do."

Brendan looked up at her. "You're going to have to stop calling me Mister, Mrs. Berry. Brendan will do fine."

"Well, that's good, thank you, as long as you call me Emma."

"I'll try to do that." He turned his attention back to the map. "Quarters, woolshed, smithy, stables, barn, stockyard," he said drawing a line around the group of farm buildings clustered together a little distance from the homestead.

"That's an awful lot. Deelie and I can help with some of those places, but we'll leave them with you for the moment. What will you do, Deelie?"

"The house, kitchen, and here, along the creek and the sheep wash," she said, pointing them out on the map. Brendan drew lines around the areas Deelie named.

"All right, I'll take what's left, the riverbank, gardens and the graveyard paddock. We each take responsibility for our own areas but help one another wherever we can. Some we can search more quickly than others." She studied the map again. "Oh, I've realised, we can't possibly search the men's quarters. That's a private area. If we need to do it, I'll have to speak to Mr. Fraser again."

"I'd better be getting back to my work," Brendan said suddenly, pushing back his chair, as if the mention of Mr. Fraser had reminded him of what he should be doing. He gathered up Liam who was half asleep on Emma's lap, his face wiped clean of tell-tale biscuit crumbs. She felt a pang of loss as the little warm body was removed.

"I can get started on searching the stables this afternoon, Mrs... er ... Emma," Brendan was saying. "And thank you for your offer to help us."

Emma wasn't yet entirely convinced Brendan wanted her help in finding a new place for the two of them, but time would tell. After lunch, she went in search of Mort and found him, a tall, gaunt man with stooped shoulders, walking up from the garden plot by the river. He carried a sack over his shoulder, a fishing rod poking from it, and a good size Murray cod, gutted and cleaned, swinging from his free hand.

"You've had a good day by the look of that lovely cod," she said.

He stopped and surveyed her, peering through white eyebrows that hung like ragged curtains over his rheumy blue eyes. Emma's fingers twitched for a pair of scissors.

"Ah, you'll be that gel from Wirramilla," he said, his upper crust British accent taking her by surprise.

"Emma Berry, Mr. Mortimer. I don't recall having met you before, though if I have and have forgotten I do apologise."

"We haven't met, but I did see you when you were here that time," he said. "And I'd heard tell the daughter at Wirramilla had her grandmother's green eyes."

"You know my grandmother?"

"It is many years since I've had that pleasure."

He walked on, Emma falling in beside him. What acquaintance had he with her grandmother that he knew her granddaughter by the colour of her eyes?

"I would like a chat if you could spare the time, Mr. Mortimer."

A wheeze that must have been a laugh shook him for a moment. "No one calls me Mister these days, young lady. Mort I'm known by on these shores."

"Very well, if you prefer it."

"As for a chat..." He turned his curtained eyes on her again, "that would depend on the subject." Not about her grandmother then?

"I need to know something about the time I was here last, when my husband died."

"Well, I'm not sure what you'd want to know, but I will do what I can. It's not often I get to chat with a pretty, educated lady. Would it by any chance come with tea and several of young Deelie's oat biscuits?"

"I'm sure the tea and biscuits can be arranged," Emma replied.

"Mort," greeted Deelie when they went in, her voice flat. "What have you brought today?"

He hung the fish on a hook near the door and opened his sack, producing a cabbage, several parsnips, some sprigs of thyme and parsley, and a knobby rhizome.

"Turmeric is this, Mort?" Emma asked, running her fingers over the rhizome. The spice wasn't common to the colonial cuisine. At Wirramilla her grandmother grew it only for its medicinal properties.

"Useful to temper the strong taste of mutton on occasion. I learned a little of its use during my days in the East. I've been encouraging young Deelie to use it."

"It does go right enough in a tatie and lamb stew," said Deelie. "For a change." She set a mug of tea and a plate of biscuits on the table in front of Mort.

"Well, now, you didn't tell me you get tea and biscuits in return for vegetables. What am I supposed to give in return for a chat?" Emma asked.

"One price will cover all," he said.

He picked up his mug and Emma noticed the way he curled his hand around it, two fingers hooked in the loop of the handle, the thumb and forefinger bent with arthritis. Perhaps there was something she could give him.

Deelie handed her a cup of tea and then busied herself by the fire. Emma told Mort the story of the lost necklace, as she had told Deelie and Brendan. He munched through several biscuits as he listened, nodding occasionally, but made no comment.

"I need to know if someone could have taken it from the homestead, during the time I was here," she said at the end. "Do you remember anyone visiting the station at that time?"

Mort raised his teacup. "I remember the time. I was busy planting for the spring harvests. I believe the gardens at Wirramilla are something special. Your grandmother's influence, no doubt. And then there's that family you have there who must be a great boon in running the place."

He gave her a sideways look at the last comment. He wasn't the first to allude to the rumour of Lucy's family having some blood relationship with the Haythornes, though the stories were probably much exaggerated. She would have to ask her grandmother about Mort, although Emma was beginning to understand Deelie's dislike of the man and thought her grandmother would have distanced herself from any acquaintance.

"You would have seen anyone who visited, being about the place all the time," Emma prompted, ignoring the comment.

Mort smiled to himself, which irked Emma. "Well, there were the chaps from the steamer, of course, the stern wheeler that was involved in the accident with your husband's vessel. The captain, I forget his name now, came up to the house several times but none of the other men I don't believe. Hugh Anderson didn't like strange men about the homestead. He was very protective of young Mary. Lovely lass."

"Anyone during the following week or so?"

He tapped his fingers on the table. "A salesman. Peddling some quack potions. You'd remember him Deelie? Tried to sell you a love potion, didn't he. Hardly think you need it now, lass."

Deelie either didn't hear or pretended not to as she attended to something on the fire.

"What about anyone overland?" Emma asked. She could check with Deelie later about the salesman.

Mort didn't have anything else to add and left shortly after, taking his fish with him.

"Oh, Deelie. He really isn't very nice, is he?" Emma said. "All those snide remarks. Does he always behave in such an obnoxious manner?"

"Likes to upset people, does Mort."

"So I noticed. Does he pester you?"

"No, no, nothin' of that sort, rest your mind. More of the leering kind. Not sure he wouldn't have been dangerous to the servant girls when he was younger, though, I'm thinking."

Emma was reminded again that Deelie was the only woman on the station. Little wonder she had taken up with Brendan O'Neill. Later that evening Emma wrote her letter to Mrs. Lockwood and put it in Deelie's hands for delivery by the first boat calling in on its way down river.

# Chapter 20

## *No Stone Unturned*

"GOOD HUNTING," Emma said to Deelie next morning, as they parted company at the edge of the creek where it fed into the river. She was to comb back along the riverbank while Deelie searched along the creek and around the sheep wash. The creek formed a natural western boundary between the built area, with its domesticated landscape, and the bush pastures. Emma hoped it would have been a natural boundary for Danny too. Brendan was continuing with the stables, so he could watch Liam at the same time.

The ground Emma was searching over was like all areas near a homestead, free of fallen timber, having been picked clean for firewood. But there was the occasional hollow in a tree or stump, or an area under exposed roots that needed to be scraped out.

Brendan had leant her a pair of thick gloves to protect her hands which she was most grateful for as she poked and prodded, scraping out leaf litter and detritus from the hidden places. Dried leaves, twigs and bits of bark crunched underfoot as she worked her way along, accompanied by the pleasant sounds of the river and the birds. If it weren't for the seriousness of the search, it would have been pleasant enough work.

Wedged under a root she found a small child's boot. She wondered what story that could tell. In another tree hollow there was a collection of bird bones and feathers. She located a fireplace, a burnt area surrounded by half a dozen stones, and an old tin billy with a rusted-out base. It was like finding the ghosts of past lives, but mostly she just disturbed the spiders, ants, centipedes and beetles that lived among the natural debris covering the ground and filling every crevice.

After about two hours she straightened and stretched. Her back ached from bending and creeping along. She had reached the timber landing, little more than a few piles driven into the riverbank to prevent it crumbling away with the constant wash from the boats, a handful of planks nailed on top. The water level was several feet below the height of the landing. She would have to get her feet wet if she were to search behind the piles, but it was a possible hiding place when the river was low, and she couldn't afford to overlook anything.

There was no one around. She had seen no sign of Mort. He might be in his garden by now, but a slight curve in the river hid it from view behind the trees.

Pulling off her boots and stockings, she hooked her skirts up into a bunch in one hand, and slid down the side of the bank, her other hand supporting her on the edge of the landing.

She gasped as her feet hit the cold water, and she worked them into the muddy river bottom to get a secure footing. With the water up to her knees she could see beneath the landing, but it was all empty pockets between the piles and the bank. If anything had been hidden there it had been washed out and disappeared long ago.

She rested her forehead on the edge of the landing. This was an impossible task. She hoped Deelie and Brendan were having more success, but of course she would have heard from them if they had. Sighing, she pulled herself awkwardly back up to the bank.

She had mud on her legs and skirt, and her feet were numb from the cold water. There was no point in putting on her boots and stockings until she had washed off the mud. She stuffed the stockings inside the boots and clambered to her feet. Mort was standing a few yards away, watching her.

Emma started. "You could have said something."

She didn't think he had been there long, but she had been sitting with legs bare for several minutes. When he didn't respond, but stood looking at her through those ridiculous eyebrows, she started up toward the homestead. Then she stopped and turned back to him.

"I meant to ask, have you ever used the turmeric you grow for medicinal purposes?"

"And what purposes may that be, Mrs. Berry?"

"For the arthritis in your hands. You boil the rhizome up into a mush and take, oh, enough to cover your little fingernail, twice a day. It should reduce the inflammation and take away much of the pain and give you some free movement in your fingers."

"Ah, the lady of the manor distributing largesse," he said, giving her a mocking bow.

"I would do no less for any animal with an affliction I had the power to ease," Emma was stung to respond, before walking on. The words of Hippocrates' oath echoed in her mind.

*I will apply dietic measures for the benefit of the sick according to my ability and judgement; I will keep them from harm and injustice.*

She had done her duty, though not with much grace. Well, even Hippocrates couldn't have liked every patient. She had washed the mud off her legs and feet and was putting on her boots in front of the kitchen fire when she heard Liam's piping little voice announcing the return of Deelie and Brendan.

"You're here, then," greeted Deelie.

"I am. Nothing to show for my time though, I'm afraid, except wet feet and a muddy dress."

"You should have let Bren search under the landing," Deelie said, when Emma explained what she had done, though without mentioning her encounter with Mort.

"I would have done that," Brendan agreed.

"I enjoyed it, if the truth be told," Emma said as she helped Deelie set out the morning tea. "Felt like being ten years old again. You had no joy in your search either Deelie, I take it?"

"No. Just some odd bits and bobs. And a tear in my petticoat from catching on a tree stump."

"I'll get you a new one."

"There's no need, really."

"Yes, there is. You're not to be out-of-pocket on my account."

"Well, thank you. The offer is kindly taken."

"I found this in the stable loft," Brendan said, producing a tin soldier from his jacket pocket. The little soldier's coat was red above blue trousers and black boots, and he carried a black gun against his shoulder. The paint was still bright.

"You didn't tell me," Deelie said, as he held the toy out to Emma.

"It's for herself we're searching."

"She's not wanting a wee tin soldier, now is she, you loony man? It'll be young Danny's all right," she said to Emma. "Two in a tin there were, bought off the hawking boat, but one went missing. Though Katy searched high and low it wasn't found."

Emma took the tin soldier in her hand. It seemed to offer some much-needed hope, some proof, making Danny's little obsession real. Brendan had recognised that, though it wasn't as obvious to the more practical Deelie. She realised he was looking at her anxiously.

"It's a talisman," she said, closing her hand over it. "You must have searched the stables really thoroughly to have found it after Katy failed."

"If what you're looking for is here, we'll find it," Brendan said. Deelie smiled at him fondly.

Half an hour later, tea and biscuits consumed, Deelie and Brendan went out to search several of the other farm buildings. Emma was left with Liam and the tin soldier. While he banged it on the kitchen floor, when he wasn't putting it in his mouth, she sat at the table with her notebook and wrote up the events since she had arrived at Merrim.

When Deelie and Brendan returned, tired and dusty and empty-handed, Liam had been fed his lunch and was napping on Deelie's bed in the alcove adjoining the kitchen. They had added the woolshed to the places that had been searched in the morning, but with no more success than before.

Emma planned to finish the riverbank past the vegetable garden in what remained of the afternoon. Deelie and Brendan had their own work to do. When Deelie refused Emma's offer to help with the chores, she had no excuse but to run the gauntlet of Mort again.

He wasn't anywhere in sight, as she made her way down to the river. She began her search along the bank from the other side of the landing, but by the time she had worked around the curve Mort was back. She waved to him as she bypassed the garden and orchard.

It occurred to her she would need to search those areas but then decided there would be little point. The area was well cultivated. If there had been anything there, Mort would have found it. He could be laughing up his sleeve at them right now. It was just the sort of thing he would do if he could, Emma was sure. She might have to talk with him again if they hadn't found it.

She eventually reached what she thought might be the north-eastern boundary of young Danny's roaming territory. It lined up with the far side of the hill on which the graveyard was located. The area here was just bush. Tomorrow she would search around the homestead itself and the grave paddock, where there were several stands of trees and scrub. They were fast running out of possible places. Of course, it would be the last place they looked, but that went without saying.

Mort hailed her as she went past the garden on her way back to the homestead.

"There are some vegetables you could take up to young Deelie if you would. Save me the trouble." He gave her a cabbage and a bunch of carrots.

She thanked him and went on her way. Deelie was surprised when she came in with the vegetables.

"Isn't he coming up for his tea and biscuits and daily annoyance?"

"He didn't say anything about it. Perhaps he just wanted me to be his servant for the day."

"That would be just like him, indeed."

Emma wondered if Mort simply didn't wish to be further reminded of her grandmother. Which made her think of home and Major Barnaby. How long would he wait before making good his threats? His visit to her father didn't auger well for his patience.

# Chapter 21

*The Needle in the Haystack*

NEXT MORNING, with Deelie and Brendan searching the other farm buildings, Emma went out to search the area immediately around the homestead. The garden that had been lush and colourful when the Andersons were in residence now sported flowerbeds empty of anything but dried stalks and weeds and unkempt shrubbery. Only a white flowering oleander bush seemed to be thriving.

Mort obviously didn't bother with anything except the vegetable garden, or else it was Mr. Fraser who didn't want him wasting his time on a garden that was purely decorative.

Emma searched under the oleander bush and the other shrubs with her gloved hands, pulling aside the dead vegetation. She found a wooden block, split from the weather, the colour so faded it could have been anything. She peered under the water tank, supported on a stand of massive tree trunks topped by thick, rough-hewn planks.

A mint plant flourished beneath the tap and a twining jasmine provided a curtain of privacy to the space beneath. The cool dimness would be an attractive place to escape to for a child. She seemed to remember Katie mentioning the tank stand. Emma's anticipation rose.

As she bent and pulled aside some of the jasmine, looking in, her breathing quickened. A child might be oblivious to the weight of the tank above, but to Emma it was very real. She stepped back, the panic that had threatened subsiding as quickly as it had come. Perhaps she could ask Brendan or Deelie to search underneath the tanks.

Then she saw the rake leaning against the kitchen wall on the far side. Grabbing it up, she began feverishly to rake out the debris. Despite several broken tines, she was able to clear the space quickly. There wasn't much; dried leaves from the jasmine, some yellowed pages of a newspaper, a blackened saucepan with burnt food in the bottom, and two more wooden blocks, in better condition and both yellow. But no jewellery box.

It had seemed such a likely hiding place. All she had left now was the graveyard paddock. She was trying hard not to give in to despondency. She decided to leave the paddock until after morning tea and went and joined Deelie and Brendan in searching the farm buildings. By eleven o'clock, the machinery shed, dairy room and stockyard had been thoroughly searched, and they were sitting over tea and biscuits again in the kitchen. On the map, Emma had put a big cross over each place they had covered.

"There's still the smithy, the yards behind the farm buildings and the graveyard paddock to do," she said, trying to sound positive. "And the storeroom, if I have to ask Mr. Fraser to let me search there."

"I will look in the smithy," Brendan said, "but it wasn't a place the children were welcome."

"Hmm, perhaps not, but I can imagine it would be a place to attract a little boy," Emma said, remembering her own fascination as a child, watching Bert Lilley work with the fire and anvil and glowing hot metal, the wait for the hiss and the cloud of steam when the piece being worked was dunked into the tub of water.

"I need to be getting on with the ironing," Deelie said, "else himself will be shouting for a fresh shirt come the morning. I can take Liam for a few hours." She looked at Emma as if unsure her contribution to the cause was sufficient.

"We could finish today, do you think?" Brendan asked. Finish, but with what result?

"Yes. And thank you, both," Emma said, "A few more hours should do it, but we'll need the luck of the Irish." As soon as she had spoken, she wished the words back. She had no intention of insulting her friends.

238 · Irene Sauman

"And us without a four-leaf clover," Deelie said mournfully, seemingly unaware of the slight derision inherent in the idea of Irish luck.

Emma didn't look to see if Brendan had a better understanding, deciding it wiser to play innocent. He went out to finish the search of the farm buildings and Emma began her search in the graveyard paddock. Even the twittering of the birds and the gentle warm breeze didn't raise her spirits as she searched. They were fast running out of places to look.

After an hour or so of scrambling around the stands of trees, she reached the graveyard itself which she had left to last. She sat on the log where Mrs. Lockwood had rested some two weeks ago, but which now felt like a lifetime, and surveyed the small collection of graves.

The stone for Sam and their infant was still fresh, but there was another large stone, weathered over the thirty years of its existence and surrounded by an iron railing. It was a memorial to members of the Wilkinson family, who had first established Merrim Station. Two young men, brothers, had drowned in the flooded river, one trying to save the other. Many early settlers learned with tragic results the dangers of the Murray, with its hidden snags and swirling currents and the freezing depths of its holes.

Of the other graves, several were marked with timber crosses in various stages of decay, the carved names and dates barely readable now, and three tiny mounds unmarked. The grave of Bridget O'Neill also had a simple wooden cross. Liam must have been a few months old when Bridget died, from the date inscribed. It was fortunate the Andersons had been in residence at the time and Mrs. Anderson was willing to help with the infant.

Emma turned from her reflections at the sound of someone approaching and saw Brendan O'Neill himself.

"I'm not disturbing you, I hope?" he asked, stopping to stand a little in front of her.

"No, not at all." She remembered her comment about Irish luck and kept her gaze on the graves. "You've finished your searches then."

"I have. Nothing to show for it of any note, I'm afraid."

"I suspected not. You would have come up here whooping and hollering if you had."

Brendan laughed. "That I would." He joined her on the log. "Do you think you can find us a new place, Emma, for Deelie and me?" he asked.

"Definitely, if you are sure that is what you want."

"It is. It'll be hard, all the same. I'll be having to say another goodbye to them when I leave."

It took a moment for Emma to register what he had said.

"You have someone else here?"

"Aye. Buried with Bridget now. Liam's twin brother."

"I didn't know that. I am sorry."

"Aye. Bridget never recovered her health after."

Emma gazed at the grave with fresh eyes. "Did he live awhile, the little boy?"

"No. He never breathed."

"Did she see him, your Bridget?"

He shook his head. "Mrs. Anderson took him away. Herself asked me after to tell what he looked like."

"And did you?"

He nodded. "He looked like Liam. Just the same. Two peas in a pod."

"I never saw my child either. It's for the best, I was told. You'll forget more easily. You are supposed to just put up the baby clothes and get on with life, as if it hadn't happened when there is this empty space inside you. You aren't yourself anymore. You are someone who has lost their child."

"They don't know what to say, I'm thinking. There are no words, not really, are there? People try to show it in other ways, in the soft voice, the sad face."

"I suppose. I do think it would help to be able to talk about it, talk your way through it, perhaps." But 'women should be delicate, let them suffer what they may.' So Trollope had one of his female characters remark, Lady Mabel Grex, she seemed to recall. Lady

Mab was speaking of lost love, but it was all the same. "Did you and Bridget talk about it?"

"Oh aye," he said softly. "The Irish are good at talking, now."

Emma smiled. "And listening." She could see why Deelie loved him. They would do well, Deelie with her energy and quickness, he with his more easygoing, thoughtful approach. Though she imagined Deelie would find that frustrating, too, at times.

They were both silent for a space.

"Well, I still have to finish my search here," Emma said, getting to her feet. "And I think this log is hollow."

"I'll do that," Brendan said.

"Thank you. You'd best have these gloves, then."

The work gloves he had lent her had been bulky on Emma's hands but not unwieldy. Brendan's hands were slim for a man. He bent to the log and reached in, scraping out the loose material onto the sand. Emma, kneeling to one side, pushed the scrapings around carefully with a finger. Most of it was splinters of wood from the log with leaves and twigs that had blown in. A tiny movement caused her to pull back, but it was only a grey slater burrowing in to hide again.

"Do you think I could have one glove back?"

Brendan pulled off the right-hand one and gave it to her. "That's as far in as I can reach from this end," he said, pulling out the last scraping.

Emma spread the last pile of material around. She picked up an odd item.

"Oh, my goodness. Look at this."

It was a piece of red wax, about half of a rounded seal. She could make out the letter "F" among some curlicues. She held it up for Brendan to see. They stared at the small piece of wax and at each other.

"Is that the seal you were talking about, then?" Brendan sounded a little breathless. "Surely, we've found the hiding place?"

"It must be it. The packet's been opened. Is the rest of it in there?" Emma scrambled to her feet and rushed to the other end of the log. "It's still solid here." She kicked at the log in frustration. Several splinters of wood fell away but there was no opening. "Can we tip it up?"

"We'd never lift that."

"We need something to reach in with."

She found a small dry branch lying under the overhanging tree and poked it into the hollow. It broke off leaving half its length inside. Meanwhile, Brendan was pulling at a branch on the tree.

Emma, giddy with impatience and anticipation, heard him curse softly as he bent the branch to snap it, and realised she wasn't the only one caught up in the excitement.

She lent her hands to the branch and pulled. It splintered, sending them both staggering, but it took minutes of twisting and tugging before the last splintery sinews gave way.

"It would have been easier to get an axe," Brendan observed, as they stripped off some of the bushy bits, leaving enough at the end to act as a brush. He thrust the branch into the hollow log.

"Be careful. You don't want to push anything further down." They'd be taking to the log with an axe if that happened.

"I'll be careful alright."

Brendan scraped out more debris, but there was less than had been nearer the opening, and most of it was wood splinters. He reached further on the next try, almost up to his shoulder. Emma leapt back with a small scream, startling him, as the shiny coils of a snake appeared before her.

"It's okay, it's okay," she managed to say, as she saw it was only a shed skin. But tangled among the coils was a small box, its honey-coloured wood showing through tattered remnants of green silk covering.

Emma stared, afraid to touch it. Conflicting thoughts raced through her mind. What if the necklace wasn't there? Or it was? Dare she believe she had found it at last?

"Is that it?" Brendan seemed to be barely breathing as he crouched beside her. He carefully lifted off the snakeskin and Emma closed her fingers on the box. It crumbled at her touch. Termites had feasted on the wood.

She brushed aside some wood splinters with her gloved hand and saw that the box was still sitting on the oilcloth it had been wrapped in, the edges now stiff and curling.

She picked up the oilcloth in both hands with the box safely held. There was a glint of gold seen through the break, and the weight reassured her the necklace must be inside. She let out a ragged breath and looked at Brendan.

"We'll take it down to the kitchen and open it there."

They started walking, quickly, but were soon running and laughing, like two excited children, slipping in the ploughed earth, hampered by the fact Emma was holding the prize with both hands and Brendan holding her arm to keep her on her feet.

"Deelie, Deelie, we found it," Emma cried as they rounded the corner of the house.

Deelie appeared from the scullery as they burst into the kitchen, out of breath but still laughing.

"What? No! Let me see."

Emma held it out to her before putting it on the table. A wail from Deelie's bedroom let them know they had woken Liam with their noise, but no one moved to tend to him. All eyes were on the item on the table. Emma opened the crumbling lid of the box, partly held together with remnants of silk covering and rusted hinges.

The necklace lay displayed, still in its shaped padding, its grandeur undiminished despite a sprinkling of termite dust. Twelve graduated emeralds, dully green in the light, six each side above a large pendant stone. Tiny diamonds formed the centre of intricate gold flowers set between the smaller emeralds and a larger gold and diamond flower hung beneath the pendant. No one spoke. Emma brushed a finger over the largest emerald, wiping off a smear of dust.

"I've never seen anything so grand," Deelie said, a little breathlessly. "You'd feel like a queen wearing it, you would. It must be worth a great deal."

"Something around six or eight thousand pound I believe," Emma replied vaguely, not daring to take her eyes off it in case it disappeared. Had she really found it? Her fingers traced the edge of a gold flower.

"Eight thousand pound on a trinket," she heard Brendan mutter.

"It does sound an obscene amount doesn't it, for something purely decorative." Especially to someone who earned around thirty pounds a year plus keep.

"It would feed all of Ireland for a month, it would," he said.

"I suppose it might."

"And what would Ireland do then? Go back to growing the taties as usual," observed the ever-practical Deelie. "I'm right glad you found it, Emma, I am indeed. It isn't a sight I ever expected to see should I live to a ripe old age."

Emma wrenched her thoughts and her gaze away from the necklace. "Thank you. Thank you both so much for your help. It's greatly appreciated."

"You'll be leaving us now," Deelie said.

"When Daniel's boat arrives. He might be several days, yet. Did you put the letter to Mrs. Lockwood on the boat that called in last night?"

"Aye, I did that."

Deelie returned Emma's smile but the atmosphere between them all was oddly constrained, as if seeing the necklace had reminded them of their different positions in life and while Emma was leaving, they would stay, nothing changed for them.

# Chapter 22

*A Twist in the Tale*

DEELIE AND BRENDAN took Liam and went off to the stable. Emma sat contemplating the necklace. Eventually, she took it out of the box and laid it on the table and began to gently clean the stones with a soft damp cloth. The relief she felt almost bordered on disbelief. She had really found it. She couldn't wait to tell Daniel. The sooner she got home and took the worry off her father's shoulders the better as well. She was impatient to be on her way now.

Deelie returned and sat down at the table.

"You mustn't mind Bren," she said, tentatively for her. "Himself remembers the stories of the famine and how the English let thousands of us die."

Emma nodded. "He's a good man, Deelie. He cares."

"He does that, all right."

Emma went on cleaning the necklace, thinking she could do a better job of it if she had a small brush or something to get into the crevices and around the fine gold work. Deelie idly poked at the crumbling box on the oilcloth wrapper.

"Fancy putting something so grand and valuable in a weak little box as this," she mused.

Emma looked at her sharply and then looked at the box.

"Fancy indeed," she said, putting down her cloth. In her excitement and relief at finding the necklace, she hadn't thought of the state of the box. Now she came to consider it, she would have expected it to have been of a hard wood such as mahogany, perhaps covered in leather, or even shagreen. The dyed shark-skin would have been highly fashionable around the time the necklace was created. Her grandmother had a small shagreen covered box, a prized possession.

She looked back at the necklace, picking it up, her gaze roving slowly over each stone.

"What is it?" asked Deelie.

Emma shook her head. She stood and took the necklace outside to examine in the sunlight. She had polished each stone but yes, there was a mark on the large pendant emerald she couldn't remove. She rubbed her finger over it again, turning it in the light. It was there, along one edge, an area slightly fuzzy with a tiny spot that seemed to have no colour.

She looked at the back, at the solid silver-coloured base, platinum Major Barnaby had said it was, and again at the stone itself. The fuzzy spot looked as if damp had gotten in between the stone and the backing.

It made sense. The poor-quality box, Lady Annabel not taking the necklace with her to England. She didn't need to take it. The original necklace was held in a bank vault, or a solicitor's safe, in London, where the ladies in the family could collect it to wear and return later. Emma knew enough about that from her readings of Trollope's novels. 'The Eustace Diamonds' came immediately to mind.

The fuzzy spot in the emerald was damp, true enough, but damp that had gotten in between the glass stone and the green foil backing that gave the glass its colour. The necklace she was holding was paste. Good quality no doubt, but paste, nonetheless.

What did it mean? If Major Barnaby wasn't aware his wife had only a replica in her possession, how would he take the news when they returned a paste necklace to him? Would he accuse them of substituting the real emeralds with fake stones?

"Emma, is anything wrong?" Deelie looked at her curiously from the kitchen door.

"No, no nothing is wrong." She couldn't tell Deelie what she had discovered. Let them believe the necklace was real and they had played a part in recovering something valuable. Besides, it seemed prudent the fewer people who knew the much-admired necklace Lady Annabel wore at the Governor's Ball was paste the better. "I could see a fuzzy spot on one of the stones," Emma explained quickly, "but it's just damp that has got in beneath the setting." She went back into the kitchen. "I'd best put this in my room."

She put the necklace back in its padded setting and gathered up the oilskin wrapper, folding it over as best she could, and saw, for the first time, some bluish streaks on what would have been the front of the wrapping. There had been an address, but the ink had run when the packet got wet. And there, still attached to the wrapping was the other half of the wax seal. She took from her pocket the broken piece she had found and put the two together. She made out the letters "FLB" intertwined in flowery script. What were the Major's given names? Frederick? That sounded right but she had no idea of the second.

The seal was the only thing connecting him to the fate of the necklace. Emma had a feeling it might be important as the thread of an idea began to tug at her mind.

MORT BROUGHT fresh vegetables to the kitchen the next afternoon when Emma was there alone, Deelie being about somewhere on her chores. She made tea and put out a plate of hot date scones she had baked as something useful to occupy herself. Mort picked one up and put it down again. So, it wasn't the light fluffy thing Deelie baked. Or Janey, or anyone else, for that matter. Emma took one, anyway, broke it in half and spread it with Deelie's freshly churned butter.

"I hear you found what you were looking for," Mort said.

"Yes, fortunately. I'm just waiting now for my brother-in-law's boat to arrive."

"Ah, yes. The other estimable Captain Berry."

Emma ignored him. "Do you know Major Barnaby out at Honey Hills?" she asked, chewing thoughtfully.

"I know of him. Never had the dubious pleasure of an association."

"Hmm." Emma wiped melted butter from her fingers. "You wouldn't happen to know his given names, by any chance?"

"Now, why would you want to know that?"

"I've seen the initials somewhere recently and was curious."

"Indeed."

"And being the educated and observant person you are, I thought you might know."

"Flattery now?" He raised his ridiculous eyebrows. Emma waited. She judged his vanity would not allow him to refuse an answer if he knew it.

"Frederick something." So, she had remembered that correctly, anyway. "And a poet's name I seem to recall," Mort mused.

"Starts with L," she prompted.

"Ah, yes. Longfellow. Presumably, his parents were hoping he would grow into the name."

"Oh, very droll," Emma said. "I wonder if they were disappointed. Major Barnaby is only about five-foot-five, but it would have depended on how tall his parents were. He may have towered over them."

"Very possibly. It depends on the stock. The aristocracy now, they are taller than the ordinary working-class Englishman."

"Because of healthier living conditions, better food and more of it," Emma said. "We seem to be growing people taller here in the colonies for the same reason."

"Breeding will out," Mort responded somewhat stiffly. He left soon after, holding his six-foot frame as tall as his stooped shoulders allowed.

"IT'S BEEN A REAL treat having you here," Deelie said that evening, after dinner. "I do miss the Andersons, all that bustle and chatter."

"Do you come from a large family yourself?" Emma asked, surprised they hadn't spoken of family before, but then much of their time had been occupied with the search.

"Aye, I do. Three sisters, Grainne, Seana, Caitlin and three brothers, too, Ryan, Eamon and Scully. I was christened Deirbhile, but everyone's called me Deelie since I can remember. Grainne came out on the ship with me. We were to start a grand new life in a new country together but…she's buried out at sea."

"Oh, Deelie. I am sorry. And you arrived here on your own?" And no letters back and forth as she couldn't write. "Does your family know about Grainne?"

"I had someone write them on the ship."

"I expect there would have been an official message sent as well," Emma said. Though who knows? It would have depended on the captain, she supposed, and there were so many young Irish women coming to the colonies as servants. "Well, when you and Brendan are settled, we will have to write to your family and tell them all about your new life. You must learn to read and write yourself, Deelie."

"Oh, I couldn't. Could I? No, I don't think I'm clever enough. Bren could learn I expect."

"It isn't about being clever. It's about being taught. Children learn, don't they?"

"I suppose they do and all." She sounded surprised at the idea. "I mind our Ryan was for sending his boys to the priest's school when they were older. Mam always said nothing good ever came from looking above yourself but Da encouraged us to try." She paused and then added a little wistfully, "I do wonder how they are all getting on. Perhaps they've forgotten about us."

"I doubt that very much. And if you learn to write, Ryan's boys will be able to read your letters and write back to you."

Deelie laughed as she pushed back her chair and gathered up their plates. "You found the lost necklace in a hollow log and if that can happen anything is possible."

Emma found Deelie pale and unwell early the next morning. When questioned, Deelie said she had a stomach upset. Emma went out and picked some leaves from the mint under the tank tap and made some mint tea. She had a suspicion there was more to the stomach upset and was strong in her admonition Deelie must have no more than two cups of the tea in a day.

By mid-morning, Deelie was feeling her usual bright self, and although the mint tea would have helped soothe the upset, Emma felt her suspicions all but confirmed. Mr. Fraser would not take kindly to his unmarried housekeeper finding herself in a delicate condition.

It was even more important now for Deelie and Brendan to find a new place. Merrim had no married quarters and Brendan's room in the stable was not sufficient for a couple and two children, although she had seen worse. A wedding wouldn't go amiss either. Something would have to be arranged.

Brendan ate lunch with them in the kitchen. After he returned to his work and Liam had been put down for his afternoon nap, Emma brought up the matter. Deelie couldn't look at her.

"We've been waiting for a visiting minister," she said, "but Mr. Fraser sent off the last one before we could ask him to marry us."

"And now it's become a bit more urgent, hasn't it?" Emma asked gently.

Deelie bit her lip as she folded and refolded the tea cloth she was holding.

"We feel we are married," she said. "We made vows to each other on the holy book. We don't feel as we've done anything wrong." This last was said with some defiance, but tears formed in her eyes.

"But you would feel better if you were properly married, isn't that right?"

Deelie nodded. "This is what I wanted, but it doesn't feel quite right. And I'm frightened. Who's to help me when my time comes? I don't have anyone here except himself."

"Well, you have me now and if you are still here at Merrim I will come and fetch you to Wirramilla when it's time, so you mustn't worry about it. And as for a minister, we'll just have to bring one for you."

Tears trickled down Deelie's cheeks as she hugged Emma, words of thanks tumbling from her.

"Does Brendan know? About the child, I mean."

"I haven't said anything to himself yet," Deelie said wiping her eyes with a corner of her apron.

Despite the vows they had made, Emma thought Deelie might be fearful that Brendan wouldn't marry her, and she would be just another fallen woman with a child to raise and no family to turn to for support.

"Wait 'til after you are properly married," Emma advised. "Then you can give him a lovely surprise." At least she hoped it would be. Having already lost a wife and child, Brendan would have fears of his own. She would have to find that minister as soon as possible.

# Chapter 23

*Threat of Mutiny*

ANOTHER FULL DAY and several other boats passed before Daniel finally arrived late the following afternoon. Emma was feeding the chickens, having taken pity on Deelie who was resting with her feet up. She heard the boat's whistle and saw the *Lisette*'s red-striped funnel. She ran down to meet it as it nosed alongside the landing, hopping aboard with a hand from Fred.

"Good to see you again, lass," he said giving her a wink.

Emma realised she had better slow down and act a little more ladylike, but she so wanted to tell Daniel her good news. Apart from the relief at finding the necklace was the chance to let him know she had been right to trust herself when he hadn't.

She picked her way up the stairs as quickly as her long skirts allowed. Daniel stepped out of the wheel-house as she reached the upper deck. She felt unreasonably pleased to see his familiar face, but his first words belied much pleasure in seeing her.

"So, there you are. You ready to go home now? Finished with your wild-goose chase?"

"I have in fact," Emma said. Why did he have to be such a bear? He'd already managed to make her not want to tell him at all.

"All this gallivanting about the colony. You seem to have had a good time, anyway, according to your letters."

And that old complaint again. She paused for a moment.

"I found the necklace."

The look on his face, his mouth open in astonishment, was worth it.

"Are you serious?"

"What do you think? Of course I'm serious. It isn't something I'm likely to joke about, Daniel."

"Where on earth was it? Did that Irishman have it?"

"Of course not."

"So, where did you find it?"

"It was in a hollow log, with a snakeskin for company."

"How on earth did it end up there?"

"It was the child I told you about in my letter, young Danny Anderson."

"I didn't give that story any credence. It was too fanciful."

"Well, fanciful it may have been, but it is what happened."

Daniel shook his head. "Where was this log? I mean, how far did you have to search? These places are measured in square miles."

"They are. Fortunately, Danny didn't roam far." Except for that one time, anyway. "It was by the graveyard."

"Good lord, really? Well. Of all places."

"Indeed." There was something poetic about it.

"Well." He said again. He seemed to pull himself together. "Grab your bag then and we'll be on our way."

"Come up and meet my helpers first. You can spare half an hour, can't you?"

"Is that necessary?"

"Yes, I can't dash off without saying a proper goodbye. It's a bit more complicated."

"Why am I not surprised. I suppose I must, as you found the dratted thing." He shook his head again, as if he still couldn't believe it. "You did well," he conceded, with some difficulty it seemed to Emma. "I didn't think it possible. I'd resigned myself to losing everything and having to start again."

Emma didn't comment. She still had to tell him the necklace was paste. They went down to the lower deck and Daniel informed the crew they would be lying-to for half an hour or so.

"Daniel, can a steamer captain perform a marriage?" Emma asked, as they walked up to the homestead.

"A marriage?" He stopped to stare at her.

"Yes, like a ship's captain at sea," she said, taking his arm and urging him on.

"That's a myth, Emma. Sea captains can't marry people, and neither can I. Who's...?"

"Really?" she said. "Bother. That would have solved one problem at least."

"Emma, for heaven's sake, what have you been up to?"

"It's Deelie and Brendan," she said. "They work here. They helped me search for the necklace and kept me sane in the process. I need to find a minister to marry them and then help them find a place for a married couple."

"Not before we leave here, I hope?"

"Daniel, really. We'll just have a cup of tea with them. And I need to thank Mr. Fraser for his hospitality."

They met Brendan and Liam on the way to the kitchen. Mr. Fraser was standing at the back door as they came up. He glared at Brendan and the boy but said nothing. Emma spoke to him, thanked him for allowing her to stay, and handed over some coins. She and Daniel joined her friends in the kitchen where Daniel was regaled with the tale of their search.

Emma and Deelie took a tearful farewell of each other, Emma promising to be in touch as soon as she had word from Mrs. Lockwood. Brendan shook her hand warmly.

Emma's last view was of Deelie leaning against Brendan, his arm around her waist as they stood waving from the landing. The sight brought a lump to her throat and memories that were painful to recall.

She joined Daniel in the wheelhouse, wanting to tell him about the necklace being paste and the plan she had come up with, but Daniel had something else on his mind.

"I've got some good news of my own," he said, eyes on the water ahead. "Knowles has been working on the *Mary B*. It's on the water. The repairs are almost complete. He's made some improvements too, off his own bat. Haven't heard of him doing that before."

Emma wasn't ready to get involved in a discussion about the *Mary B* and find herself having to admit to her deal with Knowles. Not until after they had delivered the necklace. They seemed to be almost back on good terms with one another, but it was tenuous, and she couldn't afford to have him upset with her again when the end was close enough to touch.

"That's great news, Daniel," she managed.

"I thought you'd be a bit more pleased," he said, giving her a quick look.

"I am pleased, but right now I'm more concerned about getting the necklace back to the Major."

"Well, that's easy enough. We'll just send it to him."

Send it? And run the risk of something else happening to it? No way. Seeing it into the Major's hands personally was the only way Emma was letting it out of her sight.

"I'll leave you to your work," she said, and slipped out. She would argue about it later.

It was dark before Daniel eased the *Lisette* into the bank. Emma was beginning to think he intended to travel all night and was afraid they would reach the mouth of the Murrumbidgee before she had a chance to speak to him. She joined him and Mr. Shankton and Mr. Wilson in the saloon for supper.

When they had finished their meal, the two older men pushed their chairs back from the table and lit their pipes. Daniel lit a cigarette, and Emma removed herself to an easy chair. Mr. Shankton gave her a sideways look, as if to suggest she should retire and leave the men to their talk, but she ignored the hint.

Perhaps because of her presence their conversation lagged. Eventually Mr. Shankton and Mr. Wilson said goodnight. When she was sure they had gone, not to return, Emma produced the necklace and displayed it on the table in front of Daniel, sitting down opposite him as she did so.

"So, this is what all the fuss is about," he said, leaning forward to examine it. "It's certainly handsome enough."

The stones winked and glowed in the light of the oil lamp. Outside the water lapped at the boards as the boat rode gently, and the night was alive with the persistent and monotonous sounds of frogs and singing insects. Somewhere, in a tree nearby, a boo-book owl sent its mellow musical 'book-book' into the night. It could have been any pleasant evening on the river.

"Except its paste."

He stared at her wordlessly. "Paste? After all this, it isn't even real? Are you sure? How can you tell?"

"As sure as I can be without a jeweller to assess it. See this mistiness here? It's where damp has got in between the glass stone and the coloured foil."

"Where the h..." he checked himself. "Where does that leave us?" He picked up the necklace and studied more closely the marks Emma had pointed out. "Perhaps it's just this one stone."

"I don't believe so. The box was cheap. It's almost eaten away by termites. You wouldn't put a necklace worth eight thousand pounds in such a poor box."

"So, this is fake?"

"It's a copy. And a good one. Lady Annabel wears it to the Governor's Ball each year and no one has ever questioned its authenticity." As far as Emma knew anyway. It would be considered the height of poor taste to do so, though who knew what was whispered in the privacy of the salons.

"It's obvious when you think about it," she said, leaning forward across the table. "The trustees of the Montague estate would hardly allow the original to go

to the wilds of colonial Australia would they, popu-
lated as it is with convicts as they would see it. The
original necklace would be secure in a safe in
London."

Daniel rubbed his forehead. "Barnaby can't have
known it, though. He wouldn't have gone to all this
trouble, if he were trying to do what you suspect and
replace the emeralds with paste stones."

"No, and that, by Mr. Thompson's admission, was
exactly what he intended."

"And we are going to return a paste necklace
worth, what?"

"Several hundred pounds, probably."

"To a man who believes he owns the real thing
worth thousands. He's not going to believe we
haven't had something to do with this."

"It really isn't important whether he believes it or
not, Daniel. The question is does Lady Annabel know
this is paste? I'm inclined to believe she does. In fact,
I'm as sure of it as I can be of anything. Can you
imagine the Earl allowing the youngest of his seven
daughters to have the genuine necklace over her
mother and older sisters? Perhaps all the sisters have
a replica. I don't know. Or perhaps they had one
made specially for Annabel as an added enticement to
encourage Barnaby to propose. Of course, if I'm
wrong and she doesn't know, and Barnaby spirited
this out of her jewellery case before she left, well, then

we do have a problem." She thought it extremely unlikely, but he had to know.

"The devil!" Daniel got to his feet and paced about the saloon. "I've spent the afternoon thinking this was over. The necklace was found, we'll have the *Mary B* back in a fortnight..."

"I know," Emma said quickly. "But you must realise that we need to return this directly to the Major. We need to know that it's back in his possession, paste or not. And we need to do it immediately. Lady Annabel is on her way home. How long will the Major hold off before he makes good on his threats? He's already visited my father and told him all about it."

Daniel's hand went to his head. "He told your father? About Sam and all?"

Emma nodded. "Including the threat of Sam being a party to the theft of the necklace. We need to get it back to him. Now."

Daniel looked as though he was about to explode at the injustice of it all.

"And what do we say to him? You gave Sam an emerald necklace and we are returning a cheap paste one? Just bill us for the difference?"

"I have an idea. Sit down," Emma said when he remained on his feet. "I can't talk to you while you're looming over me like that."

◇◇◇

"THIS ISN'T a journey authorised by the Company, is it Captain?" Mr. Shankton accused next morning, when Daniel informed the crew that the *Lisette* was going up the Murrumbidgee for several hours. Daniel had to admit it wasn't. "Well then, I can't go along with it."

"You will follow my orders, Mr. Shankton," Daniel replied.

"Not if it's outside the Company's orders, I won't," Mr. Shankton said, his square face obstinate.

"Is this mutiny, Mr. Shankton? Whether you are at sea or on a river the rules are the same. You follow the captain's orders. You know that."

Emma's heart sank. One thing she hadn't been able to work out was what story to tell the crew for this out of the ordinary behaviour. Daniel hadn't thought it would be an issue. The crew would follow orders.

"It's important we visit Honey Hills as soon as possible, Mr. Shankton," Emma said. "Won't you please come with us to tend the engines?"

Mr. Shankton acted as if she hadn't spoken, keeping his gaze on Daniel.

"You could at least have the manners to answer the lady, man," Fred Croaker's quiet voice broke into the tense atmosphere.

Mr. Shankton's face reddened. "You're behind this, aren't you?" he said to Emma.

She wasn't sure how to respond. She didn't want to go into the reason for the detour. Neither the Major nor Sam had acted honestly in this. Leaving most of the crew behind was meant to afford some privacy, but she should have known better than to think such an event could be glossed over. She would have to accept there would always be a question mark hanging over Sam. People must already be speculating about her own activities this past month.

"We are both behind this," Daniel said. "It concerns my brother. An expensive item consigned to his care from Honey Hills went missing when the *Mary B* sank. Mrs. Berry has spent several weeks searching for it and, very fortunately, she found it. Now we have to return it."

"Then return it on your own boat. You're going to have her back on the water when we return to Echuca. Surely you can wait that long. You must be mad to risk doing this in the Company vessel," said Mr. Shankton.

"We don't have the luxury of time," Daniel told him, his voice firm. "We have a deadline. Believe me, I wouldn't be doing this unless it were absolutely necessary."

"I won't be a part of it," Mr. Shankton insisted. "If anything happens to this boat on the Bidgee we won't get a decent post on the river again."

That was an exaggeration. Daniel would be held solely responsible.

"And what about insurance?" Shankton said. "You can be sure if you go off route the Company's insurance won't cover you for any damage. I didn't take you for reckless, Captain, but then, perhaps you are more like your brother than I reckoned."

Daniel's face darkened and he took a step toward the engineer.

"That's a low cut, Mr. Shankton," said Fred, stepping between the two. Daniel and the engineer continued to glare at one another.

"I can go on my own," Emma said quickly. "I can walk to Honey Hills. It's only five miles overland. I know it's a risk to take the boat out of its consigned course, and if it's going to cause so much trouble, I'll go by myself."

Everyone looked at her as if she'd gone mad. Then they all spoke at once.

"That be sheer folly..."

"It's all thick bush..."

"... get lost..."

"...snakes and blacks..."

"...a woman alone..."

"That's completely out of the question," Daniel's voice came clearly.

From the determined looks on the faces of the crew, including Daniel, Emma felt she would be locked in her cabin before being allowed to set foot off the boat. Only Mr. Shankton had nothing to say on the matter.

"I've never been up the Bidgee," said Shorty thoughtfully into the thick silence that followed, his legs planted firmly on the deck, arms folded across his ample chest. "I hear tell it's a twisty, narrer channel. You won't want to be doing that trip without a full crew to get you out of any trouble you fall into, Capt'n."

"Yeah," Blue agreed, nodding. "Who's going to winch you off when you get stuck on a sandbar, or pinned agin a tree?"

"Aye," said Willy.

The men were grinning at one another. There was nothing rivermen liked better than a challenge, and better still if it meant thumbing their nose at authority. Mr. Shankton's stance about what they should or shouldn't do had invited opposition.

"I can run the engine for that distance, if Mr. Shankton doesn't want to join us," Fred offered.

"I cook big lunch," shouted Ah Lo.

"We're volunteering Capt'n," drawled Willy.

# Chapter 24

## *Up the Murrumbidgee*

DANIEL NODDED slowly, looking from one to the other. "I appreciate it, but some of you are going to have to stay with the barge, in any case. We can't take it with us. Mr. Wilson, will you stay and take charge of that and the men?"

The loadmaster looked a question at Mr. Shankton. Emma found herself almost feeling sorry for the engineer. He didn't approve of the journey up the Murrumbidgee, but she doubted he wanted anyone else taking charge of his stokehold, either.

"Aye, Capt'n," Mr. Wilson agreed.

"You haven't given me much choice," Mr. Shankton said. "I'll go along, but I want my protest noted. It's on your head, Captain, anything happens to this boat."

"It always was."

Daniel looked at the rest of the crew, but no one volunteered to stay behind. The air was alive with anticipation. No one wanted to sit out this unexpected adventure.

"Ah Lo, you stay behind with Mr. Wilson and the bargemen. They will need to eat, and perhaps you can catch us some cod for supper while you're waiting, eh?"

Ah Lo said something in Chinese, which by the sound of it was just as well no one understood. The barge was soon safely moored against the bank under the shade of an overhanging eucalypt and a supply of food and drink, a tarpaulin and sleeping gear were off loaded from the steamer. The sleeping gear was only a precaution. They would have the *Lisette* back before nightfall, all being well.

Although Honey Hills was only five miles up the Murrumbidgee as the crow flies, it was more like ten by river, and they had no charts. They would be steaming by sight only. Fortunately, the rivers were high with spring rains in the north of New South Wales supporting the Murrumbidgee levels and melting snows from the Snowy Mountains to the east swelling the Murray.

It had taken Emma some time the previous night to convince Daniel to make the journey. He had suggested her father would be better placed to deal with Major Barnaby, but he was the last person Emma wanted involved. It was bad enough he even knew about it.

"Sam was your brother and my husband, and this is our business, not the business of my family," she had told Daniel, calling on his pride.

And then there was the insurance idea she had come up with. It wasn't much, but she hoped it would be enough to give the Major second thoughts about accusing them of theft. It was that which had finally got Daniel to agree to what he called her hare-brained plan.

Now, as the *Lisette*, free of the barge, turned across the Murray and moved into the Murrumbidgee against the current, she wondered if he was regretting that decision. As Shorty had said, the Bidgee was a narrow devious stream. It was not regularly cleared of snags below Balranald, because the New South Wales government wanted to discourage vessels carrying wool down to Echuca and on to Melbourne. Instead, it wanted them to use the upper part of the river to the railhead that would take the cargo to Sydney. Such was the result of the economic competition between the two colonies.

They were going to have to travel carefully. The area at the junction was swampy and thickly wooded with paper barks and river red gums. At the sound of the boat, a family of wild pigs careened through the wiry tangle of lignum bushes making up much of the undergrowth, startling a flock of galahs that rose screaming into the sky. Emma knew it would have been foolhardy to try to walk but she'd been feeling desperate.

The current was running against them at about four knots, but Daniel wouldn't allow full engine speed. He wasn't taking any risks. He and Fred watched the water ahead for the swirls and ripples that indicated a snag or rock or sandbank. It was the ones they couldn't see that were the danger. It would take them all of three hours to reach Honey Hills at the rate they were travelling.

Emma felt the air of tension among the crew, who were all keeping an eye on the river, moving restlessly around the steamer, then congregating at the fore deck.

With Ah Lo left back at the barge, Emma was relegated to the galley. Fortunately, Ah Lo had prepared mutton stew for lunch, the pot bubbling gently on the stove, the aroma of onions, herbs, carrots, and potatoes providing a homely background to the unfamiliar landscape.

As she stirred the pot on one of her irregular checks, Emma heard Mr. Shankton say something to Young James.

"But you can't." The surprise in the lad's reply caught her attention. She shivered. Would the engineer try to sabotage the trip to prove himself right in objecting to it? Without hesitating, she stepped across to the stokehold.

"Is everything all right here, Mr. Shankton?" she asked, her voice holding a challenge. Young James' wide-eyed look swivelled between them, but the engineer continued to poke at the fire and didn't reply. "I could ask Fred to give you a hand if you need some help, Mr. Shankton. It wouldn't be any trouble."

"I don't need assistance," the engineer managed to spit out.

"That's good, but it's available if you do."

Emma turned back to the galley, feeling she had got her message across. Mr. Shankton didn't know how much she'd heard, which was nothing, and it may have been nothing, but she had her suspicions. If he'd had any thoughts of sabotage, she felt they had been nipped in the bud.

Two hours after entering the Murrumbidgee, they ate and had barely cleaned off their plates when Shorty yelled.

"Channel's blocked ahead, Capt'n."

"I see it," Daniel called back. Emma heard the signal as it reached the engine room. It was immediately followed by a sudden release of steam and the *Mary B* slowed before shuddering slightly as the paddles reversed their thrust.

Half a tree blocked their way. It was only recently fallen by the look of the green leaves clinging to the branches that were above water. Removing it was not going to be a quick job. Daniel assessed the situation and gave his orders. The *Lisette* moved across to the left bank and moored.

Willy and Shorty hooked the winch chain around a solid river gum, and Blue, the strongest swimmer, clambered out along the fallen tree to attach the chain at its top end. Another length of chain was attached near the base and again secured to the nearest strong standing tree. The last thing they needed was for the fallen tree to swing around as it was winched and slide into the river, blocking the channel completely.

When everyone was clear, the steam winch was engaged. Huffing and clanking, the chain tightening, the tree began to move sideways, inch by inch.

After twenty minutes, another steamer appeared ahead of them, coming downriver. It was the little *Swallow*, hauling a wool-laden barge. There was nothing for the *Swallow* to do but heave-to and wait for the *Lisette* to clear the channel. The slim chance of getting up to Honey Hills and back without being seen was certainly dashed. Their meeting would be recorded in the *Swallow*'s logbook.

Once it had a clear enough passageway, the little steamer came slowly on, a protruding branch from the fallen tree almost sweeping her deck.

"How far up you going?" the *Swallow*'s captain called out above the noise of the winch and his own engine.

"Honey Hills," Daniel shouted back.

"You've a clear run to there then." He sounded his whistle and moved away.

"Yeah, unless another tree falls before we get there," Shorty muttered.

The winch engine was switched off and the chain unhooked, with some difficulty and cursing as it had bitten into the tree trunk in the process. Then the protruding branch had to be sawn off as the *Lisette* needed more space to pass. Shorty and Blue perched themselves precariously on the fallen tree for the task.

"You wouldn't have got through without us," Shorty said, as Emma refreshed them with cups of tea and a swig of whiskey when they'd finished. She let Shorty have his moment. They would have managed it eventually, with the help of the *Swallow*'s crew, but it would have taken longer.

Forty minutes later Emma caught her first glimpse of the two-storey Honey Hills homestead through the thinning tree belt, the white-rendered building gleaming in the early afternoon sun. Within minutes, they were tying up at the landing. Daniel, clearly relieved to have made it up safely, instructed the crew to stay on board and be ready for a quick departure.

"I hope he's at home after this," Daniel said, as he and Emma stepped onto the landing.

Emma did as well, though she wasn't looking forward to the confrontation she expected they were about to have. Dogs barked somewhere among the farm buildings several hundred yards away and someone came out to see what the noise was about, then disappeared again.

"Oh, my," she said with a small laugh. "He's put in a ha-ha."

"A what?"

"A ha-ha. A ditch to stop stock getting into the homestead grounds." The farm buildings were on the other side of the ha-ha, and she could see a curved footbridge with a gate further along.

"What's wrong with a fence?" Daniel asked.

"It spoils the view, so the argument goes. Typical of the Major to try and create an English countryside."

A woman, small and thin with greying hair pulled into a bun, appeared at the homestead door and waited as they walked up the short rise. Emma knew her as the housekeeper, Mrs. Ruskin.

"Is Major Barnaby at home?" Daniel asked her.

"He's at his lunch."

"Could you please tell him Captain Berry and Mrs. Berry would like to speak with him?"

She nodded, and they waited in the hall while she went on her errand.

"He'll probably keep us waiting at his leisure," Daniel grumbled.

"Do stop complaining, Daniel. We need to keep our wits about us."

Her own words made her realise she had been nervously checking and rechecking the necklace in her pocket, and she clasped her hands together in front of her. The housekeeper came back and invited them to join the Major in the dining room. Emma raised her eyebrows at Daniel. He scowled.

Major Barnaby stood and greeted them politely when they entered. He was not alone at the table. His youngest daughter, Abigail, a girl of fourteen, was with him.

"I expected you would have gone to England with your mother and sisters," Emma said to her after the usual exchange of greetings.

"I'm staying home to keep Father company, this time," she lisped prettily. Somehow, Emma couldn't picture the Major in the role of paterfamilias, but there must be some good in the man, and Abigail's presence seemed at least to have put him on his best behaviour. "Mother has promised I can go to London in two years, when Elise has her season," Abigail explained.

"That will be something to look forward to," Emma replied.

The Major indicated a group of easy chairs in front of the fireplace at the opposite end of the room and Emma and Daniel went across. She sat down, but Daniel remained on his feet. When the Major joined them, Emma saw both Abigail and the housekeeper had left the room, closing the door behind them. The Major took up a stance in front of the fireplace.

"Where's my packet?" he asked, his pleasant manner falling from him like a discarded cloak.

He directed the question to Daniel, but it was Emma who answered him.

"We have the necklace," she said quietly.

"Let me see it."

Emma stood and held the necklace out to him. Major Barnaby took it with a hand that shook slightly. He stared at it and then looked up sharply.

"Why isn't it in its box?"

"The box was damaged, Major. It had been hidden in a hollow log at Merrim Station for several months and was largely eaten away by termites. We were fortunate to have found it at all."

"Thousands of pounds' worth of jewellery rotting away in a hollow log? You expect me to believe that? What's your game?"

"There's no game," Daniel said stiffly, "at least not from our end. We know from the jeweller you wanted the stones replaced with paste."

"Rubbish! I sent it for cleaning. That Thompson, hah. You've made a deal with that crooked jeweller to swindle me, haven't you? This isn't the real necklace." The look he gave Emma was pure venom. She wondered, not for the first time, what his animosity stemmed from.

"The necklace you are holding is the one you gave my husband," Emma said firmly. "I am sure when Lady Annabel sees it, she will be able to confirm it." If only she could be sure.

A look of dismay flicked across the Major's face. There was a sheen of sweat on his forehead and Emma wondered if he'd been drinking.

"How can I return this to my wife without the box?" he snarled, thrusting the hand holding the necklace toward Emma. "How do I explain that?"

"Tell her your story. You were sending it to Echuca for cleaning, the steamer sank, the packet and its contents damaged."

Emma knew he couldn't tell Lady Annabel that story. She would see through it faster even than Emma had because of the customs fee. He would have to come up with something else but that was his problem.

He wiped a broad hand across his face. "I'll want the box and the wrapping."

"We will be keeping those," Daniel told him.

The Major's eyes bulged and an ugly red colour crept up his neck.

"For insurance," said Emma. "The oilskin wrapping has your seal and the box clearly fits the wrapping. Not to mention it has the address of the jeweller at Echuca." Unreadable, but he didn't need to know that. "The box itself is damaged, but still recognisable."

"It is well known you are experiencing some financial difficulties, Major...." began Daniel.

"My affairs are none of your damn business," Barnaby snarled, his face now fully red.

"You've already threatened Mrs. Berry with lies of theft," Daniel continued, ignoring the interruption, "so knowing you can't be trusted to be entirely truthful we are holding the box and the wrapping as insurance. You can tell your wife whatever you please, but be assured we know the truth, and if you try to dirty our names with lies about theft and smuggling, that truth will come out with the evidence we hold."

"You dare, sir, to stand there," blustered the Major, his voice thick with fury, "to stand there, in my own home, and accuse me of…of…of dishonesty?" His hands clenched and unclenched convulsively.

Emma flinched. He'd crush the necklace if he weren't careful.

"We need to leave, now," Emma said, taking Daniel's arm and giving it a small tug. She thought the Major was capable of anything in his current state. And they were on his home soil. He could call on help and then where would they be?

Daniel didn't move or acknowledge she had spoken.

"Daniel!" The note of alarm in her voice roused him at last.

"This isn't the end of it, Berry," bellowed the Major, as they left the room.

# Chapter 25

## *Held Up*

"DANIEL, COME ON." Emma wanted to run toward the river and the safety of the *Lisette*, but Daniel refused to be hurried, though she chivvied him.

"I won't run from any man," he said, "least of all a bullying fellow like the Major."

"He's not behaving like a man, Daniel. He's an enraged beast, a bull that's seen red. He's capable of anything. Please hurry."

"There's no need to be frightened," he said.

"I'll believe that when we're safely away. I didn't expect it to be easy but..."

"Berry!" bellowed the Major behind them.

Emma turned. Her courage almost gave way at the sight of the Major bearing down on them with a pistol in his hand, his eyes glittering. Daniel pushed her behind him.

"I want that box and the wrappings," the Major hissed as Daniel stood and faced him. "Then I'll deal with you."

With a wave of the pistol, he indicated they should continue down to the *Lisette*. Daniel tried to push Emma in front of him, putting himself between her and the Major, but she shrugged his arm away and moved sideways out of his reach. They would have a better chance of thwarting Barnaby if they didn't trip over one another.

She looked over her shoulder and saw several figures by the farm buildings. They may have heard Barnaby shout but from back there she could only hope they couldn't see the pistol. They didn't need anyone coming to the Major's aid.

"You won't get any help from there, madam," Barnaby sneered, in answer to her backward glance.

Emma bit back a curt reply. Now the danger was known, she felt an icy anger. This was all the Major's own doing. His and Sam's. She and Daniel were just innocent victims. And if there was anything she did not see herself as, it was a victim.

She thought rapidly. They would have a better chance of overpowering him once they were on board. There it would be five to his one and there was a shotgun somewhere on the *Lisette*. They reached the riverbank.

"Stop there," ordered Barnaby.

The *Lisette* was in clear view below them, but no one was in sight on the deck. Then Emma saw Fred Croaker in the wheelhouse before he quickly disappeared out the doorway on the far side. She hoped that meant he had seen what was happening and had gone to warn the rest of the crew.

"One of you will go aboard and get the box and the wrapping while the other remains here," Barnaby instructed. Emma looked quickly at Daniel. "You didn't imagine I would be stupid enough to go on board so your crew could overpower me, did you?" he sneered.

"I will stay," offered Daniel.

"Oh, no. The lady will stay," Barnaby corrected him.

He wouldn't want to be left alone with Daniel, even with a pistol. He would feel safer with a woman as a hostage.

"I don't know where to find the box," Daniel argued.

"Don't mess with me, Berry!"

"It's in the bottom of my bag, in my cabin," Emma said. Beneath her unmentionables, she thought, turning her head away as she felt her face flush. Of all the things to be worrying about at a time like this.

"Emma...?" Daniel took a step towards her.

"Step back," barked the Major.

Daniel stopped and turned back to Barnaby. "You should be ashamed of yourself, treating a lady in this fashion."

"It's all right, Daniel. I'm fine." She had seen a large rock beside the landing when she had turned her head, put there as a convenient seat she supposed, with some smaller pieces broken off at one end. Hand size pieces. "Just go. Do as he says."

With another glare in the Major's direction, Daniel went down the bank and stepped aboard the *Lisette*.

"I need to sit down," Emma said faintly, feigning weakness as she moved toward the rock. She seated herself, spreading her skirt as she did so and sliding her hand down behind it until her fingers closed around one of the broken pieces of stone. She kept her gaze on the boat. She couldn't risk doing anything until Daniel returned and she didn't want to look at Barnaby. Her quiet demeanour seemed to irritate him, however.

"Just like your grandmother," he muttered. "Sitting there all calm and composed. Interfering green-eyed old cat, sticking her nose where it doesn't belong into other people's lives."

Emma started at his words, but continued to watch the *Lisette*, her ears straining to keep aware of where he was. Not that proximity mattered when he had a pistol and then wished she hadn't had the thought.

"It's because of your grandmother I have no son," Barnaby went on, his voice rising. "Telling my wife it was dangerous for her to have more children. What else is a woman for but to bear a man's sons? Three girls." His voice dropped. "Three useless girls. What is the point of all this if I've no son to leave it to?" His voice mumbled on behind her, as if talking to himself.

So, that was his problem with her family. Her fingers closed more tightly around the stone she was holding beneath her skirt. What was keeping Daniel? It wouldn't take him this long to get the items from her bag. He must be arranging something with the crew. Oh, please don't let there be shooting. This isn't worth anyone else dying over.

"Berry!" shouted the Major, causing her to flinch. "What's keeping you man? Berry!"

"Here Major, there's no need for shouting," Daniel said, appearing again on the deck. He looked at Emma and she gave him a shake of her head to warn him not to rile the man. She hoped he understood.

Daniel stepped onto the bank. "Is this what you want?" He held out the oilskin with the remains of the jewellery box.

"Put it on the ground, and step back." Barnaby's eyes were on Daniel and what he held in his hand. As Daniel straightened up from putting the item down, Emma stood and threw the stone in one fluid movement. It struck Barnaby on the side of the jaw, and he staggered, his hand flying up, his finger tightening on the trigger. A shot rang out and Daniel dived in under the pistol, knocking the Major to the ground and pinning down his arm.

Emma was aware of voices shouting and men running. Abigail reached them first from the house but had eyes only for her father.

By the time several men arrived across the ha-ha bridge, Emma and Daniel were both bending over the Major, whom they had in a sitting position. Emma was tending the cut on his chin while Abigail helped support him. The pistol was in the hands of Fred Croaker, who was waiting discreetly on the boat, and the oilskin packaging was tucked behind the stone where Emma had been sitting.

"The Major has suffered a fall," Daniel explained. "Partially our fault, I'm afraid. One of our crew fired at a snake and startled him, causing him to lose his footing."

"I think he stepped on that small stone," Emma added, indicating the piece of rock she had thrown.

One of the men mimed drinking behind the Major's back and Daniel was only too keen to agree. Barnaby's befuddled appearance added to the belief. He was confused about what had happened, which was hardly surprising. The blow that struck him had come out of nowhere.

"Help us get him inside. He should rest," Emma instructed. Fortunately, the blow had only caused a small cut, but the Major would have a bruise and a sore jaw for some time.

Major Barnaby was put on his legs and slowly helped back up to the homestead, Daniel supporting him on one side and one of his men on the other.

"Has you father been unwell lately?" Emma asked Abigail, as they followed.

"Oh, no. Well, not unwell, really," said the girl slowly. "He does seem to have been worried about something of late. I do wish Mama were here. She would know what to do."

"She is due home soon, is she not?"

"Yes, she is on her way. She is due to reach Adelaide next week."

They hadn't been any too soon. It meant the journey up the Murrumbidgee had been warranted.

"That's good. One thing your father may have been concerned about has been resolved," Emma told her. "We returned your mother's emerald necklace he had sent for cleaning, and which was believed lost when the *Mary B* sank."

"Oh? Why would he have done that?" Abigail seemed puzzled.

"Perhaps your mother asked him to?"

"Perhaps. I suppose it needs to be kept in good condition, as it has to look like the real thing." Abigail clapped her hand to her mouth.

"It isn't the real thing?" Emma asked quietly, as the Major was helped into the hall and started up the stairs, Mrs. Ruskin following.

"Oh, Mrs. Berry, please forget I said anything," Abigail replied, turning to Emma as they stopped in the hall. "Mama has never told Papa they are paste. He doesn't know, does he?" The girl looked most distressed.

"I don't believe so," Emma said, feeling immensely relieved at Abigail's words and more than a little curious.

"Oh, good. My grandparents had a copy made for Mama when she and Papa came out to the colonies. The real emeralds are kept in London of course, and Mama would have had no opportunity to wear them as all her sisters did. We all know they are paste, but Papa has always believed they are the real set, and Mama has never wanted to disappoint him. He is a darling," she whispered, "but so proud." Emma thought Abigail was something of a darling herself but had a great deal of trouble applying that description to the Major.

"Mama has promised we girls can all wear the real emeralds when we are to be married," Abigail confided now. "How delicious is that?"

Emma said it was the nicest piece of news she'd heard in ever such a long time. She took the opportunity to slip into the dining room where she found the necklace on the mantlepiece. She gave it to Abigail to put with her mother's jewellery, explaining as she did that the box had been damaged in the accident.

For a brief moment, she was tempted to give the girl the oilskin wrapper and box, to be done with the thing, but knowing now the reason for the animosity the Major felt toward her grandmother, deserved or not, she decided it was wiser to keep hold of it.

# Chapter 26

## *Back on the River*

THE *LISETTE* MOVED off quickly downstream back towards the Murray, Fred Croaker at the wheel. Daniel went to join him in the wheelhouse and Emma took herself to the saloon. She sat down, feeling suddenly shaky. Tea with lots of sugar, that's what she needed. Daniel could probably do with some as well.

She was still trying to drag up the energy to go down to the galley and make it when Young James appeared in the saloon doorway with a tray, Blue Higgins hovering behind him.

"Mr. Croaker says as you'd likely want a cup of tea about now."

Young James put the tray on the table. As well as two steaming mugs of tea there was a plate with several slices of bread, some butter, and a bowl of plum jam.

"Bless Fred and you both," Emma said.

"That was some throw, ma'am," Young James said, as Emma heaped sugar into her mug and spread a slice with butter and jam.

"You saw it?"

"Aye. The captain gave us a quick word in case we blundered in, but we were watching, hidden like, in case we were needed see. I never knew a girl could throw like that, begging your pardon ma'am."

"My grandfather taught me to play cricket," she explained. "But women can do a lot of things, James. You must remember that." He nodded in all seriousness. Emma took a sip of tea, and a small sigh escaped her. "You'd best take the captain his tea," she said, when the lad hadn't moved.

"Oh, right." Young James blushed and left with the tray. Blue stayed leaning against the wall and watched her eat, concern etched on his face.

"I'm all right, Blue," she assured him. "Just feeling a little weary."

"Hardly surprisin'. Not every day someone holds a gun on you. Had it happen to me once. Crikey, give me nightmares for weeks after." He shuddered. "You realise you only got one life, and you want to hang onto it for a bit longer. Out here, well it can be over in a flash as it is, what with one thing or another to go wrong. Did I ever tell you about...?"

"Blue, I appreciate your concern, really I do, but I'm fine and I'm sure the captain would rather you were keeping an eye on the river right now." Just because they'd made it safely up-river didn't mean they could relax going back down. "Perhaps you can tell me about it later."

"Oh, righto."

She hoped she hadn't hurt his feelings but all she wanted to do was close her eyes. She continued to sit, not thinking, lulled by the motion of the boat and the throbbing of the engine. She had almost nodded off when she remembered the pistol. What had become of it? She got to her feet and made her way to the wheelhouse, still feeling only partly awake. Shorty looked up from his position at the near side of the steamer.

"Everything all right?" he called up.

Emma lifted her hand in a weary salute. Daniel had taken over the wheel. The boat was his responsibility after all, tired or not. She was glad Fred was there to lend a hand.

"You all right?" Daniel asked, echoing Shorty.

"Apart from feeling as if I could sleep for a week." He grunted an agreement as if he had little energy to spare for words. "I was wondering what happened to the Major's pistol."

"Dropped it in the river," he said. "Couldn't very well hand it back given what I'd said about Fred doing the shooting and didn't want to hang onto it."

"Well, that's a relief, I guess. I don't think he should have a gun near at hand in the state he's in, but what if he comes after us for it later?"

Daniel shrugged. "I doubt he will. He won't want to be reminded of any of this. But if so, it went missing in the confusion."

They lapsed into silence.

"I'll just go check on the lads, Capt'n," Fred said. "Get you another cuppa on the way back."

"Send Willy up, first," Daniel told him. Fred left by the opposite side doorway, his footsteps sounding along the deck to the stairs.

"That was some throw," Daniel said after a few minutes.

"So, I've been told," Emma replied.

"Yes, you've won an admirer there in Young James. Fred had the shotgun on him, of course. We would have been all right."

"I guessed you would have arranged something when you went on board, but at least my way no one got shot."

"That's true. Just as long as you don't get it into your head you need to go round rescuing me all the time." His tone had turned sharp.

"Why would I bother?" Emma replied in similar vein, shaken by the remark and annoyed to find herself near tears. She stepped out of the wheelhouse without another word.

Whenever she thought they were getting on well he stamped his foot over something. How were they ever going to work together on the *Mary B*? They couldn't, was the simple answer. His words echoed in her head. Why had he said that? She didn't go around rescuing him all the time, as he put it. What else had she ever done? Well, she supposed there was that one other thing. She stepped back into the wheelhouse.

"You know about Knowles?" she asked.

"I do." There he was glaring at her again, his knuckles white on the wheel.

"Why didn't you say something before?"

"I was waiting for you to tell me about it. I kept giving you the opportunity."

"I was going to tell you once we'd dealt with the necklace," Emma defended.

"You're just lucky that worked out."

"What's so bad about it anyway?" Emma said, nettled. "Knowles only has a seven and a half percent share, and at my expense, not yours. The *Mary B* could still be sitting there rotting away if I hadn't done something."

"It would have been bad enough, but I've seen the deed. You gave him his share unencumbered."

"So?"

"So, he doesn't have to pay anything toward what is owing on the boat. Which means we will be paying a hundred percent of it out of ninety-two-and-one-half percent of the profits. Although you, my dear, will be paying half of it out of your forty-two-and-one-half percent, seeing you have been the generous one."

Emma didn't care so much about the money. Her share would still give her more than she'd ever had before, but she felt crushed at the mistake.

"I knew I couldn't trust him, but I thought I had covered everything."

"You'd better leave business to me in future."

"Well, I hope you can do better at it than your brother," she snapped.

"One wrong doesn't cancel another, Emma."

"Not in your method of bookkeeping, obviously. You might want to reconsider that. You're lucky you have fifty percent of anything, Daniel, and it all rests on your brother's shoulders. The accident, the necklace, the whole mess. Stop taking it out on me. Sam was reckless before he met me."

Daniel negotiated past a sandbank before he spoke again. "Knowles thinks he's put one over me."

So, it was a matter of pride then. Men. They let their ego run their lives.

"It's only a small share. He doesn't control anything."

"Just enough to be a thorn in my side."

"Like me, I suppose."

"What is that supposed to mean?"

"Oh, come on Daniel. It's perfectly clear you resent the fact Sam gave me his share of the *Mary B*. Just listen to what you're saying. It's not just about you, Daniel, it's us. Whether you like it or not, I own a share in the *Mary B*. This affects me too."

"Except," Daniel said, his tone smug, "I have the controlling share."

Emma groaned inwardly. He did, and she had given him that. Though she wasn't sure it would have been better if they were equal owners. She could imagine the arguments and stalemates that would have resulted.

"So, what do we do now?" she asked.

"Well, I figure you are going to have to earn your keep, girl. The sooner we pay off the mortgage on the *Mary B* the sooner we can buy Knowles out and the happier I'll be. You are going to become a member of the crew. That's one less wage we have to pay out."

Emma swallowed. He wasn't going to suggest she cook, was he? Anything but that.

"What exactly do you have in mind?"

"I was thinking bookkeeper, load master, supplies officer. Anything else needed from time to time."

"A general dogsbody you mean?"

"Something along those lines."

Emma tried not to let her joy show. She was going to be back on the river.

"Well, I suppose I can manage that."

# Epilogue

## *A Wedding and A New Challenge*

"YOU HAVE BEEN so kind to us, Emma," Deelie said, tears not far away.

"It's my pleasure," Emma told her, as she adjusted the flowers she had attached to the girl's hat.

There were no special bridal clothes, although the something borrowed was a delicate lace shawl belonging to Emma's grandmother and Sal had gone to some trouble with the bouquet of mixed blooms, which included something blue in the form of plumbago blossoms. Deelie looked as lovely a bride as any.

"Now, dry those eyes or Brendan will think you're not happy to be marrying him."

As Deelie placed her hand on Edward Haythorne's arm he looked back at Emma, standing up as her friend's attendant. Their eyes met and Emma smiled a little tremulously, remembering the time not so long ago when her father had walked her out to be married.

They had talked about Sam and the trouble he had caused and although Emma knew her father was disappointed at both her choice of husband and Sam's behaviour, she also knew it was now in the past. With letters sent to everyone else involved advising them of the outcome – with a bar of chamomile soap enclosed for Clarice – she hoped never to have to think on the matter of the Montague emeralds ever again.

A murmur of anticipation passed through the little gathering as they stepped out into the garden. Daniel was standing up for Brendan, while Rose and Eleanor, Nella, Agnes Lilley, Lucy and the girls, Bea, and the *Mary B*'s new crew were all present for the happy occasion.

Except the crew weren't so new to Emma. She had been nervous, wondering how a crew would react to one of their number being a woman who would occasionally issue an order. She would technically be their senior officer after Daniel. But all that fell by the wayside when Shorty and Fred, Blue and Willy, and Ah Lo came aboard at Dutch's slip carrying their kits. She had almost cried to see their friendly faces again.

Shorty told her they figured they would have a more interesting time on the *Mary B* and show some of those Company boats what a real steamer could do on the river. He also made some comments about Blue reckoning she needed looking after, ignoring the old-fashioned look Blue threw his way. The engineer, Jake Summers, was a new crew member recommended by George Knowles. Emma hadn't decided what she thought of him yet.

The wedding ceremony was sweet and brief, presided over by Reverend Pyle whom they had collected at Euston. When it was over and the happy couple congratulated, everyone retired to the front verandah where they helped themselves to the selection of food laid out.

Emma took a cup of tea to her grandmother and learned a piece of news. Lady Annabel, it transpired, had brought Major Barnaby's nephew, his sister's second son, back with her from England.

"Annabel says the lad is taking a keen interest in the property and the Major is thinking of making him his heir," her grandmother told her.

"That's very nice, I'm sure," Emma said, careful not to let on how much she knew. "I'd heard rumours he was having financial problems. Was there any substance in that, I wonder?"

"That's been dealt with. Annabel advised him to sell the Sydney townhouse. It was an unnecessary expense. There are any number of excellent hotels available if one wants to visit the city. Quite ridiculous to have the upkeep of a whole house just for the convenience of a few weeks here and there. It's common in England of course, for the landed gentry to have a home in London as well as a country estate. The Barnaby's are hardly of that class, whatever the Major may like to think."

"I quite agree. Was he looking for an heir? I suppose he's given up on getting a son."

"Every man needs someone to inherit, child, especially a man of property. The Major's brother-in-law had an heir and one to spare, and the spare, as usual, would have gotten little. It suited everyone."

Emma realised that was as much of an answer as she was going to get. It also made her think of her brother, Joe, the spare who was needed, but didn't want the inheritance.

"And what about you and Daniel?" her grand-mother asked. "A year will have passed soon enough since you lost Sam. There's nothing to stop you marrying again. Daniel is still unattached I believe."

"Really, Grandmama. You are getting as bad as Lucy. Daniel has certainly never indicated he has any interest and that is fine by me. I have decided to leave marriage to others."

"If you say so, child. There will be many who think it not entirely proper for you to travel with him the way you are."

"Let them think what they may," Emma replied, though it stung. "We are business partners and friends, and sometimes barely even that."

"Sounds to me a lot like a marriage without the benefits," said the old lady slyly.

Emma decided this wasn't a discussion she could win and didn't respond. Daniel was much happier now the *Mary B* was back on the water. It seemed

Willy Bowman had been right on that score. As for her relationship with him, well that was a work in progress.

"I met an old friend of yours when I was at Merrim, Grandmama," Emma said. "A Mr. Mortimer. Seems he remembers you from some time back."

"I have no recollection of such a person," her grandmother responded icily, and Emma knew that story also would not be elaborated on.

Daniel came to pay his respects to Eleanor and sat down beside her. Emma smiled to herself wondering if he was going to try and convince her that not all men blamed women for their troubles. She went to talk to Bea who was helping Nella entertain young Liam. By the look of the chocolate cake around his mouth the child appeared to be enjoying himself.

"How are things at home?" she asked, as Nella took both Liam and young Billy off for a run in the garden to use up some excess energy, brought on no doubt by a surfeit of sugar. Floss, sporting a pink bow on her collar for the occasion, went with them.

"They're fine," Bea said, as they took seats in the corner of the verandah.

"Really?" She didn't sound fine.

Bea sighed. "Thomas is getting impatient with me. It's not as if he expects me to choose between him and Dad and the boys really, but it feels like he doesn't understand. I can't just up and leave them, and he won't leave Netti to take up land of his own without me. He wants us to do this together."

"That's a good thing, isn't it?"

"It should be."

"I take it Matty and Dotty haven't gotten back together then?"

"No, and he's been like a bear with a sore head. I don't understand why he stopped seeing her in the first place if he was still interested."

Emma knew only too well. She'd been afraid Matty's brief desertion of Dotty following Sam's death could end in a complete breakdown in their budding relationship. Emma didn't know Dotty well, having only spoken to the girl on the odd occasion she visited the Keogh family's drapery in Wentworth where Dotty worked. But no woman would be happy to be treated as Matty had treated her. That old promise was sending out ripples.

Nella came back with the boys, and Emma took a turn with Liam who wrapped his sticky fingers in her lace collar, while Floss sat waiting expectantly for fallout.

"How have you been?" Emma asked, knowing Nella was with child again.

"I'm feeling well," Nella replied, "but I am getting a little tired of being in this situation." She lowered her voice. "Your grandmother has offered me one of her mixtures for future use."

"Might not be a bad idea," Emma replied quietly.

Nella was back to her usual friendly self with not a word said in acknowledgement or explanation. Emma had decided the upset between them must have been due to her condition, especially if she hadn't wanted to be expecting again so soon. She'd had barely two years between each child. A not uncommon problem.

Emma's arms involuntarily tightened around Liam as she wondered if she would ever have that problem or even come close. Liam gave a little squeal of protest.

Bea held out her arms for him. "Is Aunty Emma being too rough," she cooed as she took the child.

Emma smiled. Was her friend picturing raising a bunch of little Thomases? What if big Thomas got tired of waiting? Emma felt she needed to do something. She couldn't help feeling more than a little responsible for Bea's situation.

Two days later, Mr. and Mrs. O'Neill were safely delivered to Wentworth and into the care of Mrs. Lockwood, who had honoured her offer of a job for Brendan.

Emma found herself looking forward to the new year. Joe was being transferred to the Wentworth Customs Office and Catherine was expecting their first child. Emma was planning on making the *Mary B* available to transport them and their household from Albury, though she hadn't told Daniel about that yet.

But what was the point of owning a half share in a boat — well, a forty-two-and-a-half percent share — if she couldn't make use of it, come what may?

\* \* \*

## Next in Series

### A Body in the Woodpile

WITH JOE AND Catherine safely delivered to Wentworth, Emma enlists Catherine's help in convincing Dotty Keogh's mother to look favourably on Matty as a son-in-law. In the meantime, Emma takes her place on the *Mary B* for the last journey of the season, but looking forward to the summer break is overshadowed when Hilda Zeller's body is uncovered in the woodpile and her children found, alone at their shack. Taking the children with them is the only option, but where is their father? Emma is trying to get answers, concerned about the children's future as well as the death of their mother, but with tempers on board fraying amidst suspicious accidents and falling river levels are they all just tired of one another's company? Or is something more going on? Find out in *A Body in the Woodpile*.

## About the Author

Irene Sauman writes historical cozy mysteries. Under her pen name, Rennae Todd, she writes cozy mysteries in a present-day setting.

Irene is a retired historian who grew up on a vineyard and orange orchard by the Murray River in New South Wales. She was an avid reader and started writing stories when she was nine years old (including some quite dreadful poetry).

Now living in Western Australia, she has three children and four grandchildren, and a sister who beta reads her books for plot holes and to see how quickly she can solve the mystery.

When not writing (or reading), Irene watches tennis, plays croquet, and has a reasonably green thumb, which means very little dies in her garden, unlike in her cozy mysteries.

Irene and Rennae share a website where you can learn more about their books, which are available in digital and print.

https://irenesaumanauthor.com

Follow us on BookBub to be notified of a new release.
https://www.bookbub.com/authors/irene-sauman

https://www.bookbub.com/authors/rennae-todd

# Acknowledgements

The lines of verse in Chapter 14 when Emma visits Sam's grave are from 'The Wail of the Native Oak' by Australian poet Henry Kendall.

Curr, Edward Micklethwaite, *The Australian race*, Melbourne: J. Ferres, 1886.
Jupp, James (ed), *The Australian People*, Cambridge Uni Press, 2001.
Isaacs, Jennifer, *Bush Food: Aboriginal Food and Herbal Medicine*, Chatswood, New Holland Press, 1987.
National Library of Australia, newspaper archives online: https://trove.nla.gov.au/newspaper/
Echuca Historical Society:
https://echucahistoricalsociety.org.au/
Also acknowledging all those who have written about the Murray River paddle steamers.

The fictional Wirra family would have belonged to the Latji Latji people, who lived in the region of the Murray River (near Mildura) where I have situated the Wirramilla pastoral station. I have used words from their language as recorded by E.M. Curr.